SECRETS
OF THE
GALAPAGOS

SHARON MARCHISELLO

MILFORD
HOUSE

Milford House Press

Mechanicsburg, Pennsylvania

MILFORD
HOUSE

an imprint of Sunbury Press, Inc.
Mechanicsburg, PA USA

For information about special discounts for bulk purchases, please contact Sunbury Press Orders Dept. at (855) 338-8359 or orders@sunburypress.com.

To request one of our authors for speaking engagements or book signings, please contact Sunbury Press Publicity Dept. at publicity@sunburypress.com.

ISBN: 978-1-62006-367-5 (Trade paperback)

Library of Congress Control Number: 2019952880

FIRST MILFORD HOUSE PRESS EDITION: October 2019

Product of the United States of America
0 1 1 2 3 5 8 13 21 34 55

Set in Bookman Old Style
Designed by Chris Fenwick
Cover by Chris Fenwick
Edited by Chris Fenwick

Continue the Enlightenment!

To my loving husband, Michael.

CHAPTER ONE

Laurel tugged at my flipper and pointed. I pivoted through the stream of bubbles in time to see a six-foot hammerhead shark, its flat head barely rippling the water it displaced. I could have touched its coarse, gray skin had I dared. My heart pounded. In our dark wetsuits, did we look like seals? The guides said these Galapagos sharks were not dangerous unless provoked, but who knew when one might decide to add a little tourist delicacy to its diet of fish and crustaceans?

Her dark hair floating around her face, my new friend Laurel gave a thumbs-up. I returned the gesture. I sensed her radiant grin through her mask.

The shark glided away almost as quickly as it had appeared, replaced by a school of surgeonfish, their yellow tails and silvery bodies shimmering in the sunlight. I lost sight of Laurel as I floated among them like a mermaid.

I kicked my way to the surface and lifted my head to drain my snorkel tube. As I pushed a strand of wet hair out of my face, I glimpsed the band of white skin where my engagement ring had been—until last month. *Don't think about that jerk,* I scolded myself. *Focus on enjoying this incredible cruise. And the mission: justice.* Our group had been snorkeling in the chilly waters of Gardner Bay for about an hour, and all I wanted to do now was get back on board the ship, dry off, and tell everyone over a tasty lunch of fresh seafood about our close encounter with the shark. Laurel would have shot some great pictures.

I pulled off my fogged-up plastic mask and rinsed it in the ocean. The sea had grown rougher since we'd started snorkeling, and dark clouds gathered. A wave slapped my face, sending salty water into my nostrils. I held up my right hand, the symbol for, "I'm ready to come in."

Where was everybody?

"Laurel?" She'd been swimming beside me moments ago, snapping photos of the vast display of marine life.

I scanned the water for my fellow snorkelers and the guides hovering in the inflatable black boats called Zodiacs. Laurel and I had not strayed that far from the group . . . had we?

I put my mask back on and ducked underwater to see if anyone was still swimming beneath the surface. Nothing but fish. I didn't care about the fish anymore.

The sudden sensation of being alone in the cold ocean sucked my energy. I took off my mask again, struggling to hold my head upright and tread water while I regained my bearings.

The steep volcanic outcropping where we'd congregated was on my left. It had been on my right before. I must have drifted to the other side. Seabirds squawked at me as if I had plans to disturb their nests wedged into the jagged, guano-coated crevices.

"Laurel?" She must wonder what had happened to me.

I dog-paddled around the volcanic rock and then sighted one of the Zodiacs—at least thirty yards away and headed back to the ship. A black speck in the distance must be the other boat.

"What the—?" I propelled myself in their direction, but the current pushed me back. Instead of aiding my progress, my cumbersome flippers, life vest, and wetsuit—the gear that had kept me so buoyant underwater—now weighed me down. I stopped and waved my whole arm, the sign for, "Come get me now!"

No heads turned in my direction. The boats were moving farther away.

Damn that Fernando! That self-centered excuse-for-a-guide was too busy flirting and boasting about his exploits to notice two missing passengers.

Something bumped my leg. I couldn't look.

"Hey!" I shouted at the top of my lungs. I kicked hard and sprang upward, spy-hopping like I'd seen whales do. "*Hey!*" I had visions of myself drowned in the Galapagos or devoured by a shark—a tragic end to this vacation of a lifetime, this attempt to escape the mess I'd made of my life back in Georgia. So much for ever doing any good in the world.

CHAPTER TWO

I had never felt so helpless. How long could I last before I'd sink, exhausted, to the ocean floor? Maybe I could swim to shore... And then what? Except for the blue-footed boobies and Galapagos hawks, the island was uninhabited.

My grandmother would freak out. She'd blame herself for bringing me on this cruise.

And Jerome Haddad would get away with what he did to me.

"Hey," I yelled, flailing my arms as I propelled my body above the whitecaps.

At last one of the other snorkelers turned my way and pointed. The boat changed course and headed toward me.

"Thank God! I may live to see twenty-five." I called toward the spot where I'd last seen my friend, just after the shark passed us, "Laurel, the boat is coming for us."

There was no answer. "Laurel?" I spun my head around, but there was no sign of my snorkeling partner.

Waves continued to smack my face as I treaded water and watched the boat approach. "Laurel? They're almost here." Where was she?

The Zodiac pulled alongside me. My arms trembled as I gripped the swim ladder to hoist myself up. I faltered. My frantic swim against the current had numbed my limbs.

Fernando grabbed my elbow and lifted me the rest of the way into the boat. I opened my mouth to say something snarky to him about his ability to count heads, but I didn't have enough breath left in my lungs to form the words. I clung to his sinewy, sun-weathered arms until I could seat myself on the edge of the rubber boat between two water-logged women. A survey of the other ten passengers told me Laurel was not among them.

"Giovanna! We thought you'd gone back with the other group," said Deborah Holt, the thirty-something, red-headed Australian teacher next to me. I think she was the one who spotted me, perhaps saving my life.

"Laurel . . ." I gasped, still too breathless to finish my sentence. I pointed at the water, but Fernando had already turned his back.

The outboard motor started again, and the Zodiac turned toward the ship.

Catching my breath, I cried, "Laurel! She was with me." I jumped up. The boat lurched forward, and I fell back against its rubber wall.

Fernando grabbed his radio and engaged in a crackling exchange of Spanish. He turned to me. "The other boat picked her up."

"Sure?" I looked around but did not see another boat.

Fernando patted my shoulder. "Don't worry."

"They wouldn't leave anyone behind." Next to me, Deborah reached into her backpack and retrieved a tube of sunscreen.

Reassured that Laurel was safe, I sat back, closed my eyes, and inhaled the briny sea air. *How silly of me to think we'd drown out there.* I pushed my tangled hair away from my face. The wind blew it behind me like a contrail as the boat gained speed. "We saw a hammerhead shark," I announced.

"Wow! Did you get a picture?" Deborah slathered coconut-scented sunscreen on her freckled arms and calves, exposed by her sleeveless, knee-length black wetsuit.

"I didn't, but Laurel had her camera." I gazed at the water and watched Española Island—and the volcanic outcropping where I'd last seen Laurel—grow smaller and smaller.

Our Zodiac bumped the platform alongside the black hull of the *Archipelago Explorer* and two deckhands scrambled to help us disembark. We were the last group back to the 100-passenger luxury cruise ship. The voyage was only half full this week—fortunate for me and my grandmother, who had booked at the last minute. Treating me to this cruise was her grand gesture to help me get over my heartbreak. But she didn't know the whole story. Because of *my* stupid decision, my fiancé and I had lost the dream business we'd built together—with all our savings—and he was unable to forgive me. Tim couldn't look at me now, much less marry me.

As soon as the final passenger climbed out and mounted the iron stairs to the main deck above, the crew would raise the Zodiac and prepare it for transport. The *Archipelago Explorer* was scheduled to sail to the other side of Española Island this afternoon, where we'd set out on another nature hike.

At the top of the stairs hung a locator pegboard. Each passenger and crew member had been assigned a numbered tag. I flipped my number, twenty-seven, to green, indicating I was back on board. Twenty-six, Laurel's number, was still red.

What?

I tapped Fernando's shoulder as he collected our life vests. "I thought you said Laurel was on the other boat. Her tag is still red."

With a snort, Fernando flipped number twenty-six from red to green. "That Laurel does this every day. She must think I'm her servant."

"You're sure she's back?" I rubbed the goosebumps rising on my arms as a cloud eclipsed the sun.

Fernando shot me one of those looks that warned me to mind my business and turned to help another woman unfasten her life vest.

CHAPTER THREE

I headed to the stern where the snorkelers hosed off, washed their gear, and hung up their wetsuits amid the competing smells of saltwater, rubber, and sweat.

I dripped at the sink next to one of the Roberts twins. The sixteen-year-old sisters resembled the Barbie doll my grandmother gave me when I was ten. The twins were traveling with their storybook-perfect parents from Texas. Their father, Jim Roberts, was CEO of Leisure Dreams, a well-known resort chain; I recognized his chiseled visage from the company's advertisements. Their mother, Janice, a Dallas socialite with a face made for a magazine cover, managed a multi-million-dollar children's charity. Her self-assured demeanor reminded me of Claire in my favorite TV series, *House of Cards*.

"Did you have fun today?" I asked the twin. I couldn't tell the two girls apart, and so far, had no reason to.

The Barbie flashed a pearly set of teeth ideal for a toothpaste commercial. "Awesome. All those fish. And stingrays! I lost count of how many pictures I took." Each member of the Roberts family carried a top-of-the-line GoPro underwater camera, bought new for the trip.

"I saw a hammerhead shark." *That should impress her.*

Her blue eyes widened. "Awesome!"

The twin slid a stylish cover-up over her bikini while I wrapped myself in a ship's towel. "Hey, uh . . ." I looked at the girl. I didn't know her name, and it would be rude to call her "Barbie."

"Jenny." The Barbie touched her chest. "My twin sister is Jessy. She's the one with dimples."

"Jenny," I repeated, although I hadn't noticed one had dimples and the other did not. "Was Laurel in your boat?"

"Who?"

"Laurel Pardo. Remember, the tall woman in the lounge with us last night? Telling us all that cool stuff about tortoises."

Jenny ran a finger across her forehead. The sunlight caught the sparkles in her aqua nail polish. "Dark hair? Long bangs and long nose? Isn't she some kind of wildlife photographer?"

I nodded. "She calls herself a researcher, but she takes great pictures."

"Yeah, my dad said something about her last night. Don't think I saw her today."

"You're sure? She wasn't in your boat? Picked up last?"

Jenny bit her lip as if concentration took a lot of energy. "I'm not positive. We were busy looking at photos after we got out of the water. Why?"

"She wasn't in my boat, either, and she'd been snorkeling near me."

Jenny shrugged. "Then she must have been on our boat. They wouldn't leave anyone behind."

I started to walk away, then stopped. "Fernando turned over Laurel's tag."

"He did?" Jenny picked up her beach bag. "That's weird." She frowned at the teak deck, then looked back at me. "Maybe she just forgot to turn it over herself. My sister forgot yesterday, and Fernando turned her tag over for her."

I passed Laurel's cabin on the way to my own, which was farther down the hall. I paused, knocked, but there was no answer. Ear pressed against the heavy wooden door, I listened. Was that sound of running water Laurel's shower, or was it coming from the cabin next door?

Although Laurel and I had only met a few days ago, at the beginning of this seven-day Galapagos cruise, I'd felt a blossoming camaraderie that I was certain would endure after the trip was over. Laurel Pardo, an Ecuadorian-American researcher in her late twenties—just a few years older than I— had spent years studying the wildlife of the Galapagos region, and she told fascinating stories about her experiences. She knew as much, if not more than the guides. Listening to her witty commentary helped take my mind off my troubles back home. For a few hours a day, I didn't think about being broke, single again, and forced to pry open doors to the corporate workforce I'd thought I'd nailed shut.

Shivering from my walk down the air-conditioned hallway, I arrived at my cabin. Inside, my grandmother, Michelle De-Palma, sat cross-legged on her twin bed, typing on her laptop. Michelle, who had the energy of a person half her age, had opted to skip the snorkel trip this morning to steal a few hours of relaxation.

Michelle glanced up from her computer. "How was the snorkeling? See anything interesting?"

"I almost drowned at the end. But I saw a hammerhead shark."

"I bet that was something." Typical Michelle, only half-listening. She closed the laptop and uncrossed her legs. "The Wi-Fi is slow on this ship, but I managed to download Laurel's photos and send them to Roberto." Roberto was Michelle's husband of over twenty years.

"You didn't post the pictures on Facebook, did you?"

"No, Giovanna, I just emailed them to Roberto. I haven't updated my Facebook status since we've been here."

"Good. You don't want everyone to know you're not home. Roberto will leave on a trip, and the house will be empty." Roberto was an airline pilot.

Michelle laughed. "I knew about cybersecurity before you were born, thank you."

"Right. The internet hadn't been invented yet."

"Make me feel old, won't you?"

I walked over to the bed and gave my grandmother a peck. Her cheek was smooth; her skin had very few wrinkles. I hoped

I'd inherited genes that good. "Sixty isn't old. Or excuse me, fifty-ten, as Roberto says. Or isn't it fifty-eleven now?"

Michelle smirked and then cocked her head at me. "Giovanna Rogers, what do you mean you almost drowned? You look okay now."

My eyes watered as memories of my ordeal in the ocean flooded back. "Oh, Michelle, they almost left me out there. I was so scared."

"What?"

I took a deep breath and blinked away the tears that threatened to fall. I had her full attention.

Michelle patted a spot on the bed next to her. I dropped onto the firm mattress and poured out my story.

Michelle and I headed upstairs to the Ocean Grill, the outdoor café on the top deck already buzzing with the lunch crowd, and chose a table near the rail. A warm breeze caressed our faces as the ship clipped through the waves. The smell of charcoal-grilled seafood mixed with the salty air. A few noisy seagulls hovered, searching for handouts.

A white-shirted waiter walked over and set tall glasses of ice water and a basket of fresh-baked rolls in front of us. We both ordered grilled Galapagos lobster and a green salad. I grabbed a roll and tore off a bite as soon as the waiter left.

Deborah Holt joined us at our table. She put a hand on Michelle's shoulder. "G'day, Michelle. We missed you on the snorkel trip this morning. Are you feeling okay?"

Michelle had just taken a big gulp of ice water.

I answered for my grandmother. "Michelle decided to sleep in and then catch up on email."

She finished swallowing and set down her glass. "The thought of putting on a clammy, smelly wetsuit again at that hour of the morning . . ." She hugged her torso. "Been there, done that."

Deborah eyed me. "Giovanna, why do you call your grand-mother by her first name? Don't you have some pet name like Nana or Gran?"

Michelle shuddered. I stifled a chuckle.

"Well, you look too young to be her grandmother anyway." Deborah shooed a gull who'd found a crumb near her foot. "I'd thought you were her mum, or maybe an auntie."

The youth compliment earned a big smile from Michelle.

Deborah changed the subject. "Are you two going on the hike this afternoon?"

Michelle took another sip of ice water and nodded. "I hope we see more blue-footed boobies."

The waiter returned to our table with his order pad and nod-ded at Deborah.

Deborah requested the lobster and a glass of Riesling. She shut her menu and handed it to the waiter, who headed back to the kitchen. "Laurel rang and said she wasn't feeling right, so she won't be joining us."

Michelle and I exchanged startled looks.

"Laurel called *you*?" I stared at Deborah. "Why would she call you?" That didn't come out right. As fellow native English-speaking guests on a small ship, we'd all bonded, but after our experience in the water this morning, I'd expected Laurel to call *me* instead, to find out if I'd made it back okay, to assure me that she had too.

Deborah shrugged. "Why not? She was going to give me some tips on photography this afternoon."

"Did she say what was the matter?" I picked up my water glass.

"She didn't sound like herself. Maybe she's coming down with a cold." Deborah unwrapped her silverware from the cloth napkin at her place setting. "I started to ask if we could bring her anything, but she hung up before I could get a word out."

"She seemed fine this morning." My heartbeat quickened as I gazed out at the ocean, reliving my battle against the current. "Are you sure it was Laurel who rang?"

Deborah gave me a quizzical look. "Who else would it be?"

I shook my head. Something seemed wrong.

A large black frigate bird dive-bombed the vacated table next to ours and snatched a scrap.

After the initial shock, we all looked at each other and laughed.

The waiter returned with our salads and Deborah's wine.

Michelle picked up her fork. "Where's your roomie? Sue, right?" Sue Plunkett was Deborah's travel companion, a fellow primary school teacher from Brisbane.

"Napping. She already ate."

"I guess she's not coming on the hike with us, then?" Michelle skewered a cherry tomato with a leaf of lettuce onto her fork.

"Naw. All that weight she's carrying. Zonks her out." Deborah shook her head and flared her arms around her middle to indicate Sue's girth.

The waiter returned with a pitcher and refilled our water glasses.

"I heard we might see waved albies this afternoon," Deborah said when he had gone.

"Waved what?" I sometimes strained to understand Deborah's thick Aussie accent.

"Waved albatross, also known as *Galapagos albatross*," explained Michelle. "Remember Fernando talking about them at the briefing last night? It's mating season, so if we're lucky, we might get to witness their courtship ritual."

The waiter arrived with our lobster tails, still sizzling from the grill. We watched as he deftly removed the shells from each plate and whisked them away onto his tray. Famished, I dove my fork into the succulent white meat.

After lunch, we returned to the cabin, and I couldn't resist knocking on Laurel's door again when we passed. Still no answer. I pressed my ear against the wood.

"Maybe she's sleeping," Michelle suggested. "We don't want to disturb her if she's not feeling well."

"Maybe she's not on board," I said, as we continued down the hall toward our quarters. The other boat had reached the ship first; I couldn't imagine they'd had enough time to backtrack and pick up Laurel from the water. Besides, Jenny had been on that boat and would have remembered turning around to retrieve a last-minute passenger, even if she was busy talking and looking at photos.

Not shy, Laurel would have said something to the group, made her presence known. Perhaps she would have mentioned the hammerhead shark we'd seen or given the guide a tongue lashing for almost leaving us behind.

"Do you believe they left her out there? Think of the liability." Michelle rested her hand on the brass doorknob to our cabin. "Why would they do that? They're always so careful. And who called Deborah if it wasn't Laurel?"

"Yeah, it doesn't make sense. But they almost left me. I'd feel better if I saw her." With a queasy stomach, I followed Michelle into our room.

CHAPTER FOUR

Our afternoon hike covered the rocky terrain of Punta Suarez, on the westernmost end of Española Island. Barking sea lions, nesting birds, and marine iguanas inhabited the wave-battered coastline. Dry grasses and low shrubs pushed through the stones and sand.

We arrived in Zodiacs from ship to shore for a dry landing, which meant we could disembark straight from the inflatable boat to a primitive wooden pier. This was a welcome change from the wet landings we'd made elsewhere in the archipelago, including the other side of Española Island, where that morning we'd hoisted ourselves over the sides of the boat and waded through several feet of cool water onto the sandy, pebble-strewn beach.

In the Zodiac with Michelle and me, rode the Roberts twins and their parents, along with half a dozen other tourists. The Roberts family members wore matching designer sportswear and carried expensive high-power binoculars in addition to their cameras. Mother and daughters had tied their silky blond hair with ribbons, so it didn't become unruly in the wind, like mine.

Such a happy, close-knit family, I thought as I watched them laughing together. *They have it all.*

"Is this your first trip to the Galapagos?" Michelle smeared sunscreen on her bare arms as she addressed Janice Roberts, who sat across from us.

"For me and the girls," replied Janice. She adjusted her designer sunglasses on her Duchess nose. Prada; I could read the label from where I sat. "Jim has made several business trips down here during the past year to oversee his new resort property in Puerto Ayora."

"It'll be beautiful." Jim grinned, displaying the same glistening set of teeth his daughters had. If I hadn't already known his occupation, I might have guessed he was a dentist. "I can't wait for Janice and the girls to see it."

"So, you haven't been there yet?" Michelle asked Janice.

"No, it's not ready to open." Janice eyed her husband. Was there a hint of accusation in her tone? "We were hoping it would be by the time we came down for this cruise."

Jim snorted. "Construction delays."

"I hope the pool is nicer than the one on the ship," said one of his daughters.

Jenny? Or maybe that's the other twin, Jessy? No, this one doesn't have dimples.

"I've read that most of the hotels in the Galapagos are rustic," I ventured, showing off my knowledge of his industry. "Doesn't fit the Leisure Dreams brand. How are you managing that disconnect? Are you changing the model?" I'd once attended an accounting convention at Leisure Dreams – Maui, and that hotel had been grander than any place I'd ever stayed. In my former profession as an external corporate auditor, the Leisure Dreams resort chain had been one of my firm's major clients.

Jim's face lit up as if he'd just found someone who spoke his language. "You won't believe the red tape I've had to cut through to make this resort into the jewel we have planned. But yes, it'll seem rustic compared with other Leisure Dreams properties."

"Is it going to be right in town?" asked Michelle. She passed me her sunscreen and I applied the tangerine-scented white cream to my exposed skin. "I'm trying to picture where you could put a resort."

"Sounds like you've been to Puerto Ayora before." Janice handed a tube of sunscreen to one of her daughters.

"My husband Roberto and I were in the Galapagos a few years ago. We did a cruise similar to this one." Michelle fanned her short hair up from her neck with her fingers.

"Our resort is adjacent to a new tortoise reserve," replied Jim. "On the south end of Academy Bay."

"A new tortoise reserve?" Michelle tilted her head as if studying a map of Santa Cruz Island. "Not the Darwin Research Station?"

Jim shook his head. "You should come have a look at the site when we stop in Puerto Ayora." He nodded to include me. "Friday, isn't it?"

Dieter Brüder, the stocky, balding Swiss businessman seated beside me, leaned toward Jim. He reeked of tobacco, suntan oil, and perspiration. "I'd like to hear more about your construction project. Are you still looking for investors?"

Jim turned his attention toward Dieter and lowered his voice, making it difficult for me to overhear their conversation.

"Oh look, Daddy!" squealed Jessy. Her dimples popped.

As our boat approached the landing, a sea lion and her pup swam alongside, doing underwater flips and frolicking with each other in its wake.

"We have an escort!" Michelle peered over the side of the Zodiac. My grandmother acted as excited about the friendly sea lions as Jessy.

The guide and operator tied up the boats and helped us ashore, leaving the sea lions who'd accompanied us bellowing at other sea lions lounging among the rocks and along the narrow beach. We had to be careful not to step on foot-long marine iguanas sunning themselves next to the path, their bodies draped over each other like piles of sleeping kittens. Their dark gray skins made it hard to distinguish the iguanas from the rocks.

Up ahead, I saw Fernando hover close to the twins, pointing out birds nesting with chicks in the sparse vegetation. Once the girls snapped their photos, he directed them to new subjects and gallantly offered to take shots with them posing near the wildlife. The twins spent more time arguing over who would stand in the picture next to Fernando than looking at the birds.

"What an ass," I muttered to Michelle as we trailed behind them. "He's acting like a dog in heat, and he's twice their age." I'd lost trust in Fernando when I watched him turn over Laurel's locator tag.

"You didn't seem to mind when he was sniffing around you like that yesterday."

With a huff, I turned my camera toward a male frigate bird, his red chest puffed out like an overblown balloon, part of the mating ritual. Two females watched him like judges on *America's Got Talent.* I centered the male bird in the viewfinder, then clicked.

"One of these days you'll tell me what happened between you and Tim." Michelle touched my shoulder. "Something has made you bitter toward men."

"Nothing to tell. We're over." I kicked at a stone along the dirt path. I wanted to talk about it, but it was hard. Embarrassing. Tim and I had been friends since childhood. Our relationship had turned romantic about the time I graduated from college. Now there was nothing left.

"You were engaged. Planning a wedding this summer. What changed your mind?"

"I'm a slow learner."

Michelle crouched next to a hooded lava lizard and aimed her camera. Perched on a boulder of igneous rock, the reptile held its head still, as if posing. Was my grandmother even listening to me, or was she thinking about taking pictures? "It runs in the family," she said.

"No, Tim wasn't abusive; I don't mean that." I should have known my remark would send Michelle in the wrong direction. "We weren't like you and Percy." Percy was my biological grandfather. Although he and Michelle had never married, they'd had a long and tempestuous relationship. According to Michelle, Percy once tried to strangle her. As a couple, Tim and I had been much more civil than Percy and Michelle. "I can't blame Tim. He lost his investment, too, and his reputation as a veterinarian was tarnished. It was all my fault. I never should have trusted Jerome with our venture." A lava lizard scurried between the rocks. "I just thought Tim loved me enough to get past a business failure. To face the problems together."

"I'm glad Tim—" Michelle stopped mid-sentence. "Look, some of those waved albatrosses, like the pictures the guides showed us last night." A pair of the large white birds clacked their yellow beaks together as if they were having a sword fight.

A crowd joined us and watched the albatross mating ritual, which continued for several minutes.

"I got the whole thing on video," Deborah announced. She grinned as she replayed the dance for a Japanese couple who'd wandered up late. "Like a fencing match." She stopped halfway through the video. "Look over there! Another pair are going at it now."

Amid appreciative "ahs," cameras pointed toward the action. Beaks clattered like croquet mallets striking wooden balls.

Farther down the path, we encountered blue-footed boobies. A male tap-danced his heart out while a bored female pretended to be asleep. Michelle laughed as she took their picture. "'Look at my feet,' he says. 'Aren't they a striking shade of blue?' And she says, 'So what? I have blue feet, too.'"

At that moment, the male took flight. The female looked up in surprise.

Michelle shook her finger at the bird. "I don't blame him."

I chuckled, more at my grandmother's anthropomorphism than at the antics of the boobies. "Men! They're all the same, regardless of species." Seeing all the mating birds brought back good times with Tim. Which brought me back to our break-up. I ran my thumb over my bare ring finger. *Everyone, even the animals, has someone to love.*

I turned away from the boobies and resumed my trek, leaving my grandmother to fawn over the birds.

Jim and Dieter had stopped several feet ahead of me, but the reason did not appear to be a wildlife sighting.

"Do you think she'll say something?" Dieter's raspy voice rose. "That could be a big problem for the project."

"I hope I convinced her not to. It might be——" Jim's eyes shifted toward me as I approached. His demeanor made a chameleon-like transformation. "This place is spectacular, don't you agree?" He lifted the binoculars that had been dangling around his neck and held them to his eyes.

I gave the two men a tight smile and passed them.

Michelle caught up with me. "I think I got some good shots of the boobies, but the camera never does justice to the color of those blue feet."

As we strolled along, I gazed out to sea, drawn by an irregular wave that looked like a spout. "Look over there. Could that be a whale?"

Michelle focused her binoculars toward the spot where I pointed. I saw a dark shape emerge from the water and then re-submerge. "It's a whale," she confirmed.

I sprinted ahead to Fernando and tugged his sleeve to distract him from his dialogue with the doting twins. "We saw a whale over there."

"Whale? The whales don't come to this side of the island." Fernando skimmed the horizon and turned back to his teenage admirers.

A larger spout shot from the waves, followed by a dark forked tail. "There!" cried Michelle.

Fernando raised his radio and alerted Elena and Rafael, the other two guides, whose groups had meandered farther down the path. In a few moments, the whole contingent from the *Archipelago Explorer* stood on the rocks watching, binoculars trained, cameras recording, as the whale swam down the coast, waving its tail and spouting like a fountain every few seconds. There were giggles of excited appreciation, backslapping and congratulatory words for the guides.

I was the first one to see the whale, I thought. *And Fernando basks in the glory.*

Hot and tired after our hike, we headed back to our cabin to relax for a few minutes before the next activity. The air conditioning in the hallway refreshed our weary bodies.

"Let's check on Laurel again," I suggested to Michelle. "Maybe she's better now."

The cabin steward had parked his cart in front of Laurel's room, and he'd propped open the door to her cabin.

I peered inside. "Laurel?"

Laurel's room was a mess. Clothes, gear, and papers were strewn all over the floor and the furnishings. "Whoa, she's a bigger slob than I am."

"Slob?" Michelle craned her neck to look over my shoulder. "Her cabin was spotless when I stopped by this morning before you two left to go snorkeling." She grimaced. "Looks like someone trashed the place." Michelle stuck her head further inside the room and called, "Laurel?"

Carlos, our cabin steward, appeared in the doorway of Laurel's bathroom with a towel in his hand. "Señora?"

"Sorry to disturb you, but we were looking for Laurel." Michelle maneuvered herself into the entryway of Laurel's room.

"Señorita Laurel has gone out," Carlos replied.

"Did you see her?" I stepped into the entryway. "This afternoon?"

"No." Carlos looked confused. "She isn't here."

Michelle nudged me and turned toward Carlos. "Carlos, we've been having some trouble with our toilet. Would you mind looking at it?"

While Michelle led the steward to our cabin down the hall, I stole inside Laurel's room. My heart pounded; I didn't have much time. Drawers had been left open, garments had been pulled from hangers. *What to look for?* I knew Laurel had a computer, but it wasn't on the desk. I rummaged through several drawers, finding nothing but a few undergarments. No cell phone. Where was her camera? She'd had it with her when we were snorkeling this morning. The safe was locked. Maybe she kept the camera inside. But maybe the camera was still with her... out there.

Most of the papers scattered on the floor and desk contained pictures and printed text about various species of tortoises. I picked up a magazine that lay open to an article entitled, "Tio Armando, the New Darling of the Galapagos." I skimmed the text. Laurel had said her research involved giant tortoises, hence so much literature about them in her cabin. It probably had nothing to do with her disappearance.

Behind me, a throat cleared. Of course. There was nothing wrong with our toilet.

I set down the magazine and looked at the cabin steward. "Uh, I was searching for a book Laurel borrowed from me, but I don't see it."

I edged past Carlos and returned to my room.

"Find out anything?" Michelle closed our cabin door behind me. "I kept him here as long as I could."

"Laurel had a laptop, didn't she?"

"That's how she downloaded those photos from her camera for me." Michelle walked to the desk and opened the top drawer. "I still have her flash drive."

We looked at each other.

"Is there anything on the flash drive besides photos?"

"Let's see." Michelle was about to stick the flash drive into her own laptop when there was a knock at the door. She dropped the device into her pocket, and I went to open the door.

"The sunset is gorgeous! Come on, we have to hurry upstairs to see it," said Deborah.

"Shouldn't we stay behind and look at the flash drive?" I asked Michelle.

"Maybe we'll see Laurel upstairs, and the whole mystery will be solved."

We climbed the stairs to the upper deck where we joined many of our fellow passengers, a diverse group of tourists representing a multitude of nationalities. We sipped margaritas and admired the bold shades of orange and purple that filled the sky as the sun slipped below the horizon. The onboard guitarist played lively Latin music, to which several couples were dancing.

I scanned the crowd for Laurel.

"Have you seen Laurel anywhere?" Michelle asked Deborah. "We stopped by her cabin and she wasn't in there, so she must be feeling better."

Deborah shook her head. "Haven't seen her. Glad she's better, though. No fun being sick on holiday. Sue's caught a bit of a bug now."

I didn't mention we'd found Laurel's cabin a wreck.

"I want to download some of those photos Laurel took the other day when we were snorkeling in Rábida. She got a good shot of those two penguins we saw near the shore. Right by our boat, remember?" Deborah sipped her drink. "It still amazes me that penguins are living on the equator."

"Their ancestors were brought here by the Humboldt Current." Michelle accepted a fruit punch from a tray balanced on the forearm of a passing waiter.

Deborah would not get off the subject of Laurel's photos. "Didn't Laurel put those photos on a jump drive for you, Michelle? May I borrow it when you're done?"

Michelle's hand touched her pocket.

I pressed my lips together.

"I thought I already gave it back to her, but I'll check after dinner." Michelle winked at me. "If we can't find the flash drive, I'll email you the same pictures I sent my husband. You're right; her shots of the little Galapagos penguins were National Geographic-quality."

"And we haven't seen the photos from this morning yet, with the hammerhead shark," I said. "Those should be fabulous." *And where is Laurel?*

Every night before dinner, the cruise director held a briefing, with maps and slides outlining what we could expect to see and do the next day. The cruise director and guides also answered questions and identified wildlife sighted during the current day.

When Deborah and Michelle headed downstairs to the briefing, I excused myself. "Save me a place; I'll be right there," I assured my grandmother. "After I do a quick search for Laurel."

I strolled by the pool, located on the other side of the ship from where we'd stood to view the sunset. With the sundown, the sky was dimming, but no artificial lights had yet been turned on. The pool area was abandoned except for a teenage couple, huddled together on a lounge chair, sharing slobbery kisses. I averted my eyes and kept walking.

I entered the stairwell and walked one floor down to the piano bar. The grand piano stood silent, and only one middle-aged man nursed a beer at the bar. I caught the eye of the bartender, Gonzo, and he set a cocktail napkin in front of me.

"What was that drink Laurel ordered last night? I think it started with a 'p'." I'd learned from Laurel that the way to get Gonzo to open up was to talk about cocktails.

Gonzo grinned. "A *pisco* sour. From Peru. Want one? You'll sleep good tonight."

I shook my head. "Maybe later. Have you seen Laurel?"

"Not since last night. But maybe she's with Señor Roberts."

"Jim Roberts?" *What would Laurel be doing with Jim Roberts?* "Nice looking man in his forties from Texas? Traveling with his family?"

Gonzo nodded. "He was looking for her earlier. But his family wasn't with him."

I thanked Gonzo and moved away from the bar to continue my search. *Why would Jim Roberts be looking for Laurel?* Another floor down and I'd reached the main deck. I peered through the windows of the restaurant. It was not yet open, but the staff scurried about, preparing for the dinner service. Before entering the auditorium, I poked my head into the tiny library; it was also empty.

When I arrived in the auditorium, the briefing had not yet begun, and the passengers compared notes of the day's activities. No Laurel.

I passed some of the other people who'd been on my snorkeling trip. Someone else had seen a shark. I wondered if it was the same one Laurel and I had seen.

"Did you get a photo?" I asked.

The man shook his head. "Swam by too fast."

"We saw it, too, and I think Laurel got a good shot." My eyes swept the room for my friend. Still no sign of her.

I slid into the seat Michelle had saved for me. Deborah had gone to the front row to sit with her roommate, Sue. Sue must feel better now, but if she'd come down with a bug, as Deborah had said, I didn't want to get close to her. I was glad Michelle hadn't stayed with Deborah.

A hush fell over the room as the cruise director began the briefing.

Elena Torres, one of the Ecuadorian guides, gave a presentation about giant tortoises to prepare us for the reserve we'd visit in the morning, on San Cristóbal. "This is Tío Armando," she said proudly as the slide of a tortoise the size of a Volkswagen appeared. "He's over one hundred years old and is the last of his subspecies."

After a collective sigh of despair from the audience, Helga Brüder, a middle-aged Swiss woman who always seemed to have a question or a comment for the guides, raised her hand. "What about Lonesome George?"

"He passed away in 2012 at the Darwin Research Station, the last of the Pinta Island subspecies. Efforts to breed George were unsuccessful. We're hoping for better results with Tio Armando."

"If he's the last one, isn't it too late to breed him?" asked Peter Lane, one of two Air Canada flight attendants.

"No. They can pair him with a similar sub-species to keep his DNA in the gene pool." Elena pointed a laser at the image on the slide. "Tio Armando is missing a toe on his left front foot. We're not sure how it happened, because it was that way when he was found on Floreana last year."

"Does it hurt him?" asked one twin.

"It doesn't seem to slow him down." Elena smiled at the image of the famous tortoise.

Out of the corner of my eye, I spotted a latecomer enter the room. The woman—not Laurel—slipped into a seat on the back row. The giggling teens who had tarried by the pool sneaked in behind her.

"Will we see some of the breeding areas tomorrow?" I heard Helga ask.

I turned my attention back to Elena.

"Absolutely." Elena went on to explain the conservation efforts being made in the Galapagos to slow the disappearance of more endangered species. She warned there were several other threatened subspecies of tortoises, and most of them were being bred and raised on reserves because they could no longer survive in unprotected areas.

I surveyed the room again, searching for Laurel as Elena droned on.

"The two main types of tortoise shells you'll see on this voyage are the dome and the saddleback." I glanced back at the screen as Elena highlighted each example with her laser pointer. "The tortoises who live on the larger islands where there is more rain have dome-shaped shells. The saddleback is smaller and lives in a drier climate."

"Tortoises are Laurel's thing," I whispered to Michelle. "If she's on this ship, she'd be in this briefing, taking over the discussion."

Michelle nodded. "But . . ."

"We know she's not sick in her cabin. I think something's happened to her. We have to tell someone."

CHAPTER FIVE

When the briefing was over, Michelle and I approached Daniel Ramos, the cruise director and main lecturer aboard the *Archipelago Explorer*. Black-haired and tall, Daniel projected a wisdom beyond his thirty-seven years, more like a professor than a cruise director. The son of a diplomat who'd lived all over the world, Daniel could converse articulately in six languages about Darwin's explorations, the theory of evolution, and global climate change.

"Excuse me, Daniel." I tapped his shoulder and he turned to focus his dark brown eyes on my face.

"Yes, Giovanna?" Although Ecuadorian by birth, Daniel spoke English with a British accent, the product of an Oxford education.

I lowered my voice and Michelle closed in to shield us from other passengers waiting to talk to Daniel. "I'm concerned about a guest."

Daniel pushed his glasses up his aquiline nose. "Which guest? What is the problem?"

"Laurel Pardo. I haven't seen her since this morning."

As I related the snorkeling incident, Daniel's jaw slackened, and his eyes widened.

When I'd finished, he shook his head. "That is unacceptable. The guides must keep a close eye on the guests at all times, use the buddy system, and account for everyone before leaving the area. No exceptions." He touched my shoulder. "I'm so sorry for your experience. You must have been terrified. I'll have a talk with the guides." He frowned and stroked his clean-shaven chin. "You're sure another boat didn't pick up Laurel? We use a tag locator system, and when we set sail, it showed everyone back on board."

I told Daniel how I'd witnessed Fernando turning Laurel's tag over himself, saying he knew Laurel was back on board and had forgotten to check herself in.

Daniel's eyes popped. "*Fernando* turned over Laurel's tag?"

I felt a stab of guilt at my betrayal of Fernando, but Laurel's life was at stake. "One of the other guests, Deborah Holt, said Laurel phoned her this afternoon and said she wasn't feeling well, so we figured she must be back on board. But then when we returned from our hike, we stopped by her cabin, and she wasn't in there." I described the ransacked appearance of Laurel's room without admitting I'd gone in to snoop. "She wasn't upstairs for cocktail hour, I couldn't find her in any of the public rooms, and she didn't come to the briefing."

"This is disturbing." Daniel put a hand on my shoulder again. "Thank you for telling me this. I'll speak to the guides. We'll find out for sure if Laurel Pardo is on board, and what happened out there. If we don't locate her, I'll notify the park police."

It was windy on the upper deck, so Michelle and I opted to eat in the dining room. The brightly lit restaurant bustled with diners by the time we arrived.

"Do you think talking to Daniel did any good?" I asked.

"We've done all we can for now," said Michelle. "Daniel will follow through."

"Good evening my favorite American ladies, Michelle and Giovanna." Eduardo, the gracious *maître d'hôtel*, winked. Round and almost bald except for a gray fringe above his starched collar, Eduardo fit the image of a benevolent grandfather. He escorted us to a table by the window. "Tonight's wine is my favorite Cabernet from Chile. You like?" When I nodded, he continued, "I'll have the waiter bring two glasses over to your table."

While we perused the dinner menu, the Roberts family walked in, everyone looking crisp and fresh. Janice had teased her blond hair into a bouffant style that Michelle had once nicknamed "Dallas hair." The twins wore identical cotton sundresses with a tiny floral pattern. I waved, but the family continued past our table and went to sit with Dieter Brüder, the Swiss businessman who'd ridden on our Zodiac that afternoon, and his wife, the inquisitive Helga.

Eduardo's Chilean wine had a smooth, rich taste. As I sipped it, I eyed the Roberts family, displaying all the trappings of wealth and achievement. "Jim Roberts, successful CEO, can't bother talking to a failed entrepreneur."

Michelle rolled her eyes. "At twenty-five, you're not old enough to be a failed anything."

I fiddled with my menu, even though I'd already decided what to have for dinner. "I was too embarrassed to tell you what happened with the clinic."

The waiter appeared at that moment to take our food orders.

When he had gone, Michelle looked at me, her eyes filled with compassion. "I was so impressed that you gave up a lucrative accounting job to pursue your passion. You've wanted to help animals since you were a little girl."

I snickered. "And look how it ended up."

"I'm sorry. I knew you'd lost your whole investment. You and Tim built that beautiful, state-of-the-art spay/neuter clinic, and then for it to close after only six months... How devastating." Michelle lowered her voice, "And I know about the IRS."

I pressed my fingers against my forehead. Just thinking about that fiasco gave me a migraine. "If that were all . . ."

"Good evening, ladies." Elena Torres touched the chair next to Michelle. "Do you mind if I join you?"

The guides often mingled with the guests, so Elena's gesture was not unusual. Michelle turned to me as if to grant veto power. I'd been trying for weeks to talk to her about the events leading to the loss of my clinic and the break-up of my engagement, but the timing was never right.

"Have a seat, Elena," I said with a forced smile. "Tell us more about Tio Armando."

Elena sat down. "Are you enjoying the cruise?"

"Except for a little scare on the snorkel trip this morning," I replied, picking up my wine glass again.

"Scare? What do you mean?"

I told her about almost being left behind in Gardner Bay. Elena gasped.

"I still haven't seen Laurel. Did she get on your boat?"

Elena's face stiffened. "My boat?"

"She wasn't on ours." I set down my glass without having taken a sip.

Elena grabbed a menu and scrutinized it. "I don't think so."

"You don't *think* so?"

"She wasn't on my boat. I haven't seen her since this morning."

"She wasn't on your boat, she wasn't on ours. What if she's still out there?"

Elena dropped the menu. "No. That can't be."

The waiter strolled over to take Elena's order. She chatted with him in Spanish. I didn't understand what they were saying, but I theorized they were discussing at length the preparation of each of the specialties.

While we waited for our food, Elena launched into a story she'd told us before, about working on a tortoise reserve as a teenager and then becoming a naturalist guide for cruise ships. I couldn't steer the conversation back to Laurel's disappearance. It was almost like she was avoiding the subject.

The meals came, and Elena chattered on, with Michelle feigning interest and cuing her politely. I focused on my food, and my mind wandered back to Georgia. Jerome had drained our accounts and taken off. What a mess I still had to deal with. And with no help from Tim.

The waiter brought dessert menus, but I passed, and then excused myself to take a walk outside for some fresh sea air and stargazing. I wasn't sure I could trust Elena any more than I could trust Fernando.

On the top deck, I stared over the rail at the dark ocean and inhaled the cooking smells from the Ocean Grill mingled with the salty scent of sea life. The warm breeze blew my hair across my face. Whitecaps, glistening in the moonlight, slapped the side of the ship as it cut through the water. The beauty of the night mocked my melancholy mood.

I'd always wanted to visit the Galapagos, the perfect destination for someone who loves animals and yearns for exotic travel. When my grandmother suggested a trip, it had been easy to convince her we should come here. But the demons I was trying to escape had hitchhiked all the way from Georgia, and now those stowaways were trying to surface again.

Talking to someone would be a salve if I could get past the shame. I'd almost reached the point where I could tell Laurel. But where was she now? I knew I should talk to Michelle. Michelle would understand if she'd sit down long enough to listen. I'd thought this trip would give us that time, but so far, we'd filled almost every minute.

"Have you seen the Southern Cross?" Fernando appeared beside me. Even my thoughts got interrupted.

Startled, I turned to face him. He did not appear angry, so Daniel must not have spoken to the guides yet about Laurel's absence. What was he waiting for? A woman could be marooned on an uninhabited island.

"Look here." Fernando pointed toward the sky. His other hand grazed my cheek and turned my head so I could view the famous constellation.

"This is the first time I've seen it," I admitted. "I've never been south of the equator before."

"Interesting thing about being almost right on the equator: you'll also recognize some of the constellations you're used to seeing in the Northern Hemisphere." Fernando touched my arm. "Look over there—the Big Dipper."

I smiled. "I'm not used to seeing so many stars. In any constellations."

"We're lucky to have such a clear night."

We stood side by side at the rail for a while, gazing at the glowing stars, identifying constellations, and listening to the lapping waves.

"Where's your mother?" Fernando asked. "You're usually together."

Ever since I moved in with Michelle at age eleven, most people had assumed we were mother and daughter. Neither of us rushed to correct them. At first, it bothered me, but as the years passed, I'd grown to view Michelle as a surrogate mother. "She was still in the dining room when I came out here, but she's probably gone back to the cabin by now to read."

Fernando covered my hand with his. "The night is young." His profile looked exquisite in the starlight, and I again felt remorseful for reporting his actions to Daniel. Perhaps Fernando believed Laurel came back on board.

"But I'm exhausted." I pulled my hand away and stepped back to reclaim my personal space. "You keep us busy. Snorkeling, hiking, kayaking, lectures." I sensed him moving closer again. What is it with some men?

Fernando filled the new gap I'd created between us. "You always seem to have plenty of energy." He touched my hand again. His long, thick fingers felt warm and protective.

Our eyes met, and this time I didn't move away. He was trying to seduce me, and I was enjoying it, like a shameful binge of junk food. "What time tomorrow morning do we leave for the tortoise reserve?" My question was filler; the daily program would indicate the time.

His face had grown closer. He was attractive to women and he knew it. Like a lion stalking a wounded antelope, he must smell my vulnerability. "Don't worry. I'll wake you up." His lips brushed mine.

This is wrong on so many levels, I thought, yet my lips clung to his like a magnet. His arms went around me, and he stroked my hair. He pressed his body against me, and I felt him grow hard.

We kissed again. Our tongues danced while his fingers massaged my spine. His mouth tasted of alcohol masked in peppermint. I didn't miss Tim as much as I missed *this*.

As we leaned together against the rail, his taut body covering mine like a blanket, I stared at the churning dark ocean below. At any minute I could bend over too far, swept up by passion, and plunge to my death, my body swallowed into the sea. I flashed back to that morning when I was treading water and panicking as I watched the Zodiacs head back to the ship without me.

I broke away from Fernando. "Do you do this every week?"

His brown eyes searched my face. "You're on vacation. Why not have some fun?"

I pulled back farther, in control of my hormones again. "Believe me, I'm having plenty of fun."

He put both hands on the rail, changing tactics. "That's our goal. Customer service."

A flock of frigate birds soared overhead. I'd learned to recognize them by the males' fluorescent red throats—those throats that inflated like balloons during the courting process. Even in the darkness, I could make out the glow of their red throats. "Why did you flip Laurel's tag over this morning? Are you sure she got back on board?"

Fernando's smile faded.

"Because I haven't seen her since we were out snorkeling." I gripped the rail and remembered Laurel's empty room in disarray. What was that about? Out the corner of my eye, I glimpsed one of the Roberts twins materialize from behind a wall, and then dart back, holding down the skirt of her sundress in the breeze.

Fernando turned my face toward him, his touch rougher this time. "Laurel shouldn't stick her nose where it doesn't belong."

"What do you mean?" My heart pounded.

He dropped his hand from my chin. His eyes were ablaze, no longer amorous. "And neither should you."

I backed away, still gripping the rail.

Fernando lunged after me.

"What are you—" I coiled myself into a defensive position.

He stopped, distracted by something behind him, and I ran toward the stairwell.

I didn't look back as I dashed inside and let the door slam behind me. I bounded down the stairs toward the safety of civilization.

Michelle and Elena left the dining room together. Michelle thanked Elena for her company and said she wanted to stop in the ship's library to search for a new book to read before bed.

"Is Giovanna okay?" asked Elena.

Michelle smiled. "She's just worried about her friend Laurel. She hasn't seen her since they got separated from the snorkel group this morning."

"I'm sure Laurel's fine." Elena nodded and waved goodnight.

When Michelle reached the library, the door was unlocked but the light was off. She stepped inside and fumbled along the wall for the switch. It wasn't where she thought it should be, so she moved to the other side of the door to search.

She glimpsed a glow from the screen of a desktop computer across the room. Then movement. She took a step forward. "Hello?"

Something heavy struck the back of her head. She felt the weight of it more than the pain as she crumpled to the floor.

CHAPTER SIX

My grandmother had not yet returned to our cabin. Michelle must have stopped by the ship's library after dinner; she'd already finished the paperback detective novel she'd brought with her. But the library on the *Archipelago Explorer* was not large, and the selection of recreational reading material in English, Italian, or French was limited. We still needed to look at Laurel's flash drive, to see if there was anything on it besides the wildlife photos Michelle had copied, anything that might provide a clue to Laurel's disappearance. I wished my grandmother would hurry.

I unplugged my smartphone from its charger, stretched out on the bed, and logged onto the ship's internet connection. I typed the words, "*Second Wind*" into the Google search bar and waited for the images to appear. My blood boiled every time I saw that outrageous toy.

Next, I tried "Jerome Haddad." Nothing new since my last search.

I checked my Facebook feed and Connie Haddad's profile page. *My dear friend, Connie. Not!* No new posts since yesterday. That stupid selfie of her grinning, waving from the deck of the yacht. There'd been a video, too, but it had cut off. Perhaps it never fully uploaded. I closed Facebook.

I paused, then typed the name "Laurel Pardo" into Google. The search returned a LinkedIn account, a Facebook page, and a profile for a screenwriter named Laurel Pardo whom I'd never met. And about twenty years older than the Laurel I knew. I logged off and set down my phone.

I grabbed the remote from the nightstand and turned on the flat-screen television. As I scrolled through the list of on-demand movies, nothing appealed to me. I settled for a chick flick I'd seen before. I rose and began disrobing for bed.

The desk phone rang.

"Don't freak out," Deborah Holt said. "I'm with Michelle in the infirmary."

"What—?"

"We're on Deck Two. Not sure what's up. I came down here for an aspirin and then someone from the front desk brought her in."

"Be right there." I hung up the phone, switched off the television, and threw my clothes back on.

I hurried downstairs to the tiny onboard infirmary. The area comprised an office, an examination room, and a waiting area, all emitting a trace medicinal smell.

Michelle lay on a hospital-style bed covered in white sheets in the sterile-looking examination room.

I rushed to her side and grabbed my grandmother's hand. "Michelle, what happened?"

Michelle blinked. She was awake but groggy, and otherwise unhurt. "I'm not sure. I was looking for the light switch." She closed her eyes.

I turned to Deborah. "Who found her? Who brought her here?"

Deborah shrugged. "One of those sheilas from the front desk. Julia, maybe?"

"Where's the doctor? What did he say?"

On cue, the ship's doctor entered the room, clipboard in hand. Perhaps of Indian origin, he was tall, thin, and clean-shaven. Michelle was the only patient in the infirmary. "There's no evidence of a concussion, Señora DePalma," he confirmed. "You might feel some soreness tomorrow, but otherwise, you should be fine. But please let me know if you experience any dizziness or nausea in the next twenty-four hours."

I turned to the doctor. "What happened to her?"

He tapped his clipboard. "We're not sure. She was in the library, and it appears a book must have fallen from a shelf and hit her in the back of the head. The lady who found her didn't see what happened, but she said there was a large hardback book lying on the floor next to her."

"Who found her?"

"I believe it was one of our pursers who works at the front desk, Julia Alvarez. Julia is the one who walked her down here."

"Can I talk to Julia?" I asked. "Do you know if she's still on duty?"

"Can I get out of here first?" Michelle looked at the doctor. "You said I could go?"

The doctor nodded. "I don't see why not. You'll be more comfortable in your own cabin. But please take it easy for the rest of the night."

"I'll make sure she stays out of the disco," I quipped, as Deborah and I helped Michelle out of the hospital bed.

"A book hit you on the back of the head? It just jumped off the shelf?" I unlocked the door to our cabin. "Sounds fishy."

Michelle shook her head. She winced. "I didn't see what happened. It was dark, and I was trying to find the light switch." She sank onto the bed. "But I sensed someone was in the library."

"Someone else was in the library? Who?"

"I couldn't see." Michelle puckered her brow. "I don't know what gave me the idea someone was there: a glow from the computer monitor, a breath, a page turning. And I smelled tobacco smoke."

"Smoke? In the library? What kind of smoke? Cigarette? Cigar? Pipe?" I tried to remember which passengers and crew I'd seen smoking.

"Not someone smoking, but someone who had recently smoked. Cigarettes, I think. You know how the odor clings to your clothes? But before I had time to think about it, something hit me." She reached into her pocket, moved her hand around, then plunged deeper. She checked the other pocket and then looked up at me.

The color drained from Michelle's face. "Laurel's flash drive is gone."

CHAPTER SEVEN

I convinced Michelle to crawl into bed to recuperate. I fluffed her down pillow, pulled the starched white sheet up to her chin, and tucked her in.

As soon as my grandmother closed her eyes, I tiptoed out of the cabin and headed to the front desk. The young woman on duty told me Julia would return at eight in the morning. "Did anyone turn in a flash drive?" I asked.

The woman looked perplexed, so I had to draw a picture with gestures to explain.

The woman shook her head. I wasn't sure if her negative response meant she had not seen the flash drive, or that she still didn't understand what it was.

The ship's library was located next to the lobby. Dare I? I felt like a Gothic heroine warned, "Whatever you do, don't go into that room!"

Gothic heroine at heart, I approached the library.

The beveled glass door stood open, the overhead lights were illuminated, and a steward vacuumed the carpeted floor. A faint odor of furniture polish lingered in the air. I tapped the steward's shoulder.

With a flinch, he turned off the vacuum cleaner and gave me his attention.

"Excuse me, did you find a flash drive on the floor?"

The steward seemed as perplexed as the receptionist had been.

"You know, a jump drive?"

He still looked perplexed, so I launched into my pantomime, hoping my acting skills had improved since my last attempt. He seemed to understand what I meant, but he, too, shook his head no.

"Do you mind if I look around? My grandmother was in here earlier, and she lost one. This was the last place she had it." As I spoke, I realized the flash drive could have also fallen out at the infirmary.

The book that had clobbered Michelle must have been re-shelved; it was no longer lying on the floor. I studied the collection. Which tome had been the weapon? There was a rather thick Spanish-English dictionary. The hardcover copy of Charles Darwin's *On the Origin of Species: The Illustrated Edition* looked hefty. A compilation of Darwin's correspondence looked even heavier. Did the book used to fell my grandmother have any significance at all?

I searched the floor on my hands and knees, poked my head under the table and chairs, shoved my hand under the lips of the wooden bookshelves. My fingers touched a spider web that made me recoil.

The steward crouched and joined me in the hunt.

No luck.

The steward went back to his vacuuming.

I remembered Michelle had mentioned seeing a glow from the monitor of a desktop computer nestled in an alcove. Perhaps her attacker had been using the computer, and Michelle startled him? *But why? Guests could use the library's computer. Unless he didn't want anyone to see him.*

I stood up and walked to the computer. The monitor lit when I touched the keyboard. Google was the home page. The cache had been cleared. I rummaged around the desk area for notes or papers left behind and noticed the computer's USB port was empty. I sat at the desk, picked up the mouse, and examined the programs, trash folder, hard drive, and temporary files. The last document displayed had come from a network drive. It looked like it could be a passenger list, but it required a password for access. Nothing I could guess worked.

At a dead end, I thanked the steward and left.

I stood in the lobby and contemplated my next move. The infirmary. Or perhaps I should check the restaurant, which was on this floor. Maybe the flash drive had fallen out of Michelle's pocket before she even reached the library.

The restaurant had closed, and Eduardo was just leaving. His wide lips spread into a big, friendly grin. "Señorita Giovanna."

"Good evening again, Eduardo. Do you know if anyone found a flash drive in the restaurant this evening?" I started my pantomime.

His brow furrowed. "No one turned anything in. Would you like to go back inside and look for it?"

"If you don't mind."

"Anything for you, Señorita Giovanna."

He unlocked the door to the restaurant and escorted me inside.

I checked under and around the table where Michelle and I had sat for dinner. Nothing.

"What is it you're looking for?" asked Eduardo. He ran his fingers through the gray fringe of hairs at the back of his bald head.

"A flash drive with pictures on it. It belongs to one of the other passengers."

"Pictures?"

"Yes, from our snorkeling trips."

"Oh. You don't take your own pictures?"

"I do, but Laurel's are so much better than mine."

"Laurel?"

"Laurel Pardo. The wildlife researcher we were eating with yesterday."

Eduardo nodded. "Yes, I know Laurel. One of our back-to-back passengers. She was on the cruise last week."

"Speaking of Laurel, have you seen her this evening?"

Eduardo smoothed his silver mustache. "Not since breakfast, early this morning. She was sitting with the guides at that table in the corner." He nodded toward the location. "The discussion seemed heated. In fact, I even went to their table to see what was going on, but they told me everything was fine. They were getting ready to go snorkeling, I think."

I shivered. The air conditioning was colder when the dining room was not full of people. "Did you hear what they were talking about?"

He shook his bald head. "I try to stay out of it."

There was no reason to keep Eduardo any longer from his bed. I moved toward the door. "Thank you so much for letting me look around."

We exited, and he locked the restaurant door behind us. "I hope you find what you're looking for."

When I arrived in the infirmary, I could see the doctor talking to another patient in the examination room. From what I could decipher, Peter Lane, one of two Air Canada flight attendants, had a bad sunburn and was asking for a remedy. I waited until the doctor finished with Peter and sent him on his way with an antibiotic cream.

The doctor looked up to acknowledge me. "How is your grandmother?"

"She's in bed. I think she'll be fine," I replied. "But she had a flash drive in her pocket earlier, and now it's gone. Did anything fall from her clothing?"

The doctor thought for a moment. "It wasn't necessary for her to undress for the exam, so I doubt it."

"Do you mind if I look around and see if she might have dropped it?"

"Sure, be my guest." The doctor looked at the floor, then back at me. "But might she have given this item to her friend?"

"Her friend?"

"The red-haired woman who called you. She was here when you arrived to check on your grandmother."

"Oh, Deborah." I recalled that Deborah had asked about Laurel's photos earlier. Maybe Deborah took the flash drive. Maybe Michelle even gave it to her and then forgot.

Empty-handed after my search for Laurel's flash drive, I climbed the stairs back to my floor and turned down the hall toward my cabin. *What if the person in the library attacked Michelle for the flash drive? But who knew she had it? And what was on that device to make someone attack a harmless senior citizen?*

A click jolted me from my trance. I looked up as Laurel's door closed.

I rushed down the hall and tapped on Laurel's cabin door. "Laurel? Laurel, are you in there?" I knocked again. "Laurel? It's Giovanna. I just want to know you're okay."

There was no response. I pressed an ear to the wooden door. Silence. Was it just my imagination?

The next morning, we rose at seven to allow enough time for breakfast in the dining room. We were scheduled to board the Zodiacs for the tortoise reserve on San Cristóbal at eight. While getting ready, I recounted my fruitless quest for the flash drive the night before. I eyed Michelle. "The doctor seemed to think you gave the flash drive to Deborah."

Michelle frowned. "I don't think so. Did Deborah even know I had it with me?"

"I don't know. But remember yesterday afternoon? She said she wanted to borrow it."

At the door to the dining room, Eduardo greeted us. His eyes twinkled. "Same table, ladies?"

"Why not?" said Michelle.

"Coffee?"

"Sounds great," I replied. "Thank you."

We sat in the same spot where we'd dined the night before. I made another search under the table for the flash drive in case I'd missed it last night.

"I wonder what Daniel found out after he talked to the guides." As I rose from the floor and eased back into my chair, my eyes made a cursory scan of the room for Laurel.

A white-jacketed waiter poured steaming coffee into our cups.

I added a generous portion of cream to my coffee and then poured cream into Michelle's cup before setting the pitcher back on the table. "Want me to fix you a plate?"

"Thanks. Just yogurt and fruit this morning, please." Michelle unfolded the daily program.

As I returned from the buffet with our food, Julia stopped by the table. Tall, thin, and bespectacled, she looked like she could be Daniel's sister. She wore a crisp white shirt, black straight skirt, and black pumps. Julia put her hand on Michelle's shoulder. "How are you feeling this morning, Señora De-Palma?"

Michelle blinked. "I should fall more often. Look at all the attention I get."

I set down our plates: a colorful array of fruits around a bowl of plain yogurt for Michelle, and a hot Ecuadorian breakfast of fried fish, hominy, and plantains for me. "Do you want some guayaba juice? I'm getting a glass."

Michelle eyed her breakfast. "No, thanks, honey. I have enough fruit on my plate."

I looked at Julia. "The doctor said you found my grand-mother last night and took her to the infirmary. Thank you. Can you tell me what happened?"

Julia shuddered. "I went to lock up the library for the night. When I turned on the light, there she was, sprawled on the carpet. I didn't see what happened."

"Was there a book on the floor near her?"

Julia twisted her fine facial features in thought. "I think it was that *Smithsonian Natural History* book. It's big. I didn't pay attention to the title. Señora DePalma seemed stunned, so I helped her up and insisted we go to the infirmary."

"Did you see anyone else around? Anyone leaving?"

Again, Julia looked thoughtful. "Not that I noticed."

"Do books often fall off the shelves in the library?"

"Maybe during bad storms."

Julia glanced at her watch. I couldn't think of any more questions at the moment, even though I doubted I had the whole story.

We gathered in the auditorium with our fellow tourists, waiting for the guides to assign us into groups to go ashore in the Zodiacs. Deborah Holt and her roommate, Sue Plunkett, were talking with a French family when Michelle and I walked in.

Laurel was nowhere to be found.

Deborah broke away from her group and rushed over. "Michelle, I'm so glad to see you up and about. How are you feeling?"

Michelle held out her arms and made a partial twirl.

"Deborah," I began. "Last night, did you—"

"Oh, excuse me, I have to—" Sue had waved Deborah back to their cluster.

The Roberts family entered, everyone decked out in the latest sporting gear, like they were off on a photographic safari. Janice smiled as they took seats next to Michelle and me. She had perfect teeth like her husband and daughters. A hint of shadow under Janice's sapphire blue eyes suggested not enough beauty sleep.

Janice touched Michelle's shoulder. "Michelle, how are you feeling this morning? I heard you were in the infirmary last night."

Michelle rolled her eyes. "No secrets on this boat."

I studied Janice. "How did you find out?"

Janice looked at her daughters, then her eyes swept the crowd. "Someone mentioned it at breakfast. What happened?"

Michelle sighed. "I stopped by the library to look for a good book to read before bed, and the next thing I knew, someone hit me on the back of the head."

Janice gasped. "You're kidding."

"I don't know what happened," Michelle conceded. "I woke up on the floor, and then someone led me down to the infirmary. They think a book fell off the shelf and hit me."

"A book fell on your head?" Jim had entered the conversation. "How does a book fall off the shelf and hit someone?"

"With help," I replied.

"But why?" asked Janice. "Why would anyone want to hurt Michelle?"

More guests had overheard and joined the conversation. Michelle had to retell the story at least three times, and each version grew more dramatic. Speculation abounded.

Someone looked at a watch. It was five minutes past eight o'clock, with no sign of Daniel or the guides. With the itinerary's tight schedule, they valued punctuality.

One of the Brazilian women had brought an illustrated book on tortoises which she passed around, drawing appreciative remarks from the other guests. I scanned the room again and noted Laurel still was not present. I no longer believed Laurel was on the ship. *But what happened to her? And why does no one care? Or even acknowledge she's missing? And who went into her cabin last night?*

At eight-fifteen, the crowd grew agitated. People shook their watches, compared times, rechecked the daily program. Someone stepped into the hall to see if any of the guides were on their way.

The talk became more restless. One of the French passengers mentioned that tortoises are most active in the morning, and it would be a shame to miss seeing the animals foraging.

At eight-thirty, Daniel appeared. A hush fell over the room as we all gave our attention to the cruise director. "Ladies and gentlemen, we're sorry for the delay, but I'm afraid we won't be able to go ashore for several more hours."

Several passengers started to speak at once.

Daniel held up his hand. "There's coffee and juice in here, so please make yourselves comfortable. Most of you ate breakfast already, but if you're hungry, the dining room is still open."

"Why are we being detained?" shouted Helga Brüder. "The seas are not too rough to disembark."

Daniel wiped his brow. "We've had a death on board. The police are on their way."

CHAPTER EIGHT

Everyone spoke at once, and soon the room buzzed like a hive of angry bees. Passengers fired questions at Daniel, who waved his arms like a conductor to quiet the cacophony. "I'm sorry, but I can't give you any information right now. When the police arrive, they'll share more."

"Why can't you tell us anything?" demanded Helga. "Why are the police coming?"

Daniel acknowledged her but did not respond. He turned to answer an easier question from another passenger.

I looked at Michelle and mouthed, "Laurel?" Had they found her body?

"Do the police have to come on board whenever there's a death at sea?" asked Sue, to no one in particular. "Who died?"

"I don't see that elderly Italian couple," said Deborah. "The husband was having a hard time breathing yesterday." The old man hunched over when he walked, as if every move was painful, and getting him to and from shore in the Zodiacs was challenging for the guides. I wondered why he and his wife insisted on participating in all the shore activities.

"If we're delayed getting to the tortoise reserve this morning, how will that affect our afternoon hike at Punta Pitt?" Helga asked Daniel.

"Once the police get here and start their questioning, I'll know more about any itinerary changes we may have to make," Daniel replied.

"Itinerary changes?" asked Dieter. His whole face scrunched into a frown.

"Questioning?" asked Jim. "Who will the police be questioning?"

Daniel held up his hand. "Patience, please. I'll give you more information as soon as it's available." He started for the door. "Now, if you'll excuse me, I think the police boat has arrived."

Murmurs rippled through the crowd in multiple languages, "Who's dead?" "What happened?"

"How tragic! What a nightmare."

"What if it wasn't natural causes? Why else would the police be here?"

Some of the guests scrutinized each other, some counted heads. None of the staff was in the room, except for one of the Ecuadorian kitchen workers, who came in, refilled the coffee pot, and set out a tray of sweet rolls.

I spotted the elderly Italian couple Deborah had mentioned.

"I haven't seen Laurel Pardo since yesterday morning, when we were snorkeling in Gardner Bay," I said to Helga. She had been walking around the room in circles, counting to herself in German.

"Laurel Pardo?" Recognition flickered across Helga's wrinkled face. "You're right, I don't see her. Where is she?"

"We were snorkeling together yesterday, and I never saw her get back on the ship."

Helga stuck out her lower lip. "Now that you mention it, I haven't seen her since yesterday morning, either. I looked for her at the lecture last night, but I never thought something might be wrong." Her head swiveled around the room. "I wanted to sit with her on the bus to the tortoise reserve today. She knows so much about these animals."

When Dieter walked over, Helga switched to rapid German to fill him in.

Rafael, one of the Ecuadorian guides, appeared. Usually a flirt around the younger women on the ship, he walked stone-faced to the audiovisual equipment and inserted a DVD. The lights dimmed and a National Geographic film about the

Galapagos projected against the blank white wall that served as the screen. He turned up the volume and hurried out of the room.

The film helped quell the noise, but not the speculation. I could hear passengers continue to whisper and theorize and complain.

One twin sobbed in her mother's arms. The other girl laid her head on her father's shoulder and stared at the movie. I studied them. *Why is that teenager so upset? Is she such a spoiled brat that she's crying because we're not going ashore yet?*

The film was interesting, with brilliant photography of animals we'd already seen, and more that we hoped to see. But it smacked of homework, preparation for the voyage. *Why watch a film when we're right here? I want to go out and look at this stuff.*

I found it hard to focus on the images filling the screen. The nature film was a babysitter for the passengers while the crew dealt with the police and the fallout for their negligence. What would Fernando have to say for himself? I tried to imagine how the scenario would play out. Would the police arrest him for involuntary manslaughter? What about Daniel? What about Elena? She was the guide on the other boat yesterday. The boat that didn't pick up Laurel.

Perhaps the whole crew and the cruise line itself would be held liable. They might have to cancel the cruise en route. *No.* I stopped that train of thought. *What am I thinking? Laurel is dead! I can't feel guilty about exposing those responsible.*

Someone hit the pause button on the remote, and the image of a giant tortoise remained frozen on the wall. The overhead lights came on. Daniel walked into the room.

"Ladies and gentlemen, thank you so much for your patience. This is a difficult situation for us."

Daniel held up his hand as passengers bombarded him with inquiries.

"The police are ready to begin questioning the passengers," Daniel continued. "They will interview you one at a time.

They'll need to know your whereabouts and activities last night. Please answer their questions."

Daniel adjusted his glasses, the only hint of the stress he must be feeling. "When you've finished your interview, please congregate in the dining room, where we have some snacks prepared for you. The bar will be open. Please don't come back to this room or speak with anyone who has not talked to the police yet. They have asked that you not compromise the investigation by trying to coordinate your stories."

"Why? Do we need an alibi?" demanded Dieter. "What for?"

"Are you saying the police are investigating a homicide?" Jim's tanned face had paled.

Before Daniel could answer, two uniformed police officers entered the room. The weapons holstered on their hips commanded respect. The older officer, who appeared to be in charge, came forward as if to address the crowd, then deferred to Daniel. I wondered if the officer feared public speaking or felt unsure of his English proficiency.

Daniel took control. "This is Detective Juan Estevez." He introduced the older officer. "And Detective Victor Zuniga." The younger man made a slight bow. His luscious black hair and sculpted good looks made him look more like a TV detective than a real police officer. "These officers will conduct their interviews in the library. I'll escort you there one at a time as soon as they're ready for you."

He turned to the shriveled Italian woman who was clinging to her hunched husband. "Señora, please follow the officers if you will."

Detective Victor Zuniga took the Italian woman's arm and led her out of the room.

Before the questions could start again, Daniel pressed the Play button for the film and dimmed the lights.

I fidgeted. Looking around the room, I could see that few passengers paid attention to the film. They squirmed and conjectured as they awaited their interviews. I saw a few people attempt to connect with the outside world using their smartphones, but Wi-Fi and cell service had been disabled.

"I assumed someone had a heart attack," said the Brazilian woman who'd been passing around the book about tortoises. "But the police? What does this mean?"

"I thought it might have been food poisoning," said another woman. "Maybe they want to ask everyone what they ate. You know, I felt a little sick to my stomach last night."

"I don't think the police come on board a cruise ship to investigate food poisoning," remarked another woman.

We all looked at each other with suspicion. How well did we know these people?

Michelle shivered as she remembered her mishap last night in the library. *What was the murder weapon?* she thought. *A blunt object to the head? Was I a potential victim?* She rose and headed for the coffee stand, still laid out with china cups and a shiny carafe. Even amid the chaos, the crew had preserved a luxurious feel to the ship and the guest experience.

Michelle poured herself a cup of coffee and doctored it with a generous portion of cream. She turned to find Jim Roberts behind her, ready to refill his cup. "Your daughters seem upset about this turn of events."

Jim poured coffee into his cup. Michelle offered him the cream pitcher, but he declined. "They were looking forward to seeing the property at Puerto Ayora later in the week. I hope we still stop there. Don't tell them, but that stop was my main reason for booking this itinerary."

"Mixing a little business with pleasure?" Michelle sipped her coffee.

"Have to. They're supposed to break ground for the golf course next week."

Michelle sputtered. "Golf course?" She reached for a napkin to wipe drops of coffee off her mouth.

"Eighteen holes." Jim beamed.

"What about the tortoises? I can't believe the Galapagos National Park Service gave you a permit to put a golf course that close to a reserve."

"Lots of red tape. A few more hurdles to take care of this week if we want to keep the project on schedule."

"I'm sure your place will be lovely," said Michelle. "But the world has so few pristine areas left. The Galapagos Islands are special."

"But there are already towns on several of the islands, including Santa Cruz," argued Jim. "And the resort needs that infrastructure. It will be good for the economy—a win-win."

Michelle sipped her coffee, watching him snap into smooth negotiator mode.

"Responsible tourism is what will keep these islands going for the next generation," he said. "Resorts like Leisure Dreams will bring in wealthy, high-profile travelers who will spread awareness about the delicate ecosystem of the Galapagos, and the unique flora and fauna found nowhere else."

Michelle wondered if Jim were quoting from a brochure his staff had written.

"There are still many unspoiled islands nearby, and we'll arrange day trips and longer excursions to them for our guests, so they can appreciate the wildlife."

"And I trust you've cleared that plan with the park service?"

Jim winked. "Working on it." He stirred a spoonful of sugar into his coffee. "This stuff is strong. I usually take my coffee black." He took a sip. "I have another angle to bring in so much tourist revenue, it'll be hard for them to refuse."

"I'm afraid to ask what that is."

Jim patted her shoulder. "Nothing damaging to the environment, let me assure you."

"Like a golf course?"

He laughed. "You don't stop. But you'll be happy to know we'll conform to the natural landscape wherever possible, and we'll use drought-resistant turf and recycled water."

More brochure talk. Before Michelle could respond, their conversation was interrupted. Kumiko, a middle-aged Japanese nurse, squeezed between them to reach the coffee pot. Kumiko gave a slight bow as Michelle moved away from the table.

Daniel appeared in the doorway again. He caught Michelle's eye and signaled for her to follow him.

Michelle felt her heartbeat quicken as she entered the library. She eyeballed the floor-to-ceiling shelves, wondering which book might have been the culprit that had landed her in the infirmary last night.

The police officers motioned for her to take a seat. She placed a napkin on the desk, and then set down her coffee cup.

"Señora Michelle DePalma?" Detective Zuniga confirmed. "Cabin number 327?"

"Correct."

"Señora, please tell us what you did last night. From about six in the evening until eight o'clock this morning," said Detective Zuniga. He spoke good English with only a slight Ecuadorian accent.

"Last night?" Michelle cleared her throat. Like Giovanna, she had thought the inquiry would be about Laurel's disappearance, which had happened earlier in the day.

"Please. Start at about six o'clock last evening."

Michelle told the officers about attending the briefing with the rest of the passengers, and then having dinner in the restaurant with her granddaughter, Giovanna Rogers, and the guide, Elena Torres. "Oh, and after the briefing, Giovanna and I spoke to Daniel, the cruise director, about our concerns for a missing passenger."

"A missing passenger?" The two officers looked at each other.

"Yes, Laurel. I thought—"

"Laurel?" Detective Zuniga scanned the passenger list.

"I believe her last name is Pardo. Laurel Pardo." Michelle knit her brow. *Isn't this inquiry about Laurel's death? Why do they have to look her up?* "One of the guests. Back-to-back cruising; I heard she was on the previous voyage too. Isn't she—?"

Detective Juan Estevez tapped his pencil at a name on the list.

Detective Zuniga turned to Michelle. "Laurel Pardo is not missing. We interviewed her this morning."

CHAPTER NINE

What? Michelle stared at the police officers. "Laurel Pardo is not missing?"

Detective Zuniga looked at her as if she were a demented old fool.

Michelle gazed at her coffee cup on the table. *Could Giovanna have imagined the whole episode in the water and Laurel's disappearance? No one else on board seems to think Laurel is missing. And now these detectives say they've interviewed her.*

During the first few months after Giovanna moved in with Michelle and Roberto, at age eleven, she had struggled to separate fact from fiction, but Michelle had attributed the twisted truths—and outright lies—to Giovanna's method of coping with the difficult circumstances that had uprooted her life. Michelle was busy dealing with the discovery that she was a biological grandmother, and Roberto was reeling from the shock of meeting new family members.

Giovanna's father had died before she was born, and when her mother went to prison, Giovanna had nowhere to go. Michelle and Roberto were relative strangers, and not used to living with children. Even though Michelle had tried to welcome Giovanna into their home, the child must have sensed she was cramping the couple's carefree lifestyle.

No, thought Michelle. *It's been more than a decade now. Giovanna has grown into a thoughtful, level-headed young woman. She doesn't lie anymore.*

She looked back at the officers, who were waiting for her to finish the accounting of her whereabouts. "Okay, well that solves the mystery. We had no reason to worry." Michelle knew better than to ask the police officers anything about their interview with Laurel. She was the one being questioned. "After dinner, I headed to the library to find a book to read in my cabin."

"You were alone?" Detective Estevez asked. His accent was thick, and it took Michelle a moment to process the question.

As Michelle related her tale, she wondered if her story seemed as improbable to the police officers as some of Giovanna's childhood yarns. It sounded implausible now, even to her.

"Someone hit you over the head?" Zuniga clarified, his whole face a squint. "Do you have any idea why someone might do that? Did you see the person?"

Michelle shrugged and shook her head. She didn't mention Laurel's flash drive.

"What time did this happen?" Zuniga asked.

"After I left the dining room. Around nine."

"And your granddaughter, Giovanna Rogers? Where was she during this incident?"

Michelle studied Detective Zuniga, who seemed to be asking most of the questions, perhaps because he had a better command of the English language. He had intense brown eyes and a small mole on his smooth cheek, a beauty mark if he were female. He wore a neatly pressed khaki uniform and his thick, shiny black hair hung almost to his collar.

"My granddaughter came down to the infirmary, and then we returned to our cabin together."

Estevez whispered something to Zuniga. Detective Estevez appeared to be in his late forties, portly with a thick head of salt-and-pepper hair. The little English he had spoken so far had been heavily accented.

"Señora, where was your granddaughter before she came to the infirmary?" asked Detective Zuniga.

Her first attempt at answering the question about Giovanna's whereabouts must not have satisfied the officers. "Deborah Holt, one of the other passengers who stopped by the infirmary while I was there, reached Giovanna in our cabin by phone."

The two officers conferred again in whispered Spanish. Michelle had studied Spanish in high school, and she spoke fluent French and Italian, so she could get by when traveling in a Spanish-speaking country. But she could not decipher enough of these officers' rapid, muffled jargon to follow their conversation.

"And after you returned from the infirmary?" asked Detective Zuniga, back into English.

"I went to bed and slept until morning." *No need to mention Giovanna going to look for the missing flash drive.*

The crowd in the auditorium thinned as the morning ticked away. The scene brought back memories of middle school, waiting to be chosen for a soccer game, and hoping I wouldn't be last. How had Michelle's interview gone? I wished I could talk to my grandmother, but those who had already been interviewed were kept separate from those yet to have their turn.

I hadn't been able to figure out what system the police were using to question the guests. The order was not alphabetical, nor numerical by cabin. For a while, it appeared they spoke to the older passengers first. They took Michelle. Helga and Dieter Brüder had had their turns. But then the police had interviewed both twins and some of the younger guests. Perhaps the system was random, and they grabbed the person closest to the door when ready for another potential witness.

The film replayed. I was bored. The smell of a fresh pot of coffee made me queasy.

Also, I couldn't bear to watch the footage again describing how many of the boobies who hatch twin chicks abandon one of them to die of starvation, because the food supply could not support raising both. How did a mother choose between her two children?

And the part of the film about the goat eradication project angered me. Even if the goats destroyed native flora and fauna, they had lived on the islands for hundreds of years and had a right to exist, too. *Why does man get to decide which species deserve to live or die?* The islanders' attitude toward goats paralleled public opinion about feral cats in Georgia: vermin, annihilate them. *And how many more cats will be born now, only to die in over-filled shelters, because I lost my spay/neuter clinic?*

I stood up and paced. Although the auditorium was large enough to hold all the guests at once, it felt confining, even as the crowd dwindled. I wanted to sneak into the dining room and talk to Michelle, find out what she'd learned about Laurel's demise.

Deborah Holt and Janice Roberts still awaited their turns, and we'd all run out of casual conversation.

Janice's smile had dimmed, and her face looked tired. "Don't you feel like a wallflower?" Her Texas accent was stronger than I remembered. As Janice picked up her almost-empty coffee cup, her hands shook.

"I can't imagine you as a wallflower, Janice," said Deborah. "But I'm used to being the last one chosen. Ever since I was a little girl."

Janice rummaged in her fanny pack, pulled out a bottle of pills, and popped a handful into her mouth.

I studied her. "Are you okay, Janice? Your fingertips are turning blue."

Janice shivered. "It's cold in here, don't you think?" Her words slurred as if she had not swallowed the mouthful of pills she had taken.

"No," replied Deborah. "I think it's kind of warm."

"Can I get you some water, Janice? Maybe a sweet roll?" I asked. The woman, always so put-together and confident, seemed to be fading before my eyes.

"Just water," Janice murmured. "Thank you."

When I returned with Janice's water, Daniel appeared like a specter in the doorway. He gestured for me to follow him. It was my turn.

My heart thumped as I walked into the library. Daniel closed the door behind me.

At last, I could tell the authorities what I knew about Laurel's disappearance. Perhaps I'd be the one to supply the missing pieces of the puzzle that would bring those responsible to justice. I flashed my most charming smile to calm my nerves. "*Buenas días.*"

Neither officer returned my smile or greeting. Maybe I'd mangled "*Buenos días,*" one of only about three Spanish phrases I knew.

"Señorita Giovanna Rogers, cabin number 327?" Detective Zuniga's brown eyes skimmed my features like a camera making a mug shot.

I lost the smile. I seated myself in the empty chair in a too-cozy circle.

"Señorita, please tell us what you did last night. From about six in the evening until eight o'clock this morning." Detective Zuniga flipped his notebook to a new page.

I started to tell them about the snorkeling trip, about how Laurel and I had become separated from the group and had almost been left behind, and how I hadn't seen Laurel since, even though no one else seemed concerned.

Detective Zuniga held up his hand. "You went snorkeling last night?" He raised one perfectly formed eyebrow.

I replayed the initial question. "Last night? You're asking what I did last night?"

"Yes, please," said Detective Estevez.

I told them I'd dined with my grandmother, Michelle, and then the guide Elena had joined us.

"How did Elena seem?" asked Estevez.

"How did she seem?" I frowned. "I'm not sure what you mean. Normal. Perky. She chatted about her childhood visits to the islands, and how she moved here and became a guide when she was in her teens." I didn't admit my mind had strayed a lot during our dinner conversation and thus I didn't remember much of it. How was I to know it might be important? My attention strayed again as I watched the photogenic Detective Zuniga take notes.

"What did you do after dinner?" Detective Zuniga's deep brown eyes met mine as if they could read the inappropriate thoughts of me ripping his clothes off that were dancing in my mind.

His steady gaze made me look away. "I took a walk on the open deck to look at the stars."

"Which deck?" Zuniga asked.

"Five, and then I went up to six."

"Near the pool?" asked Zuniga. The eyebrow arched.

"The pool is on that deck, but I couldn't see it from where I was standing."

Detective Zuniga wrote something down and then looked into my eyes again. "Was anyone with you during this after-dinner stroll?"

I cleared my throat. "I ran into one of the guides, Fernando. We talked for a while. He showed me the Southern Cross."

"Fernando Ferrar?" asked Estevez. His eyes widened.

"I suppose that's his last name. I don't know of any other Fernando on this ship."

"And what is your relationship with Fernando Ferrar?" asked Estevez.

"Relationship? We just met when I came on this ship three days ago."

"How did Fernando seem when you were talking?" Detective Zuniga's dark eyes bored into mine. I wondered what Fernando had told them about me during his interview.

I felt a blush creeping up my neck. Did the officers need to know about Fernando making a pass? Would that help their investigation into Laurel's death? "Uh, fine, I guess. He knows a lot about the constellations." I remembered his tongue had tasted of alcohol, masked by breath mints, but the guides drank in the evenings and mingled with the guests at cocktail parties; I felt no obligation to mention it.

"You just talked about the stars?" Zuniga's voice had a hint of sarcasm.

"Did you have any . . .?" Estevez started the question but looked to Zuniga to supply the rest.

"Did you have a disagreement?" Zuniga finished. One eyebrow arched, he looked at me. "Perhaps about the constellations?"

I cleared my throat again. Even if my story would get Fernando in trouble, I owed it to Laurel to be honest. "We parted on a foul note. I mentioned Laurel Pardo, and how I hadn't seen her since we were snorkeling yesterday morning. Fernando said Laurel and I shouldn't stick our noses where they don't belong." I winced. Was it betrayal?

Detective Zuniga's brow furrowed as if my answer had not been what he'd been expecting. "What do you think he meant by that?"

"I don't know. Maybe Laurel knew something that someone didn't want her to share."

The detectives looked at each other and conferred again over the passenger list. "This information," began Zuniga. "Do you think Fernando knew what it was?"

I shrugged. "I'm not saying Fernando killed her. But..." I looked at the detectives' puzzled faces.

"Señorita Rogers." Detective Zuniga tapped his pen on his notebook. "Fernando Ferrar is the one who is dead."

CHAPTER TEN

I sprang from my chair. "Fernando? Dead?" I didn't realize I was standing until Zuniga motioned for me to sit back down.

A chill seeped into my bones despite the warmth of the small library. Fernando had annoyed me with his arrogant disregard for Laurel's safety, but I'd never wished him harm. I could still feel his soft lips against mine, taste his minty tongue in my mouth, feel his nimble fingers caressing my body. "How?" I breathed. "What happened?"

"The crew found him face down at the bottom of the pool early this morning," Zuniga replied. He watched my eyes as if he could see inside my brain and read my memories.

"Did you kill him?" asked Estevez. He enunciated each word.

"What?" I blinked. "Me?" *Did he fall? He must have fallen. But how? Fernando was not careless. Yes, he'd been drinking, but he was far from drunk when I saw him.*

Zuniga gave Estevez a sharp look. "We're still investigating the circumstances of his death." He then turned to me. "Did you see where he went after he told you to mind your own business?"

"He may have gone toward the pool." A twin had poked her head around the corner while Fernando and I were kissing but if I mentioned that, I'd open a discussion I'd rather not have. "I didn't pay attention." I paused. "He was wearing knee-length khaki shorts and a T-shirt, not swimming attire, when I saw him. Was he found in his clothes?"

Estevez grunted as if to remind me who was asking the questions.

"And where did you go next? Did you stay outside on the deck for a while? Or did you follow him?" Zuniga consulted a deck plan as he spoke.

"I stayed there for a few minutes, watching the waves. Flocks of frigate birds flew overhead like they were following the ship."

"They do that. They aren't able to dive for their food, so they have to scavenge." Zuniga rose and leaned closer to spread the deck plan in front of me. He smelled of soap and a pleasant aftershave I didn't recognize. Our hands brushed for a second as we shared the paper. "And when you left the rail where you were stargazing with Fernando, which way did you go?"

I studied the ship's deck plan, trying to concentrate, afraid I'd remember something wrong and cast more suspicion on myself. The frigate birds had come by while I was still with Fernando; I'd headed down the stairwell as soon as the conversation went sour, to get away from him. But it was too late to amend my story. *And what difference does it make now anyway?*

My hand shook. *Fernando, dead?* I jabbed my finger at a spot on the Deck Six floor plan. "We were standing here. Then he went that way." I tried to remember my route back to the cabin, hoping I was not confusing my movements last night with steps I'd taken earlier in the day, or the day before. "I went down this stairwell."

"You did not go by the pool, then?" asked Zuniga.

I shook my head to break the magnetic pull of Zuniga's eyes.

"Did you see him again after he left you?" asked Zuniga.

He left you. That phrase sounded so final, so cold. For a second, I thought about Tim. But I'd been the one to leave Fernando. He'd scared me. I'd wanted to get away. "No, that was the last time I ever saw him," I said. "I went back to my cabin. And then I got a call that my grandmother had gone to the infirmary."

Zuniga kept writing. He didn't seem surprised. But why would he be? He had already interviewed Michelle. "Who called you?"

"Deborah Holt, one of the other passengers." I thought for a moment. "She said she'd gone to the infirmary for some aspirin and saw Michelle. Someone else found Michelle and took her down there."

"Michelle?" Estevez asked, his brow creased.

"Michelle DePalma, *su abuela*," Zuniga said to Estevez. With his pencil, he tapped the name on the passenger list and then turned back to me. "And did you stay in the infirmary until your grandmother was released?"

I told the detectives about my conversation with the doctor, and how I had walked Michelle back to our cabin.

"And this passenger, Deborah Holt? Did she go with you?" asked Zuniga, giving me that penetrating gaze again.

"She left the infirmary when we did. I assume she returned to her cabin. Hers is down the hall from ours."

Zuniga nodded and wrote. "So, after you accompanied your grandmother back to your cabin, where did you go?"

I presumed the detectives knew about my late-night quest for Laurel's flash drive. They had questioned the staff first; someone must have mentioned an encounter with me. I recapped my itinerary in chronological order, careful to include everyone with whom I'd come in contact, fueling my alibi—and perhaps multiple alibis. I didn't mention seeing someone slip into Laurel's room, as I couldn't identify that "someone."

"This flash drive," said Zuniga. "What was on it that was so important?"

"Photos from our outings the first two days." I met his eyes. Soulful eyes like a puppy I'd once rescued from the side of a freeway. "It belongs to another passenger, and my grandmother felt awful about losing it."

"Photos only?" asked Zuniga.

"I assume so. I never saw them. Laurel gave the flash drive to Michelle right before we left to go snorkeling."

"You don't think this flash drive might contain this 'secret information' that Laurel and Fernando knew?"

I disregarded Zuniga's mocking tone and leaned forward. "Did *you* find the flash drive?"

Zuniga and Estevez looked at each other. Estevez whispered something to Zuniga.

Zuniga turned his attention back to me. "Do you think the person who knocked out your grandmother in the library took the flash drive?"

My breath caught. "It crossed my mind. But no one knew she had it."

Zuniga nodded. "So, the infirmary was your last stop? You didn't go back upstairs, perhaps to the pool?"

"The pool? No. My thought was to retrace Michelle's steps, to see if she might have dropped the flash drive along the way." As I spoke, I realized I had not retraced Michelle's steps *before* dinner, which would have included the auditorium and Deck Six, where we'd watched the sunset with Deborah. If I'd gone up there to look for the flash drive, I might have passed by the pool, where Fernando met his end. But I didn't. Did they believe me? *The police don't care about finding Laurel's flash drive; they want to know where and when I last saw Fernando alive.* "The infirmary was my last stop. After I spoke to the doctor, I went back to my cabin and stayed there the rest of the night."

"So, again, what time was it when you last saw Fernando Ferrar alive?"

I had not paid attention to the time, and now it sounded like an important detail—perhaps the difference between being accused of murder or freed as an innocent witness. "Around nine-thirty."

I watched the detectives' faces as Zuniga wrote. Was that a good answer?

I was exhausted by the time I joined the other passengers in the packed dining room. Lunch was being served, but I had no appetite. Laurel was still missing, and Fernando was dead.

Michelle sat with the French family, engrossed in animated conversation. She had lived in Europe when she was in her twenties—two years in France—and since then, she'd seized every opportunity to keep her language skills polished.

"*Mais vous parlez très bien*," Claudette, the forty-something apple-cheeked wife, assured Michelle, and Michelle beamed at the compliment for her French proficiency.

"*Surtout pour une Américaine*," her lanky husband, Jean-Marc, agreed.

I smiled, not understanding a word, but guessing they were praising my grandmother's linguistic abilities. Both my mother and Michelle had encouraged me to study French, but I'd never had an aptitude for foreign languages. I suspect my refusal to even try had been rebellion, and I regretted it now.

Michelle switched to English, and the Francophones obliged. Their English was competent, although not as good as Michelle's French. I felt like the ugly American, demanding that everyone speak my language.

Jacqueline, the couple's ten-year-old daughter, eyed me suspiciously and then buried her head in her mother's shoulder. Claudette stroked the girl's curly brown hair and looked at me. "*Normalement*, she like to *pratiquer* her English with strangers. But today, hard. She want... she *wants* to see the tortoises. And now . . ." Claudette gestured around at the chaotic dining room, abuzz with conjecture and complaints.

"This trip . . . lots to tell in school," said Jean-Marc. "But perhaps . . ." He waved his hands, struggling for the right words. "Perhaps too much adventure."

"I still can't believe he's dead," I said. I looked at Michelle but included the French guests in a polite sweep with my eyes.

"They told you who died?" asked Claudette.

I swallowed and looked from face to face. Even Michelle seemed mystified. "No one knows who's dead?"

Jean-Marc puffed his cheeks in disgust. "No, the police want to know where we were last night. We all went back to the cabin after dinner. *Fini*. Not much to talk about. They told us nothing."

Michelle touched my shaking knee. "What did they tell you?"

I pressed my fingers to my temples. "I felt like a suspect."

"A suspect?" Michelle gasped. "But why?"

"Who was it?" demanded Claudette. "Who is dead?"

"Fernando." My voice broke. "Fernando Ferrar, the guide."

"Fernando! Oh la, la!" moaned Jean-Marc.

Claudette's hazel eyes watered as she stroked Jacqueline's hair. "Oh, no. Fernando was Jacqueline's favorite. What happened?"

"But how?" asked Jean-Marc. "*Un accident?*"

"They don't know yet. That's why they're interviewing everyone on board," I tried to explain. I didn't like being in the spotlight, but I was the one with the most information. "He was found at the bottom of the pool early this morning." I cupped my face in my hands.

Claudette gasped, and she and Jean-Marc retreated into rapid French between themselves. Jacqueline sobbed, and Claudette rocked her against her chest.

Michelle leaned her face close to mine. "Why did they tell you who's dead, and not the rest of us?"

"They think I could have done it." I mouthed.

"What? You?"

In a hushed voice only for Michelle's ears, I began to recount my interview with the police.

"I didn't know you'd seen Fernando last night." Michelle flinched. "Oh, Giovanna."

"Nothing happened," I declared. "And I didn't kill him. He was alive when we parted. Rebuffed, but alive."

Michelle took my elbow and we rose from the table. She nodded toward the French family. "*Pardonnez nous.*" She steered me through the crowd and out the restaurant door. A few passengers loitered near the entrance to the public restrooms; we edged past them. No one prevented us from climbing a flight of stairs and walking onto the promenade deck.

I welcomed the warm sunshine against my back after the morning of dim, air-conditioned rooms. I took a deep breath of sea air. "Are we allowed to be out here?"

"If we're not, someone will tell us."

We walked to the stern of the ship near the dive equipment washing station. A forest of wetsuits hung in the breeze.

Michelle stopped at the rail and looked out to sea. "Tell me more about you and Fernando. Did you know he'd be up on Deck Six when you went for a walk after dinner?"

"No."

"Running into him was a coincidence, then?"

"It's a small ship."

"Were you happy to see him?" Michelle looked at me. "I could tell you were attracted to him from the first day of the cruise."

I stared at the waves. In the distance, I saw a splash, perhaps a large fish leaping out of the water. I pointed.

"I think that was a shark," said Michelle. "The hammerheads jump like that."

"He kissed me," I admitted. "And I liked it."

Michelle pressed her forehead against her hands.

"But then I couldn't get Laurel out of my mind. The episode in the water, the trashed cabin. I accused Fernando of covering up her disappearance."

"I'm sure that went over well."

"It broke the mood."

"Do you think Daniel had talked to him yet?" Michelle leaned against the rail, then turned back to me.

"He didn't mention it, but if Daniel had already talked to him, Fernando would have said something unpleasant to me right away."

"He wasn't angry with you—"

"Not until I brought up Laurel. Then he told me to mind my own business." I brushed a strand of hair off my face. "I decided it was time to part company, and that was the last I saw of him."

"And that's what you told the police?"

"It's the truth."

"Did anyone see you with Fernando?"

"I'm not sure. One of the Roberts twins poked her head around the corner while we were, uh, you know."

"Those two seem smitten with him. With both Fernando and Rafael. To the chagrin of their parents, I'm sure." Michelle looked at me. "Wait. You don't know about Laurel—"

The wind shifted, and a strong odor of tobacco tickled our nostrils. We spotted the source, coming from behind the hanging wetsuits: Dieter, puffing on a cigar.

Michelle and I exchanged frantic glances; our illusion of privacy shattered. How much of our conversation had Dieter heard?

ichelle smiled as Dieter stalked toward us. "Good afternoon, Herr Dieter. I see you escaped the madhouse, too."

Dieter took another puff on his cigar. Neither of us mentioned the big, red "No Smoking" sign on the wall behind him.

Michelle turned to me. "You didn't get any lunch yet, did you, Giovanna? You must be hungry."

"The young man had it coming," said Dieter. He had taken the cigar out of his mouth and twirled it like a baton. "But his enemies picked a bad time."

"His enemies?" I repeated. "On the ship?"

"Someone got to him. Fernando Ferrar was not a careful man."

"How do you know Fernando had enemies on the ship?" asked Michelle.

Dieter caught his cigar ashes in his calloused hand. I wondered about his next step: pocket, for proper disposal later? Overboard? The teak deck?

I heard footsteps approaching from the other side of the wetsuit rack. The three of us looked up to see Daniel come around the corner.

Daniel stopped when he reached us and placed his hands on his hips. "We need everyone back in the dining room now."

All the other guests had assembled when Michelle, Dieter, and I followed Daniel back into the stuffy dining room. The room was not designed to hold everyone at once, and it felt over-crowded. Good thing the ship wasn't full. The two police officers chatted with Eduardo, the maître d', and Detective Estevez popped the last piece of a seed-covered roll into his mouth.

"Ladies and gentlemen, I think we're all here now." Daniel gave a sideways glance to us stragglers, and I pressed myself against the wall to appear as inconspicuous as possible. My eyes panned the room for Laurel. *So much for "we're all here."* With all the hubbub, I wondered if Daniel had had time to report Laurel's disappearance to the authorities.

Silence fell over the room as everyone turned their attention to Daniel.

"Ladies and gentlemen, we apologize for the inconvenience this morning. We know this was not what you expected, not what you paid for, and not what you deserve on a luxury cruise." Daniel was back to his smooth, professional demeanor. "But as you know, we had an unusual event—a death aboard the ship—and the proper procedure is to call the police."

He turned to Detectives Estevez and Zuniga, who each gave a nod. "While these detectives were questioning everyone, their colleagues were examining the scene. They have removed the body and will take it back to Puerto Ayora, where the medical examiner will do further tests."

"What does this mean for our cruise?" demanded Helga.

"And who is this 'body'?" cried a middle-aged man. "When will you tell us what happened?"

"I heard it was a guide who died," said a woman.

"Was it murder?" demanded another woman.

"Please." Daniel held up his hand and made eye contact with the woman who had spoken. "We lost one of our best tour guides last night, Fernando Ferrar."

A hush descended over the audience.

"Fernando was born and educated in Quito, but he came to the islands when he was only sixteen," Daniel continued. "He fell in love with this place, as most people do when they come to the Galapagos. He earned his naturalist certification and worked as a free-lance guide for over a decade, for some of the best cruise lines. We were lucky to have him working with us this past month, and we'll miss him very much." Daniel's eyes watered as they swept the crowd. "As I'm sure many of you will."

Mumbles of sympathy and regret rippled among the passengers.

Daniel cleared his throat, but his voice quivered. "Early this morning, one of our deckhands found Fernando at the bottom of the pool. The man pulled him out and several people attempted to revive him, but he was already deceased. As I mentioned, we had no choice but to call the authorities."

A low murmur rumbled through the crowd.

"I will let Detective Zuniga tell you about their preliminary findings." Daniel stepped aside to yield the floor to Detective Zuniga.

I felt my heart pound. Staff members stood at all the exits. There was no avenue of escape. Would there be an arrest? A Perry Mason moment? Was he looking at me?

Detective Zuniga made another nod to the crowd, almost a bow. Most of the guests gave him their full attention. I expected a man as good-looking as Zuniga to strut, but he didn't; it was almost as if he didn't realize how handsome he was. Unlike Fernando, the deceased.

"Ladies and Gentlemen, thank you so much for your cooperation this morning. We realize it hasn't been easy, and we apologize we couldn't tell you everything right away. But that is the nature of an investigation." Zuniga's brown eyes smoldered as he looked from face to face, perhaps finding some who had been less cooperative than others. I felt those eyes meet mine for a second and their heat forced me to shift my gaze to my feet.

"At this time, we haven't found any evidence of foul play in the death of Señor Ferrar. We'll know more when we meet you at Puerto Ayora on Friday." After a dirty look from Detective Estevez, Zuniga tossed his head of thick, black hair and continued, "But for now, Señor Ferrar's unfortunate death appears to have been caused by an accidental fall. We're very sorry for your loss."

I detected a twist in Zuniga's mouth as he spoke, and something about his tone when he said the words, "accidental fall" did not ring true. And what was that glare between him and Detective Estevez about?

Zuniga stepped aside to return the floor to Daniel.

"I've spoken with the staff at the tortoise reserve, and they've agreed to accommodate us this afternoon. So please, if you'd still like to go ashore, we'll begin disembarkation in ten minutes."

"Hallelujah," cried Helga, picking up her camera and fanny pack.

There was a rush to gather belongings and exit the dining room.

"I need to go back to the cabin for a minute," I told Michelle. "Shall I meet you in the auditorium?"

Michelle nodded, and I hurried down the hall.

I almost bumped smack into Daniel. "Sorry."

He stepped aside. "Excuse me."

Before I continued on my way, I ventured, "Daniel, did you ever find out if Laurel Pardo is on board? I still haven't seen her."

His face froze.

"And I saw someone go into her cabin late last night. I didn't get a good look at the person, but I'm sure it wasn't Laurel."

A bespectacled Asian man tugged at Daniel's arm and launched into a question. As if I hadn't been standing there at all, Daniel turned to address the interruption and then walked in the other direction with the man.

I stared after him. *What was that?*

I stopped outside Laurel's cabin, listened, and knocked. No answer, no sounds of life coming from within.

Back in my cabin, I picked up my smartphone and tried to log onto the internet, but the Wi-Fi connection was still down. I sat on the vanity seat to freshen my makeup. I stared at my haggard face, took a few deep breaths. After my interview with the police, I'd had a disturbing vision of being handcuffed and moved without due process to some third-world prison. Relieved that I was not a suspect, I was free to continue my vacation as if nothing had happened.

Except something *had* happened, and it seemed the officers had closed the investigation too quickly, like a gift-wrapped package with a fancy bow. *Where is the justice for Fernando? And what about Laurel? Why does no one care that she's missing?*

The seas had grown rough, and as we descended the steep steps to board the Zodiacs, the boats rose and fell several feet with each swell. The guides had to study the gap between the stairs and boat and urge each passenger to board when the two were level. I held my breath and made a perfect landing on the Zodiac, as did Michelle at the next swell.

Both an elderly Japanese woman and Joseph, one of the Air Canada flight attendants, stumbled upon entering the Zodiac. Instead of rushing to steady them, as Fernando would have done, Rafael just stared and left it to the rest of us to help our fellow guests to their seats. *I miss Fernando*, I thought. *Dead. Fernando is dead.*

Michelle and I found ourselves again on the same Zodiac as the Roberts family. The family had changed clothes, and all appeared in much better spirits. In fact, our whole group of tourists had snapped back into vacation mode after the exasperating interruption of a death inquiry.

"Do we get to meet Tio Armando?" asked Jessy, who was wearing a scoop-necked, sleeveless pink chemise. All smiles, her dimples deepened as she spoke.

"When is he moving to our place?" asked Jenny. Clad in an oversize Metallica T-shirt, she fiddled with the settings on her camera and then snapped a few shots at the other passengers in the boat.

I noticed a sharp look between Jim and his daughter.

"Now, Jenny, we haven't worked out those details yet." Jim's Colgate smile radiated toward all who may have overheard.

"So that's the angle you were talking about?" Michelle said to Jim. "Tio Armando?"

My ears perked up and I tuned in to their conversation.

Jim's face reddened and he lowered his voice. "They're searching for new quarters for the animal. I've made an offer to accommodate him on our resort property."

"And I'm sure you'll have researchers on staff, and experts who will monitor all his needs." Michelle gazed skyward. "A one-hundred-year-old specimen, the last of his sub-species?"

"We're only in the preliminary talks. I'd appreciate it if you'd keep this quiet for now."

"Your daughter brought it up."

"Jim, look at those funny-shaped fishing boats." Janice tugged her husband's sleeve and aimed with her camera. "That one reminds me of an ark."

Jim trained his binoculars at the harbor, full of fishing boats, where Janice was pointing. The conversation with Michelle about Tio Armando had ended.

We disembarked at the pier of Puerto Baquerizo Moreno, a large fishing town on the southwestern coast of San Cristóbal. Puerto Baquerizo Moreno was the oldest settlement in the Galapagos, founded in the mid-nineteenth century. The main streets were paved, but none of the buildings rose higher than a few stories.

"Let me guess: the main industry here is fishing." I sniffed the air, pungent with the stench of diesel fuel and fish in various stages of life and death.

"Right," replied Michelle. "But tourism is catching up. Look at all the hotels and shops along the waterfront."

Small tourist buses picked us up for the forty-five-minute ride to the tortoise reserve we would visit. As we boarded, Jessy pointed at a souvenir shop. "Will we have time to shop?"

Rafael winked and boosted her up the steps of the bus. "We're late, but for you, I'll see what I can do."

I settled next to Michelle and groped for a seat belt, but there were none. Peter and Joseph sat in front of us, Helga and Dieter were across the aisle, Deborah and Sue spread out in the back of the bus. The Roberts family sat up front, and Rafael, standing next to the driver, flirted with the twins. *I wonder what Jim and Janice think about that. What are they talking about that's keeping them from noticing what's going on with their daughters?*

I turned to my grandmother. "Just before we left, I asked Daniel if he'd reported Laurel missing yet." I examined my chipped nails, in need of a fresh coat of polish. "He blew me off. Can you imagine? What's up with that?"

"Oh, Giovanna," Michelle began. "With all that was going on this morning, I didn't tell you." She turned in her seat to face me. "The detectives claimed they interviewed Laurel. They'd marked her name off a passenger list. She's not missing. That's why Daniel didn't report the incident. He must have found her on board."

I threw up my hands and looked around the bus again. "Then, where is she?"

"I don't know. There aren't that many people on our ship. But who was I to argue with the police?"

"All the passengers were together in the same room. Twice. Laurel wasn't in there."

"Maybe she was in the infirmary. Deborah said she wasn't feeling well."

"Michelle, you were in the infirmary last night. Did you see her? I didn't."

My grandmother looked away and sighed. "This conspiracy theory you've cooked up isn't healthy."

I stared out the window as we left the small town and increased our speed on the two-lane asphalt road. The tropical vegetation passed in a blur, some lush green, but most cactus-like, more suited to the arid climate. "You don't believe me."

We rode in silence for a few moments.

"What if someone impersonated Laurel?" suggested Michelle. "The police would not have known the difference."

"I didn't notice any new faces among the passengers. Perhaps it was someone who works on the ship?" I fiddled with my hair, which was escaping from the ponytail I'd tried today. "I don't like what's going on. A woman disappears, and everyone pretends it didn't happen. Even covers it up. Call it a conspiracy theory if you want to."

"Excuse me, Rafael." Helga's abrasive voice hushed the private conversations taking place among the rest of us. "Why are you not telling us about the terrain?"

Rafael, who had been making Jessy giggle about something, looked annoyed at the interruption.

"You have already delayed us this morning. The least you could do is tell us about what we are seeing." Helga leaned toward the front of the bus and glowered at Rafael. "Young man, do you know how much these passengers have paid for this cruise?"

Rafael sobered and picked up the microphone. As if reading from a script, he began talking about how San Cristóbal, the easternmost island in the Galapagos archipelago, had been formed from three now-extinct volcanoes. It was named after St. Christopher, the patron saint of seafarers.

"What about El Junco?" asked Helga. "Will we see that lake today? We should be near there."

Rafael blinked. He conferred with the bus driver, then spoke into the microphone, "El Junco, a lake inside a volcanic crater, is the only source of fresh water in the Galapagos. And no, we won't be able to see it from the road." Jessy tickled him and he waved the microphone at her in a mock threat.

Helga looked at Michelle and me. "This young man is useless as a guide. I will write a complaint. All he can think about is those pretty young girls. And their parents should put him in his place."

We arrived at the Beagle Galapaguera, a small family-owned tortoise reserve on the southern end of San Cristóbal established in the seventies as a breeding facility. There were several more famous tortoise reserves on San Cristóbal, but the Beagle Galapaguera had become the preferred destination for cruise ships and tour groups since the discovery of Tio Armando, the last surviving member of the Floreana giant tortoise sub-species. Tio Armando had been found about a year after the demise of Lonesome George, long-time resident of the Charles Darwin Research Station on Santa Cruz Island, last survivor of the Pinta Island sub-species, and one of the most popular tourist attractions in the Galapagos.

Nice windfall for this place, I thought. Tourist dollars had allowed the Beagle Galapaguera to build a brand-new interpretive center and add five acres of gravel-paved trails through semi-natural tortoise habitat, and large state-of-the-art pens where they raised young tortoises.

When Rafael announced a restroom break our group scattered—some to the restrooms, some to the gift shop, others to the interpretive center.

As soon as the twins and their parents were ready, Rafael started down the trail without waiting for the rest of our group to reconvene. I looked around for Michelle, then we trotted together after Rafael. He stopped at a sign marking an endangered plant and read to the twins, even though the signs were written in English as well as Spanish. Janice and Jim huddled away from the group, still inattentive to their daughters' interactions with the flirtatious guide. A few others from our bus struggled to engage with Rafael, but after he ignored them several times, the rest of us gave up.

Elena's group was touring the tortoise breeding area next to the building. Michelle and I opted to join them.

"Young tortoises stay in their pens until they're around five years old," Elena explained. "It's too dangerous to release them before they're big enough to fend off predators."

"What predators are here?" asked Kumiko.

"Dogs, goats, cats, pigs, even man. Man brought all those animals here."

"*Quelles mignonnes!*" cooed Jacqueline, the young French girl, pointing to the pen full of adorable baby tortoises.

"Cute, aren't they?" Elena agreed, with a smile. "These babies were born last month."

Amid ohs and ahs, we all peered into the pen holding the tiny tortoises, small enough to fit into a child's hand.

Elena moved from pen to pen, explaining the giant tortoise breeding program. Researchers had divided the animals by age, like grades in an elementary school. "These juveniles over here will be ready for release next year." She indicated a group of tortoises close to a foot in diameter. "They won't reach their full size until they're almost forty years old, though."

"How old are those . . . how do you say . . . 'juveniles'?" asked Jean-Marc.

"They're almost five years old. But even though we release them, we'll continue to monitor them."

Helga and Dieter slipped into Elena's group, and we started down the trail. Elena walked backward part of the time to keep her followers in view. If she'd noticed a few additions, she didn't seem to mind.

"There are fourteen sub-species of Darwin's finches throughout this archipelago," she said. "You can tell them apart by their beaks, which have adapted to the environment where they live. The depth of the beak fluctuates by several millimeters, depending on drought conditions in their habitat."

She pointed out a finch sitting in a bush next to the trail. It fluttered away as soon as someone's camera clicked.

Gravel crunched under our tennis shoes as we followed Elena along the trail, binoculars poised, cameras ready. Right before we crossed a marshy area on wooden planks, we spotted our first giant tortoise.

Everyone stopped, in awe of the massive animal in its natural habitat, a slow-moving five-hundred-pound boulder. The tortoise seemed oblivious to us. Two sticks of green protruded from either side of its mouth as it chomped on tall grasses.

We watched the tortoise finish its snack and then lumber down a narrow ditch lined with shrubs. The creature moved faster than I'd imagined it could.

"Look!" cried Jean-Marc.

Another giant tortoise, larger than the first, approached from the opposite direction. The passageway was not wide enough for them both. We waited for the confrontation as the two beasts advanced toward each other.

The impasse came. Neither tortoise could move further without running into the other. Their necks stretched out of their shells, their toothless mouths open like serpents about to strike.

Their heads thrashed about in a kind of dance as each vied for dominance. Jacqueline giggled as she tugged at Claudette's sleeve. "*Ils ressemblent à E.T.*"

The stand-off continued as we watched. Some tourists snapped pictures or recorded videos. Then the larger tortoise reared onto its hind legs, its scaly front flippers extended like wrinkled boxing gloves, and lunged toward the smaller one. The smaller tortoise retracted its head and lowered it beneath its carapace, a gesture of submission. Then it moved forward, butting its shell against its upright opponent.

The large tortoise resisted, but the smaller one kept pushing. As the larger one struggled to keep from flipping on its back, the smaller one pressed its way underneath. The hind legs of the larger one dangled from atop the shell of the other tortoise as it propelled itself forward, under the momentum of the opponent passing below.

In a moment, the tortoises had changed places and faced in opposite directions. The larger one turned its beak as far as it would go to the side without turning around as if to ask, "What just happened?" and then each tortoise continued on its way.

We all laughed. Tourists chattered and showed off their photos to one another as the group began moving again.

"Interesting way to solve problems," mused Jean-Marc.

By the time we finished the trail with Elena's group, Rafael's group had returned to the interpretive center. Elena clapped her hands. "And now, I'm sure you all want to meet our star attraction, Tio Armando."

We followed Elena to a large pen near the entrance of the reserve. A prominent sign with a color photo of the giant tortoise broadcasted the spot.

The tourists gathered around the enclosure. There was a lot of vegetation inside, a lot of hiding places, but I couldn't detect any movement. People craned their necks and strained to peer around each other, searching for the famous resident.

"Where is he?" said Helga. "I don't see anything."

"Yes," said Jenny. "Where is Tio Armando?"

Elena's face froze.

"No giant tortoise in that pen," said Peter.

Elena held up a finger. "One moment. I'll find out." She headed back toward the offices where I watched her flag down one of the uniformed custodians of the tortoise reserve.

I looked at Helga. "It wouldn't matter so much, except last night, she hyped up Tio Armando. Got everyone excited about seeing the last survivor of a sub-species."

Elena returned, still looking disconcerted. "Tio Armando is not here. He was moved to Santa Cruz yesterday."

CHAPTER TWELVE

Michelle stared at Jim while the rest of us milled around the empty enclosure. "You pulled it off?"

Jim's face looked as perplexed as Elena's. "I'm not sure what's happening." His eyes focused on one of the staff members who had been talking to Elena. "Excuse me."

Elena and Raphael ushered their groups toward the buses waiting to take us back to the ship.

"Sir," Rafael told Jim, "the bus is ready to load."

"Don't leave without me," Jim called over his shoulder. He and the staff member disappeared into an office together and closed the door.

I nudged my grandmother. "What was that about?"

"While we were cooped up in the auditorium this morning, Jim told me more about the resort his company is building on Santa Cruz. He thought he had enough money and power to feature Tio Armando as an attraction at the property." Michelle eyed the closed office door. "Now it appears his plans have gone awry."

I shrugged. "They said they'd shipped Tio Armando to Santa Cruz. Isn't Jim's resort property in Puerto Ayora?"

"From his expression," Michelle said, "Jim may have lost to a higher bidder."

"Seems like exploitation to me," I said. "Under the guise of preserving an endangered species."

"Ladies, please, the bus is boarding." Rafael tried to round us up like a mother goose with her goslings.

Elena's bus had already left, and everyone but Jim was waiting on ours. Janice alternated looking at her watch and eyeing the interpretive center. The twins tried to entertain Rafael with their photos, but despite his earlier attentions, he seemed pre-occupied. Like Janice, his eyes kept darting to the entrance.

The driver leaned over and said something to Rafael. Rafael picked up the microphone and announced, "Ladies and Gentlemen, we'll be on our way in a moment. We're waiting for one more passenger. I'll see what's taking so long." He replaced the microphone and then hopped down the steps of the bus.

Five minutes later, Rafael returned with Jim, red in the face, but in better spirits. The rest of us applauded as he boarded the bus.

"We're missing our cocktails," called Deborah, and several others laughed.

Jim gave a little bow before he sat down with his family.

To prove he has a sense of humor, I thought. From my vantage point, I detected a scowl creeping over Jim's face as soon as he turned away.

"I wonder what he found out," said Michelle. "I hope they told him these giant tortoises are not for sale."

The bus ride back to the pier was quiet. Helga and Dieter fretted over the late hour, as our scheduled afternoon hike at Punta Pitt, on the other side of San Cristóbal, would not take place. They fumbled with their programs, shaking their heads and wondering aloud what other changes Daniel would make to the itinerary.

When the bus reached the pier, Jessy made another half-hearted request to visit a souvenir shop.

Rafael scowled, placed both hands on her narrow shoulders, and turned her toward the waiting boats. "You had time to buy postcards at the gift shop."

The seas were calm for the short boat ride to the ship. En route, a few passengers commented about giant tortoises and speculated on the whereabouts of Tio Armando. No one mentioned Fernando or his untimely demise. Or Laurel and the fact that she had not been with us all day.

I unlocked the door to our cabin. "I wonder if the Wi-Fi is back up." The battery in my smartphone was almost dead, so I plugged it into the charger. Wi-Fi was so spotty on the islands, I wondered why I'd even bothered to bring it along on our excursion.

"I want to see if I got a message from Roberto." Michelle set her backpack on the bed.

Seated at the desk, I opened Michelle's laptop. "It's up." I began typing into the Google search bar as soon as the screen illuminated.

"What are you researching?" Michelle passed me at the desk as she walked to the closet. "You've been on the internet a lot since we got here."

"Sorry. Here, check your email." I took my hands off the keyboard.

"Go ahead and use the computer while I get dressed."

As soon as Michelle went into the bathroom, I rose to retrieve a stack of papers from the bottom of my suitcase and brought them over to the desk. I consulted my notes, typed more entries into the search engine, and wrote additional notes on the papers.

The bathroom door opened. I shoved the papers into the desk drawer and typed, "Tio Armando" into the search bar. Michelle came out of the bathroom and I smiled. "I wanted to find out more information about that giant tortoise."

Michelle peered over her shoulder. "What did you find?"

"Nothing yet about where they moved him, or even the fact that he's moved. Here's his picture." I pointed to the screen. "Too bad we didn't get to meet him. Elena had us all excited."

Michelle cocked her head. "Why this sudden interest in Tio Armando? Two days ago, you'd never heard of him."

"But now I have. I want to learn more. I want to make this trip an enriching experience."

Michelle laughed. "What were you really researching?"

I lowered my head toward the desk drawer where I'd stashed my papers. The drawer wasn't closed, and papers protruded from the opening. I might as well spill. "Jerome." When Michelle's response was a baffled glance, I continued, "Haddad. My ex-business partner." I spat the last phrase; the word "partner" tasted worse than spoiled milk.

"At the spay/neuter clinic?"

"Yes." I sighed and turned to face my grandmother. "I should have done a thorough audit and found his crooked dealings before I ever thought about going into business with him." I rose and ushered Michelle to take her seat at the desk. "Ironic, isn't it? I made my living as an auditor. I was becoming an expert in financial forensics. CFOs trembled when they saw me coming. And yet when I started my business, I ignored due diligence."

"Don't beat yourself up. He was charming. He brought in funding, didn't he?"

"Ha. So, I thought. Tim didn't trust him. I should have listened to my fiancé." I paced the carpeted floor. "It was such arrogance to think that shyster couldn't fool me." Talking about Jerome could work me into a fury.

"How did you get mixed up with that man anyway?" Michelle had only met Jerome once, at the clinic's grand opening. I hadn't ever talked about him much with her. Maybe I should have. Maybe she would have steered me away. She was a better judge of character than I. Impatient to get going with my project, I didn't want any naysayers.

"His wife Connie and I were friends in college," I explained. "That was years before they married. Connie met Jerome-the-Conman later when she went to law school. She interned at his firm, and they fell in love."

"And she convinced you to go into business with Jerome?"

"She recommended his firm, yes, to help me with the financing. Said she and Jerome were both big animal lovers. I trusted her." I stared out the window, watching the lapping waves, remembering my years at the University of Georgia. "Connie used to help me feed the stray cats around our dorm and drive them to the vet to get fixed. But she and Jerome the Jerk don't even own a pet now."

Michelle touched my hand as I paced past the desk. "A lesson learned. But it's over." Her eyes swept to the cracked-open desk drawer. She pulled the drawer out and lifted the stack of papers I'd been hiding. "Or maybe not."

I took the papers from Michelle. I sat down on my bed and Michelle moved next to me. "Some of these dealings are recent, so I couldn't have known about them when we founded the clinic together." I showed Michelle an article from the *Miami Herald*. "His card house is collapsing. But there were signs. I ignored them." I shuffled through more papers. "Look at the 501(c)(3) he partnered with to collect our donations until we got our own exemption. Owned by—guess who? His wife, Connie—my former friend. They get zero stars on GuideStar. All their income goes to administrative expenses, which means big fat salaries for Jerome and Connie Haddad. Nothing to programming. They don't even have a program. Unless you call swindling people a program."

"How can they get away with it?"

"They shut down as soon as someone gets suspicious and opens an investigation. Make a fresh start under a new name. Like those telephone solicitor scammers who change their phone number every time someone blocks their calls or files a complaint. I tried to check out his organization, but it was too new and small to be listed with Charity Navigator. Who was I to judge? We were a new nonprofit, too, and very small."

Michelle touched my shoulder. "Roberto and I know how much you wanted that clinic to succeed."

"I should have listened to Tim, waited until I could raise more funds on my own." I shook my head. "Look at the finance company where Jerome 'invested' our endowment, my life's savings. JerCo Investments, LLC. I should have realized 'JerCo' was code for Jerome and Connie. Sounds like the jerks they are.

Donors thought they were helping animals in the county, but they were contributing to the lavish lifestyle of Jerome and Connie Haddad, with my encouragement." My cheeks burned as I relived my nightmare. Asking for money. Making promises. Looking city officials in the eye. I was toast. How could I ever face that community again? "JerCo Investments was also servicing the mortgage on our building, putting the taxes and insurance payments into escrow. But everything went into the pockets of those scumbags."

Michelle stared at the papers I'd thrust at her. "What a crook!"

"There's more." I picked up another sheet. "Here's a copy of his bankruptcy filing. His biggest creditors? At the top of the priority list? JerCo Investments, the law firm of Haddad & Haddad, and J.C. Corporation. All owned by you-know-who. And J.C. Corporation went under because of a bad loan to JerCo Investments made on behalf of my clinic, and they're suing us over it. Their lawyers are Haddad & Haddad. We have to pay their court costs. Can you believe the gall?" I showed Michelle the list of creditors that went on for pages and pages. "So many people screwed."

Michelle shook her head. "He's despicable."

I thumbed through more papers. "He likes the charity business. Decided it's easy to take advantage of people's generosity. Wealth distribution—to him. Look at C.J. Children's Fund and J.H. Ministries. More bogus nonprofits founded and run by the Haddads. Posted a bunch of phony five-star reviews about how compassionate they are, how they've changed people's lives. Forgot to file tax returns, though, and then they shut down, but not before collecting hundreds of thousands of dollars in donations." I slapped the papers against my knee. "I could strangle him with my bare hands."

"Giovanna! You don't mean you'd strangle him, do you?" Michelle bit her lip. "Wouldn't it be more satisfying to see him behind bars?"

"I'd love to see him suffer a prolonged, painful death." I gritted my teeth. "If only the authorities could catch him. But I'm the one on the hook for the shortfall at the clinic. And the taxes." I squeezed my head between my palms, remembering the threatening letters from the IRS, the cold, institutional lack of understanding, and my frustrated quest to bring Jerome Haddad to justice. Were not his dealings illegal? Couldn't someone hit him with a penalty for fraud? "You won't believe how hard it's been to get any government agency interested in pursuing that slippery slimebag. So many loopholes. So many jurisdictions. It's no one's problem but mine. And now he's protected under the umbrella of bankruptcy." I pointed to another creditor on my sheet. "Look at his last purchase before he filed for bankruptcy. An ocean-going yacht."

Michelle glanced at the paper and shook her head. "So, has he sailed off into the sunset?"

I returned to the computer and flipped to the page I'd been viewing while Michelle was in the bathroom. "The *Second Wind*. Here's a photo." I glared at the image—the ostentatious toy that had brought down my clinic. "He's too far away for you to see the smug look on his face."

Michelle studied the photo. "Nice yacht."

"And he'll never pay a dime for it. One hundred percent financed by JerCo Investments, using my building as collateral." I was a whistling tea kettle.

"What can you do now?"

I tapped the computer screen. "I've been tracking the route of the *Second Wind* through social media." Typing a few characters, I brought up Connie's Facebook account. "Look, she posted another update yesterday."

Michelle's facial features drooped. "Honey, if there's nothing you can do about it, let it go. And don't let anyone hear you talk about killing someone, even in jest. The authorities are still investigating a homicide on this ship. I know they said it looked like an accident, but . . ."

"He's here."

"Here?"

"Well, Puerto Ayora."

"Puerto Ayora? Jerome Haddad sailed to the Galapagos?"

I put on my Cheshire smile.

"And you knew this when?"

I kept smiling through bared teeth.

Michelle groaned. "I was giving Jim Roberts a hard time about having ulterior motives for bringing his family here on vacation. I never realized he wasn't the only one." She stared at me. "What do you expect to accomplish by tracking Jerome here? What will you do if you find him?"

I cleared my throat. "Get justice."

"Justice? How?"

I looked back at the screen. "If I know Jerome, he's running some kind of scam here. I'll stop it."

Michelle's mouth dropped. "How?"

"I don't know yet."

Michelle glanced at her watch. "You better get changed now, or we'll be late for the briefing."

While Giovanna was in the bathroom, Michelle stared at the pictures of the *Second Wind*. She felt sick to her stomach about what Jerome and Connie Haddad had done to her granddaughter. She wished she and Roberto had become more involved in the venture. Maybe they could have lent Giovanna the money she needed and prevented this disaster. But she hadn't asked.

When Michelle had met Jerome Haddad at the clinic's grand opening, he'd stared at her with eyes the color of glacier water—a stark contrast to his dark hair, dark beard, and olive skin. Looking into those piercing eyes reminded her of a boy she'd known in high school—Paul Malin—who was now serving a life sentence for the kidnapping, torture, and murder of his ex-girlfriend and her fiancé.

Even more disturbing was the way Jerome had looked at Giovanna, like a predator stalking his next meal. And Giovanna had seemed oblivious.

Jerome struck Michelle as one of those too-good-to-be-true smooth talkers, like a television evangelist. Giovanna had been secretive about her business partner, and Michelle had not asked questions. She had let her granddaughter be a grown-up.

With a sigh, Michelle logged into her Gmail account. As she had hoped, there was a message from Roberto. He and the cats were fine, although everyone missed her. It had not rained since she left, so he'd turned on the sprinklers to keep her azaleas alive. The sun had shone on his last layover in Germany. He'd impressed the neighbors with the photos Michelle had sent from the Galapagos, and now everyone wanted to visit there.

Roberto's last line in the email was confusing. Michelle read it again. She didn't remember telling Roberto anything about Tio Armando. Was she getting dementia? Her mother had suffered from Alzheimer's in her later years, and Michelle often feared she would one day meet the same fate. She panicked at any memory lapse, thinking it might be a potential symptom.

I came out of the bathroom to find my grandmother hunched over her computer. "Tell Roberto I said hi."

"He sends you his love." Michelle beckoned me over. "What do you think he means by this?"

I leaned across her shoulder and read aloud the last paragraph of Roberto's message. "'Interesting stuff about Tio Armando. Do you know if it's true?'"

Michelle looked at me, brow creased. "How would Roberto know about Tio Armando? I didn't tell him anything about that giant tortoise."

I bent closer to the computer screen. "Check your Sent Messages file."

CHAPTER THIRTEEN

I backed up and watched my grandmother navigate to her Sent Mail folder. "Here it is." She clicked on her last message to Roberto. "With all the attachments."

I surmised that when Michelle had attached the photos from Laurel's flash drive to her email message, she must have selected multiple files at a time. In between photos, she had accidentally included a Word document from the same folder with the photos. Now she clicked on the lone Word attachment and together, we watched the hourglass as we waited for the file to open.

"This connection is so slow," I muttered.

"Patience. We're out in the middle of the ocean."

The document opened. I'd been holding my breath, and I released it in a puff.

Text appeared on the screen. Our heads collided as we again bent over the computer, skimming the article. The words, "Tio Armando" appeared.

There was a knock at the door.

Michelle glanced at her watch. "We're late for the evening briefing."

The knock grew louder. Deborah's voice called, "Michelle? Giovanna? Are you in there?"

"We should find out what's in store for the rest of the cruise." Michelle threw me an apologetic look.

I went to answer the door while she closed the laptop.

"We're coming, Deborah." I opened the door.

Deborah held up a flash drive. "You were through with this, weren't you, Michelle?"

"Is that Laurel's?" Michelle joined us at the doorway and eyed the device in Deborah's hand.

"It fell out of your pocket at the infirmary last night," Deborah explained as she handed the flash drive to Michelle. "I was going to give it back to Laurel after I downloaded the photos I wanted, but I thought I'd check with you first."

So, Michelle's attacker didn't take the flash drive. Then what was the motive for knocking out my grandmother?

"Thanks. I'd like to give it back to her myself since I'm the one who borrowed it." Michelle started to drop Laurel's flash drive into her pocket, hesitated, contemplated the desk drawer across the room, then opted for the pocket. She edged Deborah and me into the hallway and closed the door to the cabin behind us.

"Speaking of Laurel, have you seen her?" I asked Deborah, as we walked toward the auditorium.

"Not since yesterday," replied Deborah. "I've stopped by her room a few times, but there's never any answer. Odd that she wasn't in the auditorium this morning, either, while the police were conducting their investigation. She must still be sick."

"I haven't seen her since we were in the water," I said. "And she wasn't in her room when we got back from our hike yesterday afternoon. She wasn't in the infirmary last night. Are you sure Laurel was the one who called you?"

Deborah's response was a blank look.

"What did Laurel say to you when she called yesterday?" pressed Michelle. "I mean, what specific words did she use?"

Deborah scrunched her face. "I don't remember. Something like, 'Hey, it's Laurel, I feel awful. Tell everyone I'm staying in this afternoon.' And then she hung up before I could ask her anything."

"You said her voice sounded funny, like she wasn't herself," I reminded her.

"The voice was husky. Almost masculine." Deborah thought for a moment. "She said she was Laurel, so I just assumed . . ."

Michelle and I looked at each other.

Deborah put her hand over her mouth. "You think something happened to her?"

Daniel had already begun speaking when the three of us slipped into the back of the auditorium. Sue tapped her watch and gave Deborah a sharp look.

"Ladies and gentlemen, as you know, we've had to make some changes to our itinerary due to circumstances beyond our control." Daniel glowered at us latecomers. "The police have asked us to arrive in Santa Cruz earlier than planned, so we'll be available to clear up more questions about the death of our colleague, Fernando Ferrar."

Sympathetic sighs punctuated some groans and grumbles.

"But we have several expeditions planned for you, on and around the island, so don't worry. You'll still get to see plenty of wildlife and beautiful scenery."

Helga waved her program in the air. "Does this mean we will not go to Punta Pitt?"

"I'm sorry, Madame, but all cruise lines reserve the right to alter their schedules when necessary, and we can't guarantee specific wildlife sightings. But most of the animals in the Galapagos thrive on more than one island, so you have the chance to see many of the same species in various locations." Daniel pushed his glasses up his nose. "We're committed to giving you a first-class adventure vacation."

Mumbling from the guests ensued.

Daniel turned away from the audience and pressed a clicker. A map of the Galapagos Archipelago appeared on the screen. With a laser pointer, he marked our current position, reviewed where the ship had been so far and then focused on the island of Santa Cruz. "We'll stop tomorrow morning for a dry landing on Plaza Sur, off the eastern coast. You'll have an excellent opportunity to see some large land iguanas and Galapagos

Shearwaters. After a two-hour hike, we'll proceed to Puerto Ayora, earlier than we had expected."

The next slide projected pictures of the small black and white birds—Galapagos Shearwaters—which, Daniel explained, had a range as far north as western Mexico.

"Will we visit the Darwin Center tomorrow afternoon, then?" Jean-Marc interrupted. "I read that tortoises are most active in the morning."

"We're still scheduled to visit the Darwin Research Station the following morning," Daniel replied. "The ship will overnight in Puerto Ayora."

Jim looked elated. Janice frowned.

"Will we have time for shopping in Puerto Ayora?" asked Jenny. "The guides wouldn't let us stop at the stores in the last town." She grinned at Jessy, who dimpled at the suggestion.

Daniel smiled. "Plenty of time for shopping in Puerto Ayora. We'll be there longer than scheduled. But we'll also arrange a snorkeling trip tomorrow afternoon for those who are interested."

My heartbeat quickened at the mention of another opportunity to snorkel. Closing my eyes, I could still feel the panic of watching the boats move farther away from me and Laurel while I treaded water and fought the waves invading my nose and mouth. Would I ever want to snorkel again?

"Once we arrive in Puerto Ayora, we'll know more about what activities we can offer. Do you have questions about the tortoise reserve you visited today? Or anything else you've seen so far?" Daniel turned off the slide projector.

"Yes. Why did they move Tio Armando?" asked Dieter. "We thought we'd be able to see him today."

Daniel looked agitated. His eyes swept the room and locked on Elena.

"How do you lose a 250-kilo animal?" Dieter demanded.

Elena rose and came forward. She took the microphone from Daniel. With an apologetic glance at her boss, she turned to the audience. "No one told us until this afternoon that Tio

Armando would be moving." She addressed Dieter. "Señor, he's not lost. They said he's been taken to Santa Cruz, which as you know is our next island. We're trying to find out where he is and arrange for you to visit him."

"Is he at the Darwin Center?" asked Helga. "That would make the most sense if they want to breed him. It would be a shame to let another sub-species die out. Like poor old Lonesome George."

"The Darwin Research Station does not have him," Elena replied. "We were hoping they did, but a private sale is being arranged."

I watched Michelle steal a glance at Jim, but he kept a poker face. The twins looked at their dad, but he remained impassive even to them.

"First Laurel, now Tio Armando?" I whispered to Michelle. "Like Dieter said, how do you lose an animal that huge?"

"I can't wait to read the rest of that report," said Michelle.

The crowd poured out of the auditorium and dispersed to the restaurants. I suggested to Michelle, "How about having dinner upstairs at the Ocean Grill? It will be faster than the dining room, and I don't think it's as windy tonight." I'd vowed not to let Michelle out of my sight until we'd examined the contents of Laurel's flash drive, which we already knew contained more than vacation photos.

Helga and Dieter approached us while we were waiting for the elevator. "I learned something curious about Laurel Pardo today," Helga said. "Remember you told me you had not seen her since the last snorkel trip?"

The elevator doors opened, and the four of us got in, along with two Japanese tourists. Helga placed her finger on her lips and looked at me during the ride to the top level of the ship.

"Won't you join us?" suggested Dieter, as we walked out of the elevator toward the Ocean Grill.

I looked at Michelle. Neither of us could resist the prospect of hearing what Helga had discovered. "Sure," Michelle agreed.

The temperature was pleasant, the air still. The charcoal-tinged aroma and the sizzle of grilling meat reminded my stomach that I had not eaten since breakfast.

A white-jacketed waiter escorted us to a table for four. He pointed to a chalkboard that listed the specials for the evening and then took our beverage orders.

"How is the lobster prepared tonight?" asked Michelle.

"Over pasta in a light lemon cream sauce," the waiter replied. "Number two on the board."

"Sounds good. That's what I'll have."

"Me, too," I said. "I never tire of lobster."

Helga shook her head. "I don't like lobster much, and these little ones in the Galapagos are not as tasty as the North Atlantic lobsters." She studied the chalkboard. "What is the sauce you serve with the beef filet? I cannot read the handwriting."

"Béarnaise," replied the waiter. "I can bring it on the side if you're not sure you'll like it."

Helga waved her hand. "Your cook doesn't know how to make a proper béarnaise. How about a *champignon* . . . er . . . how do you call it? A mushroom sauce?"

The waiter wrote on his order pad. "Señora, I will check with the cook."

"And no garlic," she instructed.

The waiter nodded and kept writing. He turned to Dieter. "And for you, Señor?"

"I'll have what she's having." Dieter patted his wife's shoulder.

"Señor, is that the beef with the béarnaise sauce, or with a special mushroom sauce?"

Dieter raised his eyebrows. "Surprise me."

Enough about the sauces! I threw Michelle a helpless glance and we exchanged surreptitious eye rolls.

"I'll bring both sauces on the side," the waiter said, unfazed. "Will that be all?"

When no one responded, he left with our orders.

At last! "So, Helga," I said, "what did you learn today about Laurel Pardo?" *And don't tell me you saw her. Laurel, the only guest no one will acknowledge is missing.*

"I've looked for her, too, and you're right, I don't think she's on this ship anymore." With a furtive glance around her, Helga leaned across the table. "This afternoon, I overheard the kitchen help talking. When the police were here this morning questioning everyone." She lowered her voice. Her Swiss-German accent grew stronger, and I had to strain to understand. "Daniel asked one of the young ladies to pretend to be Laurel Pardo."

"What?" Michelle had been about to unroll her silverware, and she dropped it, making a thud against the wrought-iron table.

"*Daniel* asked someone to pretend to be Laurel? To lie to the police?" I shrieked. I set down my napkin and started to rise.

Helga put a warning finger over her lips.

I looked around at the other diners and then sat back down.

"Why would Daniel do that?" Michelle said. "Last night we reported to him that Laurel was missing, that she might never have come back on board after the snorkel trip yesterday morning."

"And what did he say to that?" asked Dieter.

"Daniel told us he'd talk to the guides, conduct an onboard search, and then notify the Galapagos National Park Service if Laurel didn't turn up." Michelle fiddled with her silverware.

Helga glanced around the restaurant again and then whispered, "He told the young lady to wear a bathrobe and no makeup and to tell the police detectives she had been sick in her cabin all afternoon and evening. I heard the interview was short."

"And then the young lady left the ship this afternoon, at Puerto Baquerizo Moreno," said Dieter. "Her family lives on San Cristóbal."

"Which kitchen worker—?" I began.

The waiter brought our drinks. "The salad bar is open if you'd like to start there," he advised us. "Your main course will be out soon."

I was impatient to extract more information from Helga, but Helga and Dieter rose and headed for the salad bar. Michelle and I followed.

"I don't know what some of these things are," complained Helga, as she picked up various vegetables with a tong and examined them before putting them on her plate or rejecting them. "Why can't they just bring us a proper salad?"

When we were all seated again with our salads, Michelle raised her wine glass. "To finding the truth about Laurel."

The four of us clinked our glasses.

"The people on this ship are covering something up," declared Dieter. "Someone killed a guide, and a guest is missing."

"Dieter, *Schatz*, they said it was an accidental fall." Helga took a bite of salad.

Dieter sipped his Cabernet. "Then why are the police still asking questions? Why must we alter our itinerary and head to Puerto Ayora a day early?"

I gulped.

"Do you think they used a substitute to minimize disruption?" suggested Michelle. "Who knows how long the police would have detained us if it turned out a guest was missing, and no one had reported it?" She stared at her wine glass. "Daniel must not have reported Laurel's disappearance."

I shook my head. "I don't think he ever planned to. You should have seen the look on his face when I asked him today." I looked at Dieter. "What's your theory about why Laurel vanished?"

Dieter puffed his cheeks. "Maybe she and Fernando Ferrar were involved with something illegal."

Michelle and I exchanged incredulous glances.

Helga thumped the side of her husband's head. "*Dummkopf.*"

"What do you think happened, Helga?" I asked.

Helga huffed. "Negligence. You remember, Giovanna, they almost forgot you yesterday. They didn't pick up all their passengers before they left the area. There ought to be a serious fine for that." She kneaded her forehead. "I hope poor Laurel swam to shore or got rescued by another boat."

The waiter arrived with our meals. The lobster pasta was still steaming, and the sweet lemon cream sauce smelled heavenly. I picked up my fork.

Helga stared at her steak. "What is this? This meat is overcooked." She leaned toward Dieter, who was making faces at his plate. "How is yours?"

He pushed his plate away. "Let's go downstairs. Maybe we can get a decent meal from the main restaurant."

Michelle raised her eyebrows as our dinner companions excused themselves and left the table. She picked up her fork and stabbed a chunk of fresh, grilled lobster coated with creamy sauce.

I smiled. "The pasta is delicious. Hurry and eat so we can go read the rest of that document."

We hurried back to the cabin as soon as we'd finished dinner. I put the chain on the door while Michelle inserted Laurel's flash drive into the USB port of her laptop.

I fidgeted while the computer booted up and recognized "new hardware."

CHAPTER FOURTEEN

Michelle and I waited at her computer. At last, the flash drive's files came into view.

"Here's that document we were reading about Tio Armando," said Michelle. "I must have sent it to Roberto by accident. Looks like Laurel misfiled it in the Photos folder."

"What's this one?" I pointed to a folder called Research. "It looks interesting."

Michelle clicked on it.

The folder contained photos of the Beagle Galapaguera, the tortoise reserve we'd just visited on San Cristóbal. The timestamp was a week old. Laurel had taken shots of Tio Armando in the now-empty enclosure from various angles, much more detailed than the images we'd seen in Elena's presentation last night. He had a long, wrinkled neck, beady little eyes, and flat, pinkish nostrils above his beak—not unlike the two giant tortoises we'd watched sparring at the reserve today. Except Tio Armando was missing a toe on his front left foot, as Elena had mentioned in the briefing.

Michelle studied the screen. "Jacqueline was right. He reminds me of E.T."

There were photos of more giant tortoises at a different reserve—one we had not visited. The label read, *Isla Isabela.*

"After a while, they all look alike," I said.

"Don't let Elena hear you say that." Michelle wagged her finger. "Although these tortoises have similar shells."

I squinted at the screen to compare photos. "If you say so."

There were several documents full of notes: times and dates, measurements, interview synopses written in Spanish. Another file contained a report of DNA test results from a lab on the mainland, comparing two animals. We skipped through the bars and dots of the analysis to the summary, which concluded that the two animals were genetically related.

"One of these samples is labeled *Tio Armando*," I observed. Michelle and I looked at each other.

"What does that mean?" I asked. "Tio Armando is not—?"

"Let's look at that other document," said Michelle. "The one Roberto saw, that we were reading when Deborah knocked on the door." She went back to the misfiled document, and we re-read Laurel's article.

Tourism had declined after the death of Lonesome George, the giant tortoise who had been the most famous attraction in the Galapagos. Interest in conservation had waned. People seemed to be taking a more fatalistic attitude, believing nothing could be done to stop climate change and the gradual extinction of many species. Corporations with deep pockets were putting more pressure on the national park service and the Ecuadorian government to allow increased development.

Then Tio Armando was discovered, living on an obscure tortoise reserve on San Cristóbal, the Beagle Galapaguera. The naturalist who had brought him there for rehabilitation claimed to have found the giant tortoise, almost starving, on the island of Floreana. Scientists had performed DNA testing and proclaimed Tio Armando to be the only remaining member of a Floreana sub-species thought to be extinct for more than a century.

The marketing campaign began. Tio Armando put the Beagle Galapaguera on the map. Cruise ships visited, bringing busloads of tourists to photograph him. Investors poured more money into giant tortoise research. Laurel had come to the Galapagos as part of that wave.

A bidding war had begun, as several other reserves boasted superior breeding programs and proposed to relocate Tio Armando to their properties. The goal was to breed him with a similar sub-species to keep his genes in the pool—an experiment they had tried unsuccessfully with Lonesome George. And now a resort being constructed near Puerto Ayora by the

American company, Leisure Dreams, was vying for the privilege of housing Tio Armando.

"Jim Roberts," Michelle said. "I told you that's why he's here."

"'Showcasing a beloved symbol of a near-extinct species will bring awareness to the public about the special and precarious ecosystem in the Galapagos,' said Jim Roberts, CEO of Leisure Dreams." I read. "What a crock!"

As part of her research program, Laurel had made a trip to Floreana, searching for more survivors of Tio Armando's sub-species. She revisited the location where he had been found, trying to determine how he alone had survived there so long, undetected. She had also visited some little-known giant tortoise reserves on Isabela Island. There she discovered a colony of tortoises that bore a strong resemblance to Tio Armando. She collected tissue samples and sent them to an impartial lab on the mainland for DNA testing.

"Tio Armando has a family." I whistled. "He's not lonesome, like George."

"That must have been what Roberto meant in his email," agreed Michelle.

According to most of the correspondence in the folder, Laurel's findings were not well received. Angry emails contained accusations that she had faked the tests. Laurel ran new DNA tests, at a different lab, and they yielded the same results.

I couldn't tell if she had finished the article; it just stopped. Laurel might have been at a loss about her next steps. She had expected the discovery to be welcome, proof that Tio Armando's sub-species was not quite as endangered as everyone had feared. She had found candidates for the breeding program. Instead, her information was viewed as a disruption to an income stream. The world cared more about money and publicity than knowing the truth.

"I wonder how many people she told about her discovery," said Michelle. "The cruise line built up Tio Armando in their brochures. They might not want people to find out he's just another giant tortoise."

Michelle and I looked at each other.

"Do you think this research could be the reason Laurel is missing?" I asked.

"And what did Fernando have to do with it?" Michelle stared back at the screen.

I remembered my last encounter with Fernando on the deck. "He knew something."

That night, I dreamed I was swimming underwater, propelling myself through reefs with my flippers, surrounded by sparkling fish and undulating anemones. Laurel's distorted face appeared, and she pointed desperately at something. I turned to spot a giant tortoise with a missing toe struggling to reach the surface, its leathery appendages paddling against the current, its heavy carapace sinking like an anchor. *But giant tortoises are land animals,* I thought. *Tio Armando is not a sea turtle. What's he doing in the ocean? We have to help him.*

Fernando's face appeared, his features also distorted underwater. A trail of blood trickled from the middle of his forehead down the bridge of his nose. He held up both hands, blocking my path and preventing me from reaching the drowning tortoise.

I turned back to Laurel for help, but she was gone.

I jerked awake. The darkened cabin was quiet, except for the wheeze of my grandmother's snores. I smirked. Michelle had always claimed she did not snore. *I should record her*, I thought, but remained in my bed and drifted back to sleep, dreamless this time.

Michelle and I ordered coffee and croissants for breakfast in our cabin. Michelle accepted the tray from the room service steward at the door and carried it to the coffee table.

I picked up the china pitcher and poured cream into each cup. I looked at Michelle. "More?" We both liked lots of cream in our coffee.

"A little." Michelle took the coffee pot and finished filling our cups, then sat down on the couch. "Jim Roberts will be surprised when he finds out Tio Armando has relatives."

I lifted my cup to my lips and sipped the hot coffee as I sank to the couch. "You're not thinking of telling Jim about Laurel's research?"

"You don't think he'd want to know?"

I set down my coffee and grabbed a croissant. "I think we should be careful about who we tell. Look what happened to Laurel. And Fernando."

Michelle leaned toward the table to butter her croissant. "I see your point, but I don't think we're the only ones who know about Laurel's research."

"Maybe no one knows we know." I pulled the end off my croissant and popped it into my mouth. Flakes tumbled down the front of my shirt and onto the floor.

Michelle handed me a napkin and then finished spreading guava jam on her own croissant. "Deborah Holt had the flash drive for a day. Do you think she or Sue looked at anything besides the photos?"

I finished chewing, patted my mouth, and then tore off another piece of croissant. "Deborah is a busybody. I'm sure she looked at everything there. And I wonder about the guides."

"You think they know?"

"Eduardo told me he saw Laurel sitting with the guides in the dining room the morning she disappeared. They were arguing." I shuddered. Poor Laurel. No one wanted to listen to her.

"Arguing?" Michelle raised her eyebrows.

"And Fernando made a strange comment to me when we were out on the deck." I set down the rest of the croissant. "The night he died." I'd lost my appetite.

Michelle chewed, looking at me.

"He said Laurel shouldn't stick her nose where it didn't belong." My eyes strayed to the window. "And neither should I."

Michelle winced. "Fernando is dead. They say it was an accident. Laurel is missing, but no one has acknowledged it." She took a sip of coffee. "We need to find Laurel."

After breakfast, we made a dry landing on Plaza Sur, a tiny wind-blown island off the eastern coast of Santa Cruz formed centuries ago by lava streaming up from the ocean bed.

As soon as I disembarked the Zodiac and climbed up the crude stone steps from the rickety pier, I almost tripped over a three-foot land iguana basking in the middle of the path, its brownish-yellow body camouflaged against the arid soil. It raised its scaly head to blink a sleepy eye at me. Once I recovered from the shock, I snapped a close-up to capture the moment. I looked at the iguana as if he could understand me. "Sorry, Mr. Iguana. Go on back to your nap."

"Look, those iguanas are eating cactus," called Jenny from down the path, her camera already in action. She was wearing a loose green T-shirt with the face of an iguana covering her chest.

"The prickly pear cactus is the land iguana's main source of food and water," Elena explained. "No part of the plant goes to waste."

"What is all this red ground vegetation?" asked Michelle as we walked alongside Elena. "When my husband and I were here a few years ago, this island was greener."

"This *Sesuvium* is an ice plant, and it's green during the rainy season. In the dry season, its foliage changes colors—orange, red, purple—like you see now."

Elena whirled to address Jessy, who had strayed off the path and was poking a dozing land iguana with a selfie-stick, angling to get an extreme close-up. "Miss, please do not harass the wildlife. It's against the law. And stay on the path, please."

Janice stiffened and whispered something to Jessy when she rejoined our group. Jessy stuck her tongue out as soon as Elena turned her back, then dimpled as Jenny snapped her photo.

Our group hiked along the rocky trail, stopping to photograph iguanas, sea lions, Swallowtail Gulls, and Galapagos Shearwaters. I noticed that Elena kept a watchful eye on the twins as she lectured about the flora and fauna to those of us who were listening.

"No giant tortoises on this island," remarked Deborah, as she strolled up behind Michelle and me.

Michelle raised her eyebrows.

Deborah blushed. "I guess you read what was on Laurel's flash drive."

"Have you told anyone else?" Michelle shielded her mouth with her hand as she spoke to Deborah.

"I showed Sue the photos. Don't know if she saw anything else."

"Sue didn't come on the hike this morning?" I looked around for Deborah's friend.

Deborah shook her head. "Too strenuous."

"Oh, how cute!" Michelle cooed over a sea lion nursing her tiny chestnut pup as they snuggled beneath a rock outcropping for shade.

Deborah snapped a photo. "Can't wait to show Sue what she's missing."

The three of us dropped back from the rest of the group, but we didn't notice another straggler until we turned away from the mother seal and her pup. Jim Roberts, his camera hanging around his neck, gave me a faint smile. "You three hang around with that tortoise researcher . . . what's her name? Laura? Laurel?"

"Laurel," I confirmed.

"Laurel." Jim touched his camera. "I haven't seen her for a couple days. Do you know if she's still on the ship?"

"I haven't seen her since we were snorkeling buddies in Gardner Bay," I said. "Fernando told me the other boat picked her up. Was she on your boat?"

I thought I saw Jim twitch at the mention of Fernando.

"She wasn't on ours," Deborah said to Jim.

Jim recovered his composure. "I don't remember seeing her on our boat, either."

"She's gone," I said, watching Jim's face.

"Gone? What do you mean, gone?"

"Jim, were you thinking of talking to Laurel about Tio Armando?" asked Michelle. "She might have known who else had an interest in buying him."

"I wasn't trying to *buy* him," Jim insisted. "I thought I offered that tortoise the best home, all in the interest of conservation and research."

Michelle suppressed a chuckle. "Of course. And the fact he's a star because he's supposedly the last survivor of his sub-species doesn't matter?"

Jim's nostrils flared. "*Supposedly?*"

"Did the manager at the Beagle Galapaguera tell you where he went?" pressed Michelle.

Jenny skipped up to her father. "Daddy, come see the baby chicks." She tugged on Jim's sleeve and pulled him down the path, away from us.

I turned to Michelle. "What are you doing?"

"Don't you want to find out how much he knows?"

"I thought we agreed to be careful," I said.

"Sounds like Jim Roberts may have a motive to make Laurel disappear," suggested Deborah.

Michelle and I exchanged a bewildered glance.

Deborah defended her assertion. "Well, she turned up information that could hurt his business."

"Or save it from going in the wrong direction," said Michelle.

Deborah raised her eyebrows. "If you say so."

The three of us resumed our trek down the path to catch up with the group.

We passed Helga and Dieter, who had stopped to photograph some nesting Swallowtail Gulls. The avian pair stood guard over a white egg hidden under an overhanging rock. Their identical black, white, and gray plumage made it impossible for the untrained eye to distinguish male from female.

Helga looked up from her camera as we passed.

"How was your dinner in the dining room last night?" I asked. "Was the food any better than upstairs?"

"It was good." Dieter adjusted his camera lens.

They joined us as we resumed our stroll down the path.

"Jim Roberts was just asking us about Laurel," Michelle ventured. She ignored my sharp look.

Dieter huffed. "Jim Roberts!" His lip curled.

"Why the sour face?" Michelle turned to him. "I thought you were talking the other day about going into business with Jim."

"We looked at his plans for the resort in Puerto Ayora." Helga snorted, "A golf course? No."

"We're interested in investing in property here on the islands," Dieter agreed. "But more like a bed and breakfast or a cottage hotel. Something friendly to the environment." He scowled. "Jim Roberts? The man is a fool."

"Did he tell you about—?"

I yanked Michelle's arm and redirected my grandmother toward the rocks. "I thought I saw a whale out there."

"Where?" Michelle grabbed the binoculars dangling from her neck.

"Didn't we agree to be careful?" I whispered. "We don't know who we can trust."

CHAPTER FIFTEEN

The *Archipelago Explorer* set sail for Puerto Ayora as soon as the last group of us had re-boarded.

"I'll talk to Eduardo before the dining room opens for lunch," I said to my grandmother. "Maybe he knows about the Laurel impersonator."

"Be careful." The way she said it sounded like she was mocking my earlier admonitions.

Michelle went back to our cabin and I headed for the dining room.

Eduardo stood in the doorway, perusing some paperwork. "Señorita Giovanna," he greeted me as I approached.

"Hello, Eduardo. Can I ask you something?" I knew he was getting ready for the lunch service, but when he looked up and smiled, I took it as an invitation to plunge in. "A young woman working in the kitchen, who left the ship on San Cristóbal ..."

A waiter walked over and said something in Spanish, to which Eduardo gave a sharp reply. He then turned his attention back to me.

"I heard that, when the police came, Daniel asked this girl to—"

Eduardo shook his head and waved the papers in his hand. "Señorita Giovanna, I know nothing about this person." His benevolent eyes had lost some of their twinkle and his smile had vanished. "Please excuse me. The dining room will be open in about twenty minutes, if you'd like a table then."

I slammed the door to my cabin.

"No luck with Eduardo?" Michelle turned from the mirror and faced me.

"Let's go eat upstairs."

"Good choice. It's nice out." She set down her comb.

"What is everybody hiding?"

Michelle shook her head and sighed. "Maybe Eduardo doesn't know anything."

Lunch at the Ocean Grill turned out to be a pleasant choice. I began to relax, take deep breaths of fresh sea air, and bask in the warm breeze as we cruised. Fresh-grilled lobster tails were on the menu again.

A large splash off the starboard side of the ship interrupted my reverie.

"Wow, did you see that?" I cried. "It was a huge fish, and it jumped straight up!"

The waiter, balancing a tray with our food on his shoulder, looked where I was pointing. "A shark," he said. "Or maybe a manta ray." He turned back to the table and set our plates in front of us.

I caught the waiter's attention again. "Hey, can I ask you about a girl in the kitchen? You know, when the police were here."

The waiter's face hardened. "*Buen provecho.*" He stepped away.

I stared after him, open-mouthed.

There was another large splash in the distance.

"Did he say that was a whale?" asked Joseph, one of the two Air Canada flight attendants, who was sitting at the next table. He was a petite man, neatly manicured, with fine cheekbones, large dark eyes, and long lashes.

"The waiter said it might have been a shark," I replied. "Or maybe a ray."

"A shark?" Peter, the other flight attendant, got up and walked to the rail, his binoculars raised. "Was it trying to catch a seagull or something?"

"What do you think we'll be doing this afternoon?" Joseph, already over the shark sighting, addressed Michelle and me.

Michelle shrugged. "I suppose they'll make an announcement at the lecture after lunch."

After staring at the water for several minutes, during which the animal did not jump again, Peter sat down. He tossed a shock of strawberry-blond hair off his forehead and picked up his fork.

"Did you remember your sunscreen?" Joseph said to Peter, loud enough for us to hear.

Peter whipped a tube out of his pocket with his other hand. "Yes, Mother."

"Doesn't do you any good if you don't put it on," said Joseph. He picked up his fork and brought a tiny mouthful of salad to his pursed lips.

Peter set down his fork, opened the tube, and sloshed a generous amount of cream on his red face and then, stretching his lanky body like a cat, he rubbed some over his fair arms, already turning pink.

"Eww, you could have waited until we finished eating," said Joseph.

Peter shared a sly smile with me as he capped the tube and then wiped his hands on his napkin. "I heard the police want to talk to some of the passengers and crew again about Fernando."

I felt a chill as a cloud blocked the sun.

"Who told you that?" asked Michelle. "I thought they determined Fernando's death was an accident."

"We heard it from Daniel himself." Joseph sipped his Chardonnay, holding the stem by two fingers.

"So, they don't think it was an accident?" Michelle took a drink of ice water. Sometimes Peter and Joseph liked to joke around.

Peter and Joseph exchanged conspiratorial glances.

"We have our own theory about what happened to poor Fernando," said Peter.

Joseph nodded. "A woman scorned."

I played with my food, my appetite gone.

"What woman?" asked Michelle.

Peter and Joseph looked at each other again.

"That's the million-dollar question." Peter grinned. His lips were chapped white from the sun.

"That might be what it'll cost to make it go away." Joseph chuckled.

Jean-Marc, Claudette, and Jacqueline arrived and claimed a nearby table that other guests had just vacated. Jean-Marc greeted Michelle as they passed. "*Salut, Madame.*"

"*Salut,*" Michelle replied. She launched into an animated conversation with them in French, and I couldn't comprehend what anyone was saying. I hoped she was asking something inconsequential, like how the family had enjoyed Plaza Sur.

As her parents were getting seated, a beaming Jacqueline came over to our table and held her digital camera toward Michelle, showing off pictures she'd taken of iguanas on the island. At least I assumed that's what she was showing my grandmother; she didn't bother to show her pictures to me.

Joseph leaned across the aisle to join the conversation with Michelle and the French family, his French-Canadian twang giving a lilt to certain words.

I looked at Peter, who was not saying much.

He caught my eye. "Never much good at French," he mouthed, pointing to his chest. "Just squeaked through my language test when I got hired at Air Canada."

I smiled, feeling less excluded. "May I see your binoculars?"

Peter and I walked to the rail and watched the waves. The outline of Santa Cruz Island filled the horizon on the starboard side.

"Boobies." Peter tapped my shoulder, and I trained his binoculars in the direction he was pointing. "They look so different when they're flying. Like ducks."

"That's because you can't see their bright blue feet." I took the binoculars away from my eyes and handed them back to

Peter. "I feel like the ugly American when Michelle goes off in French like that."

"You? Ugly? Not a chance." Peter put the binoculars back around his neck. "Where did your mother learn French? It's unusual for an American to speak so well. She has very little accent."

I didn't bother to correct Peter's reference to Michelle as my mother. "She always liked to study foreign languages in school, and then she lived in France for a couple years when she was in her twenties."

"*Voilà*, then. That's what you should do if you want to learn another language." He winked. "And get a lover while you're there. You'll learn it fast."

I covered the smile that crept over my lips. My friends often said they had a hard time picturing their parents or grandparents having sex. But Michelle? I could totally see her with a French lover.

A pod of dolphins swam by, arching their sleek gray backs over the waves and playing in the ship's wake. Peter and I leaned over the rail and pointed with excitement, and several other passengers got up from their tables to look.

I watched Michelle chattering away in French after the dolphin sighting. *I hope she's not spilling what we found out about Laurel and Tio Armando.*

After lunch, we headed downstairs to the auditorium, where Daniel gave a lecture on climate change. He referenced a map that illustrated how the gradual warming of the oceans over the last century had affected the flora and fauna of the Galapagos.

"We were lucky to see those penguins the other day," he said. He looked around the room. "At least, I heard that some of you saw them." He flipped the slide to a picture of a Galapagos penguin, which elicited a collective "ah" from the audience. "In another decade, there may be no more penguins in the Galapagos."

"Maybe penguins weren't meant to live in the Galapagos in the first place," snickered Jim Roberts, who was sitting with his family behind Michelle and me. "It's right on the equator, for God's sake."

Janice elbowed him as I turned around to confirm the identity of the speaker. Michelle turned around too.

"What?" Jim deflected his wife's jab. He caught Michelle's eye. "Global warming is propaganda by the government to justify new taxes on business. The climate will change regardless, as it's been doing for millions of years. Taxes and regulations won't stop it."

I noticed several nearby passengers look their way.

"Daddy!" Jenny buried her face in her hands.

"Some people refuse to believe the science if it interferes with their plans for development," came a male voice.

Daniel continued his talk without engaging the comments from the audience. He showed a few more charts and then changed the subject. "Tomorrow morning, we'll be visiting the Charles Darwin Research Station, just outside Puerto Ayora."

More slides flashed across the screen as Daniel discussed various conservation projects sponsored by the Darwin Foundation.

Jean-Marc raised his hand. "Will we see Tio Armando when we visit the Darwin Research Station tomorrow?"

Daniel cleared his throat. "We don't have any information about Tio Armando's whereabouts. We'll try to find out more this afternoon, once we reach Puerto Ayora."

"The children will be disappointed if we cannot see Tio Armando," said a woman.

Daniel pushed his glasses up his nose. "This afternoon, we've arranged a snorkeling trip. I think the children will enjoy that."

He projected more slides onto the screen, showing different fish species we could expect to see on the snorkeling trip, which would take place off Isolete Caamaño, a nearby islet. "The Galapagos is one of the only areas on earth where you can see pelagic species of fish so close to shore."

"Pelagic species?" asked Peter. In a lower voice, he added, "Is that a good thing?"

"Pelagic fish live in deep water—neither in reefs nor on the bottom," explained Daniel. "Examples are hammerhead sharks, tuna, manta rays. No guarantee you'll see all of them, but you have the chance. Some of you have already seen rays and sharks on our previous snorkel outings."

I pictured the hammerhead shark Laurel and I had marveled over when we were snorkeling in Gardner Bay. The last time I saw Laurel.

"You may also see marine iguanas near the rocks and the ubiquitous sea lions," Daniel continued.

"What if we just want to shop in Puerto Ayora?" asked Joseph. "Some of us might have had enough of the sun." He put his hand on Peter's shoulder.

"Certainly," Daniel replied. "We'll offer continuous Zodiac service to the pier throughout the afternoon and evening. There are plenty of stores along the main waterfront that will welcome your business."

"What if we want to snorkel *and* see the town?" asked Dieter.

"We can arrange that, Señor Brüder." Daniel shut down the presentation. "Let one of the guides know when you're ready to leave the snorkeling area. And since we're here overnight, some guests may prefer to eat dinner in town or to sample the nightlife. There are many excellent local restaurants."

We gathered our things and moved toward the exit.

Daniel held up his hand. "We'll begin disembarkation in about twenty minutes. Those who wish to go snorkeling, pick up your gear and meet Rafael on the port side. For those who wish to go into town, we'll meet on the starboard side."

He wrapped the cord around the projector and put it back in its case. "Before we leave, I need to speak with several of you." His eyes searched the room, and I felt them stop on me like the ball on a roulette wheel. "Giovanna Rogers, Janice and Jessy Roberts, can I please have a moment?"

I felt a bitter taste at the back of my throat and gulped. Michelle reached for my hand.

I crossed the room to join Janice and Jessy, who stood beside Daniel. He finished putting away the projector and then explained, "The police have a few more questions for us regarding the death of Fernando Ferrar."

I stopped by the cabin before we had to leave for town. I opened the desk drawer and retrieved Laurel's flash drive. If I had to talk to the police again, I wanted them to know about Laurel, and the documents on the device provided a motive for her disappearance.

The cabin door opened, and Michelle entered, carrying her wetsuit. "It's almost dry." She hugged it to her chest and sniffed. "Even though these suits hang out in the sun all day, they get clammy inside when they're used frequently." She set the cropped wetsuit down on her bed. "But since I skipped the last snorkel trip, mine had more time to air." She picked up her bathing suit. "What did Daniel want?"

I held up Laurel's flash drive. "When I talk to the police again this afternoon, I'm taking this with me." I slipped it into my pocket.

Michelle frowned. "You have to talk to the police again? About Fernando?"

I nodded.

"Janice and Jessy, too?"

I nodded again.

"At least you won't be alone."

"What if they try to make me look guilty?" A wave of panic hit me. "Remember, I told you I thought I saw a twin stick her head around the corner while I was with Fernando? What if she thinks she saw something? What if she tells the police I killed Fernando?"

"I thought the police concluded that Fernando's death was an accident."

I took a deep breath. Right. "Maybe they want to find out if Fernando had any connection with Laurel's disappearance like I suggested in my first interview." I patted my pocket. "I'll feel much safer when the police have this flash drive, and the motive for someone to silence us is gone."

Michelle carried her bathing suit into the bathroom. "But now we know that no one hit me over the head to get the flash drive. Deborah picked it up when I dropped it in the infirmary."

"Someone still hit you. And we don't know who. Or why."

As soon as the bathroom door closed, I opened Michelle's computer. The internet was down. I closed the lid. Jerome Haddad, my treacherous ex-business partner was likely in the Galapagos by now, and I'd have liked to find out what he was up to. Connie's last post was two days ago. Maybe I could find a Wi-Fi signal in town. I grabbed my smartphone.

The bathroom door opened, and Michelle came out wearing her swimsuit.

"What did you tell those French people and Joseph about Tio Armando?" I asked.

"Don't worry, I didn't say a thing." She picked up her wetsuit and stepped inside.

"But I heard someone say 'Tio Armando' a couple times." My fingers drummed the lid of her computer.

"Jean-Marc was wondering if he'd be at the Darwin Research Station tomorrow." Michelle zipped up her wetsuit.

"And you didn't tell him one of our fellow passengers is in a bidding war to put Tio Armando on display like a carnival freak?"

"The conversation moved quickly. We didn't go there." She picked up a towel.

I studied my grandmother. In some ways, Michelle seemed wise, like a grandmother should be. But sometimes she acted so naïve, it was amazing she had survived unscathed for so many years. I had an uneasy feeling about Michelle going snorkeling this afternoon without me. Who would protect my grandmother? I closed my eyes and tried to banish the image of myself treading water, sucking in waves, watching the boats head back to the ship. "Be careful in the ocean this afternoon, you hear?"

I started for the door, but then rushed back to give my grandmother a hug. "Stay close to the boat. And keep an eye on Rafael; he's not the most reliable guide."

Michelle patted my shoulder. "Don't worry about me. And good luck with the police."

CHAPTER SIXTEEN

Michelle sat next to Jim and Jenny Roberts on the boat ride to Isolete Caamaño. She watched them stare stone-faced at the waves as the Zodiac rose and fell with the swells. The Roberts father and daughter didn't project the same sparkle they'd had when the cruise began, when the family was all together.

"I'm surprised you're not out overseeing your resort property," Michelle said to Jim. "I thought this stop was what you were waiting for."

Jenny turned bleary eyes to her father.

"I hope to get out there later." Jim cleared his throat. "My wife's little detour to the police station has complicated matters."

"I wonder what the police want to ask that they didn't cover already." Michelle turned in the boat to face them.

Jim looked down. Jenny winced.

Michelle could tell they'd heard her, despite the noise from the Zodiac's outboard motor. "Giovanna ran into Fernando on the upper deck not long before he had his accident. I imagine that's why the police want to speak to her again. Maybe to get a better timeline of his last movements. Did Jessy see him, too? Or Janice?"

Jim buried his face in his hands. "Who knows what that woman does?"

Michelle knitted her brow. "But you share . . ."

Jenny touched her father's shoulder and then looked at Michelle. Her eyes watered.

Jim pulled Jenny's head onto his shoulder.

Deborah Holt, seated on the other side of Michelle, nudged her. "They're separating," she confided. "I heard them talking about it this morning."

"What?" Michelle spun toward Deborah.

"I heard this vacation was a last-ditch effort to make it work." She nodded, with a glance at Jim and Jenny. "So sad."

Several passengers leaned to the side of the Zodiac and pointed at a pair of brown pelicans who nose-dived into the water in pursuit of a meal. The conversation shifted to the wild-life.

Michelle kept Giovanna's admonition in the back of her mind and stayed in the middle of the pack of snorkelers. She and Deborah agreed to be buddies. They swam through schools of angelfish and surgeonfish, the water crackling with the electricity of underwater life. They watched a large parrotfish nibble algae off the coral. A blue damselfish poked its head out of an underwater crevice. Although the vibrant marine life was spectacular, the water was not as clear as other areas where they had snorkeled.

Periodically, Michelle lifted her face above the surface and waved at Rafael, then raised her hands and locked them over her head to signal that she was okay. The water around the boat rippled with the kicks of the snorkelers' fins.

Michelle was catching her breath again when Jean-Marc surfaced, excited. "We saw a giant manta ray! Did you see it?" He pointed, gestured for her to come along, and then plunged back underwater.

Michelle swam after Jean-Marc. Deborah followed. In a moment, they were rewarded with a ringside view of the dark shape, a stealth bomber gliding through the water, its wingspan at least ten feet across, its long, thin tail guiding it like a rudder.

Jenny and Jim swam nearby, and Jenny snapped multiple shots of the ray with her underwater GoPro camera. She twisted her lithe body like a gymnast to capture the best angles.

Michelle felt a tug on her leg. She turned to find Jacqueline clinging to her, tiny fingers clawing at her wetsuit. The snorkel mask covered the child's face, but her movements conveyed fear. Jean-Marc and Claudette were swimming several yards away.

Michelle took Jacqueline's arm and steered her to the surface. "*Qu'est-ce qui se passe, ma petite?*" *What's the matter, little one?* Jacqueline was about the same age Giovanna had been when they'd met—when Michelle had first learned she was a grandmother—when she'd had almost no experience relating to a child.

"Batman! *La grande bête!*" Jacqueline cried, her blue lips trembling. "*Le diable!*"

It took Michelle a moment to realize Jacqueline feared the giant manta ray, which, she had to admit, projected a specter-like aura. Yes, maybe it even looked like the devil. "*Calme, ma petite. Ne t'inquiète pas. Il est parti maintenant.*" *Don't worry, it's gone now.*

Jacqueline relaxed her grip a fraction, and Michelle signaled Rafael that they were ready to get out of the water. The operator propelled the boat to them, and Michelle boosted Jacqueline aboard. She followed, with Deborah behind her.

"Was the water a little murky?" Rafael asked.

Michelle and Deborah looked at each other and shrugged. "Maybe a little," said Michelle. "What's normal for this spot?"

"I've been on the radio with some of the other boats," said Rafael. "A large yacht ran aground here late last night, and there might have been a fuel spill. They're investigating—" Another transmission interrupted and static muffled Rafael's words.

Jean-Marc and Claudette had both surfaced, panic-stricken as they looked around for Jacqueline.

Michelle waved to get their attention.

Claudette caught her eye, and Michelle pointed at Jacqueline, unmasked and wrapped in a towel. "*Voici*," Michelle mouthed.

The grateful French couple dog-paddled to the boat, and in a moment, they were aboard and reunited with their daughter.

"*Merci beaucoup, Madame*," Claudette thanked Michelle, stroking Jacqueline's wet curls.

"*Il n'y a pas de quoi*," Michelle replied. *It was nothing.*

Rafael spoke into the radio in Spanish and then turned to the passengers in the boat. "We have to go. They've found a lot of damage to the yacht's tanks, and fuel is leaking fast. The park service is closing off this area as a precaution."

He blew his whistle and then called to the remaining snorkelers, "All aboard. Time to go!"

Word circulated, and the others made their way back to the boat. Michelle was pleased to see Rafael counting heads. She was counting too.

Helga shook water off her goggles as she sat down in the Zodiac. "It was a little muddy down there. Not so nice as Gardner Bay."

Jim was the last passenger aboard. As he stepped onto the Zodiac, there was a huge splash off the other side.

Jenny, GoPro still in hand, aimed and started shooting.

Jacqueline buried her face in Claudette's shoulder. The manta ray they had spotted earlier—or perhaps one of its companions—breached into the air like a whale, not thirty feet from the boat. The Zodiac dipped and swayed back and forth, spraying the passengers with seawater.

Jim grabbed Helga's shoulder for balance.

"*Mon Dieu!*" cried Jean-Marc.

"*Wunderbar!*" exclaimed Dieter.

"Wow," said Jim, shaking as he lowered himself into the Zodiac.

Rafael took a bow. "I arranged for that."

"Bravo," said Jean-Marc, playing along.

As soon as everyone settled, the motor revved, and the Zodiac began to move. Rafael said something to the operator, and they changed course. "We're going to check out the shipwreck, if you don't mind," Michelle heard him tell Jim and Dieter. "It's not far from here."

The warm wind ruffled Michelle's short hair as the boat sped through the water. They rounded the small island, and the air became thicker with gulls and a strong odor of guano and boat fuel. Someone spotted another manta ray jumping farther out, sending waves of excitement among the passengers. They reshuffled themselves in the boat and combed the horizon for another photo opportunity.

Jenny showed around the video she had taken with her Go-Pro. Michelle agreed with her fellow passengers that Jenny had done an excellent job of capturing the close encounter with the manta ray. "I'll post it on YouTube and share the link with everyone," Jenny promised, her eyes sparkling.

More boats had appeared in the area: curious fishing vessels, another Zodiac full of snorkelers, a tourist yacht. Park service and police boats patrolled the perimeter of the crash site. Rafael's radio crackled again.

Someone on the deck of an official-looking boat shouted in Spanish into a megaphone.

"They want us to leave," Rafael groused. He nodded to the boat operator. Michelle suspected that, if Rafael were not responsible for a boatload of tourists from a respectable cruise line, he would have defied the order.

The operator turned the Zodiac around.

Jim trained his binoculars on the crash site.

Michelle shielded her eyes from the sun and squinted, trying to make out the shape of the capsized yacht surrounded by rescue boats.

"What do you see?" asked Dieter.

"Nice yacht," said Jim. "Too bad they ran aground. Looks like a lot of damage."

"Here in the Galapagos, they'll hold the owner accountable for any environmental damage the accident has caused," said Rafael.

"Oh, yes, they must have destroyed a reef," said Helga. "Their fuel spill will be toxic to the wildlife."

"It's just a little yacht," said Jim. "I can't imagine it causing an environmental disaster like the Exxon Valdez in Alaska." He readjusted the binoculars. "People tend to over-react. Even the area where the Valdez sank has almost fully recovered."

"Are there any people on the boat?" asked Deborah.

"I don't see anyone." Jim stared through the binoculars. "I can read the name now: *Second Wind*."

"*Second Wind*," Michelle repeated. "That name sounds familiar."

Jim offered her the binoculars. "I like it."

I sat next to Daniel on the Zodiac ride from ship to shore. It was no surprise the police would want to speak more to Daniel, as Fernando had died on his watch. But I didn't expect to see Elena on our boat, seated on the other side of Daniel.

Emboldened by our proximity to law enforcement, I ventured, "So, Daniel, you never answered me yesterday. Did you report what I told you about Laurel Pardo?"

"There hasn't been any sign of her." He adjusted his sunglasses on his long nose.

"Did you report her missing?"

"I told you I did."

Not really. I sucked on my lower lip. "When the police were interrogating us about Fernando, they told my grandmother they'd interviewed a woman on board who claimed to be Laurel Pardo. But how could that happen if you reported Laurel missing?"

Daniel touched his glasses again.

I waited, giving Daniel my "auditor" look, which had always been effective with reluctant accounting managers. When Daniel didn't answer, I added, "I guess that's why we're on our way to talk to the police again, instead of snorkeling by Caamaño Islet with the other passengers."

Daniel turned to face me. "You deserve to know what happened."

"Thank you. I've felt like a fool. The only one who can't see the invisible passenger who everyone pretends is still on board."

Daniel gave me a half-smile. "After I talked to you, I learned we had a young woman on board, the sister of one of our kitchen workers, who was not part of the crew and not on our passenger manifest. Her name was also Laurel. Laurel Perillo. She was planning to leave the ship in Puerto Baquerizo Moreno the next morning, and she did. Her sister, who I fired, thought it was okay for her to hitch a ride without clearing it with anyone."

I shrugged, maintaining my auditor countenance. *And? What does that have to do with reporting Laurel Pardo missing? A missing passenger. The longer the delay, the greater chance of a deadly outcome.*

Daniel's eyes darted around the boat. He lowered his voice. "After I called the police to investigate Fernando's death, I panicked about the discrepancies in our manifest. A stowaway, and a missing passenger. It was simpler to ask Laurel Perillo to stand in for Laurel Pardo during the passenger interviews, so as not to complicate the situation further. In exchange, I agreed not to prosecute her for trespassing." With his erudite accent and professor-like manner, Daniel's explanation almost sounded logical. "Otherwise, we would have been detained much longer, and our guests would have become more restless."

"So, when did you report Laurel Pardo missing?"

The expression on Daniel's face said it was none of my business, but he answered anyway. "I know what you're thinking. Not until we arrived in Puerto Baquerizo Moreno."

"Not until morning? A little late to save her from drowning."

A flock of gulls flew overhead, squawking as if they agreed with me.

"Right after I talked to you, I ran into Rafael, and he said he'd seen Laurel Pardo on board after they'd returned from the snorkeling trip. It wasn't until the next morning that he corrected his statement. That's why I waited to report her missing."

"What?" Elena turned from her conversation in Spanish with the two deckhands who had found Fernando's body in the pool. "You reported Laurel Pardo missing?"

Daniel turned to Elena. "Well, yes. You told me you hadn't seen her on board."

Elena gaped.

As we approached the pier, Daniel addressed the boat operator, then turned back to me. "I told you I had to investigate before I could file the report. We take a missing person very seriously. I had to make sure Laurel Pardo was not on board. And I had to hear Fernando's explanation."

"What did Fernando say?"

The boat bumped the dock and shore workers began securing it.

"I called a meeting with all the guides, but Fernando was a no-show." Daniel rose to help us disembark. "I never got a chance to speak to him."

A police van waited at the pier to pick us up and drive us the few short blocks to the tiny stucco police station. Crime was uncommon in the Galapagos, and a group of people being led into the police station attracted attention from passers-by. I felt like I was doing a perp walk.

Sitting on a hard, wobbly chair in the sweltering, cramped lobby of the police station, I missed the luxurious trappings of the *Archipelago Explorer*.

Thin-lipped, I smiled at Janice and Jessy Roberts, mother and daughter clinging to each other like frightened kittens at a pet adoption. I flashed back to the glimpse of a sundress darting around the corner while Fernando and I stood together at the rail. The twins had dressed alike that evening, so I didn't know which girl I'd seen; Jessy must have confessed to seeing Fernando. *What's she going to say about me? And why is Janice here? Because Jessy is a minor? Moral support and alibi for her daughter? Or perhaps an encounter of her own?*

Seated across the room, Elena focused on cleaning her short fingernails with a toothpick. I was tempted to lend her my nail file. I wondered what Elena and Fernando had known about Laurel's research, and whether that knowledge had led to violence. Why was Elena singled out for more questioning, but none of the other guides? *What does Elena know about Laurel's disappearance? She seemed surprised when Daniel said he'd reported Laurel missing.*

Detective Victor Zuniga came out of the small office to greet our group from the *Archipelago Explorer.* His dark hair shone, his smooth cheeks were clean-shaven, and despite the suffocating heat, his brown uniform still held a crease. "Thank you for rearranging your schedule," he said, more gracious than he'd been during the interrogations on board the ship. He was even better looking than I'd remembered.

"You didn't give us much choice, Señor," said Daniel.

Zuniga suppressed a smile. "I promise it won't take long. I just have a few questions about the timeline. And also, about another matter that has come to our attention."

Daniel swallowed. "No disrespect intended, Señor. I believe this is everyone you asked for."

Zuniga scanned our faces and turned back to Daniel. "You can be first." He ushered Daniel toward his tiny office.

A young woman brought a tray of water in plastic cups, which she distributed to us involuntary guests. I took a sip. Lukewarm, but at least it was wet.

Daniel grabbed a cup on his way into Detective Zuniga's office. I noticed a slight tremble as Daniel raised the cup to his lips before Zuniga shut the door.

He has plenty to answer for, I thought.

I sipped my water, wishing I'd brought something to read. I took out my smartphone. My cellular service didn't work in the Galapagos, but maybe there was Wi-Fi. My phone detected three locked networks. I doubted anyone would offer me the password for the one at the police station.

I glanced around at my fellow suspects, witnesses, or whatever they considered us. Curiosity gnawed at me. Was Detective Zuniga not convinced that Fernando's death was an "unfortunate accident" as he announced on board the Archipelago Explorer? I remembered Zuniga's face when he delivered the news; his expression had hinted dissatisfaction with the onboard investigation's conclusion.

I wonder if the autopsy revealed something suspicious. My heart pounded. *Am I a suspect, or a witness?*

Talking to the others about the case, tipping my hand, seemed imprudent. If Fernando's death had been a homicide, I didn't want to reveal any personal information they could construe as motive or opportunity and thus deflect attention toward me and away from the killer.

I stole a glance at Janice, sipping her water and staring at the bare walls. Not a blond hair out of place, makeup still dry. Janice always looked so polished, despite the inner turmoil she must feel now. Being the wife of a CEO and the head of a multi-million-dollar charity gave her plenty of experience acting poised.

Even before the cruise, before having any idea we'd meet, I'd known about Janice and Jim Roberts. I'd helped with some of the audits my accounting firm had done of Leisure Dreams, and I'd even sat in a meeting with Jim once. I doubted he'd remember me though, because the group was large, and I had not spoken.

And Janice's charity, the Big D Children's Literacy Foundation, was one I'd studied as a model when I was planning my nonprofit spay/neuter clinic. She had founded the Big D Children's Literacy Foundation over two decades ago, when she was around my age, as a grassroots campaign to help low-income children in the Dallas area learn to read. Now it had grown into a four-star-rated organization on Charity Navigator with branches all over the United States. Having a wealthy business executive as a husband must have given Janice a boost.

Since the cruise began, I'd wanted to pick Janice's brain about the workings of a successful nonprofit. But so far, I'd been too embarrassed about my dismal failure with my clinic to broach the subject. Jim and Janice Roberts perched high enough above me on the social ladder to regard me with disdain. As long as I kept quiet about my life beyond the cruise, I could pretend to be an equal.

But now that we were captives together in a Puerto Ayora police station, far-off charities seemed a much safer topic than discussing the investigation into Fernando's death. I addressed Janice, "You know, I've read a lot about your work with the Big D Children's Literacy Foundation. I'd love to hear how you got started."

Janice's face lit up. Even Jessy's mood appeared to improve as her mother began talking.

I smiled. Picking charities for the topic had been the right decision.

Janice related how she had become involved when one of her college sorority sisters confessed she'd had to teach herself to read, the first in her family. Inspired by her friend's struggle, Janice had persuaded their sorority to organize after-school reading programs in some of Fort Worth's poorest neighborhoods. The venture became so successful and popular that Janice continued the work after graduation and recruited children who had thrived in the program to join forces and spread the word. Other cities heard about her success and asked for help founding their own chapters.

"Sounds like you followed your passion." I tried to keep the envy out of my voice.

"Oh yes," Janice agreed. "It wasn't always easy. There was one point when I thought I'd lose it all, but we got through it." Her blue eyes darkened but then regained their luster. "And there's never enough funding."

I raised my eyebrows. "Funding has been a problem?" *With all the rich friends you and Jim must have?*

"There's so much competition for donations," replied Janice. "So many worthy charities to choose from. And some people tell us they won't donate to us because education is the government's job."

"I thought I had it tough starting an animal charity," I said. I hadn't intended to mention my nonprofit experience, but somehow the words slipped out. "People would rather donate to save children with terminal diseases than to spay cats and dogs to prevent pet overpopulation and keep healthy animals from being killed in shelters."

"I love animals!" Jessy grinned at me.

I smiled back. It was my first real connection with the twin.

"We support animal charities," Janice agreed. "We donate to several every year, and we rescued our dog."

I stifled a chuckle. *A rescue dog.* As a teenager, I'd helped Michelle and her friends as a volunteer at the Pecan Point Humane Society. Those women were true animal rescuers who trapped and socialized kittens from feral colonies, pulled and rehabilitated abandoned pets from kill shelters and hoarding situations, and picked up lost dogs and cats reported roaming on the highway. When working pet adoptions, I often heard people bragging about "rescuing" an animal, when all they'd done was adopt it from a shelter or rescue group. Some volunteers objected to the terminology, but I'd never begrudged the adopters their right to consider themselves rescuers, too.

"That's great," I said. "I'm glad you didn't buy one from a puppy mill."

"Never," said Janice. "We saved our Buster from death row at the Arlington animal shelter."

I smiled. Adopters wanted to be heroes, and they were. Organizations like the Pecan Point Humane Society depended on them, so they could make room to rescue more animals. I was impressed that the Roberts family had chosen to adopt a mutt from a shelter when they could have purchased a designer dog from a breeder.

"What kind of dog?" I asked Jessy.

Jessy produced her phone and started to show me a picture, but before I could get a good look at the dog, Zuniga's office door opened, and Daniel emerged.

Zuniga crooked his finger at me.

My heart thudded. I gave Jessy a grim smile and rose. I felt like I was walking into a minefield.

CHAPTER SEVENTEEN

The straight chair facing Detective Zuniga's desk was no more comfortable than the chair in the lobby, although it wobbled less. The view from the new chair was better. Instead of looking at the bare, grimy walls and wondering which spots were moving insects, I was facing a drop-dead gorgeous police officer.

A police officer who might suspect me of murder.

I finished my water and searched for a place to set the plastic cup. My hand trembled, just as Daniel's had when he entered the detective's lair.

Detective Zuniga held out his hand for the cup. Our fingers grazed as the empty cup changed hands. "Can I get you more?"

I shook my head, ready to start the interview so I could remove any suspicions the police might have about my involvement in Fernando's death. "Where's Detective Estevez?"

"Today, my colleague is on San Cristóbal, in Puerto Baquerizo Moreno." Zuniga raised an eyebrow. "Do you miss him?"

"No." *That didn't come out right.* I'd posed the question as an ice breaker. Zuniga acted as if I'd tried to make a joke, and it had fallen flat.

"Señorita Rogers, I'd like to review your statement again. About the time you were with Fernando Ferrar." Zuniga settled back behind the plain steel desk. His swivel chair squeaked. "When I'm finished, please let me know if you remember anything else." He reread what he'd jotted in his notebook, which took me back to the much more comfortable library on the cruise ship, where I'd thought I'd be giving evidence about Laurel's disappearance.

I watched his luscious lips moving as he read.

He reached the end of my statement and looked at me. His lips had stopped moving.

"Uh, that about covers it." I shifted my gaze from his lips to his brown eyes. *Like chocolates.*

"Did you see anyone else while you were talking to Fernando? Maybe someone walked by? Maybe off in the shadows? Another part of the deck?"

I hesitated to betray Jessy after she'd acted so sweetly and tried to show me a picture of her dog. Why make trouble for an innocent teenager who had been in the wrong place at the wrong time, not unlike myself. "I glimpsed someone peering around the corner. But I couldn't tell who it was." That was true. I had not known which twin it was.

"Man or woman?"

"Female. She was wearing a sundress."

Zuniga wrote. "Did you hear this woman say anything?"

"It was a glint in my peripheral vision." I shut my eyes, trying to replay the scene on the deck, my last conversation with Fernando. "Like she started to come in our direction and then maybe changed her mind."

"And where was Elena?"

"Elena? I don't think it was Elena who I saw." Our eyes met, and I held his gaze.

"You said you had dinner with Elena. Did she leave the dining room when you did?"

"No, she and my grandmother were ordering dessert when I left the table."

"And did you see Elena again that night?" Zuniga consulted his notes. "Perhaps when you were searching for the missing flash drive?"

I remembered seeing someone enter Laurel's cabin when I returned from my search for the flash drive. Could it have been Elena? I didn't see enough to tell if it was a woman or a man. Just a door closing. "No. I didn't see her again that night."

"And Daniel? Did you see him anywhere on the ship after the briefing?"

"No." I pushed a strand of hair behind my ear. Maybe it had been Daniel entering Laurel's room. But why wouldn't he have answered when I knocked? He knew I was looking for Laurel, and he must have been, too, if he'd gone into her cabin to search for clues. The office felt stuffy, despite a small fan running at full speed in the corner. The air smelled musty. "Most nights, Daniel shows up in the dining room, but I don't remember seeing him while I was there. Nor afterward."

"And during your late-night search for the flash drive?"

"I didn't run into him. But I wasn't looking for him."

"What about Señora Roberts?"

"Janice?" The question surprised me. Wasn't Janice just here to accompany her minor daughter?

Zuniga nodded. "Janice Roberts."

"I saw the whole Roberts family in the dining room. They came in right after Michelle and I did." Closing my eyes again, I tried to visualize my exit from the dining room that evening. Jim and Dieter had been engrossed in conversation, but I couldn't recall seeing Janice and the girls, nor Helga, at their table when I passed it. "I can't remember if Janice was still there when I left."

"Did you know their suite is beside the pool?"

It made sense the Roberts family would not be staying in an ordinary tourist cabin on a lower deck like most of the other guests. I looked at Zuniga again. "They've never invited me to their quarters."

There was something sensual about the way Zuniga touched the back of his pen to his mouth in thought, tapped it against a crooked tooth. Was it chipped, too? Or only a little out of alignment? Words were coming out of his mouth again.

"The female who poked her head around the corner. Could she have been one of the Roberts women?"

"I suppose so."

"And this woman had gone by the time you left Fernando and went downstairs?"

"I don't remember seeing anyone else."

"And you're sure you didn't pass by the pool?"

"Positive."

Zuniga closed his notebook.

I breathed a sigh of relief, glad the interview had concluded. No handcuffs had appeared. I leaned forward, ready to rise from my chair.

Zuniga held up a hand. "There's something else I'd like to talk to you about."

I squirmed in the rigid chair.

"When we were on board the ship, you mentioned a missing passenger."

"Laurel Pardo. She's like the invisible passenger." I sighed. "Everyone tells me I'm crazy and she's not missing. According to my grandmother, you interviewed Laurel. But I haven't seen her since that morning we were snorkeling. And Daniel—"

"I know."

"You …" I looked into Zuniga's eyes. Gone was that accusing assessment that had made me so uncomfortable in my first interview with the police. "You believe me?"

Zuniga nodded, and again, his smile was almost warm. The crooked tooth, which rendered the smile a little off kilter, added character. "We interviewed the wrong person."

I blinked. Did Daniel confess on his own? Or did the police figure it out?

Zuniga picked up another notebook. "Daniel admitted a stowaway named Laurel Perillo stood in for Laurel Pardo when we were conducting our interviews. He had not yet reported Laurel Pardo missing and didn't want to complicate our investigation by not being able to produce everyone on the manifest."

I would have loved to eavesdrop on that interview. From the look in Zuniga's eyes, he was skeptical about Daniel's story.

"My colleague talked to the young lady again on San Cristóbal after she disembarked the *Archipelago Explorer*."

"Did she know the real Laurel Pardo is missing?"

"No, but she sends her apologies to your grandmother."

What's he talking about? "My grandmother?"

"I believe there was an incident in the library."

"Oh." I clasped my hand over my mouth. "It was that woman?"

"Señorita Perillo claims she was at the computer, trying to add her name to the ship's manifest, and Señora DePalma frightened her." Zuniga made a cynical face. "She hopes your grandmother was not hurt."

"She seems okay." *One more mystery solved. Now if we could just find Laurel. The real one.*

"Good. Since the young lady's efforts to legitimize her presence were unnecessary. Little did she know that, in a few hours, the cruise director himself would invite her to impersonate one of his paying passengers."

"Did you find out who turned her in?" *Maybe Fernando discovered the stowaway, and she killed him. That woman was strong enough to knock someone unconscious and impulsive enough to do it without provocation.*

Zuniga raised his eyebrows as if to remind me I was still a witness in an investigation, not a partner in solving the crime.

"I mean, that could be a motive." I pushed a sticky strand of hair behind my ear. "And she has the strength. I know you announced on board the cruise ship that Fernando died of an accidental fall, but here we are, still talking about it."

As Zuniga watched my face, his expression was unreadable. *Annoyed? Amused?*

"I'm not telling you how to do your job."

"Thank you, because we don't have any openings. There's a long waiting list for law enforcement positions on the islands." Zuniga stroked his smooth upper lip.

I stifled a giggle. "No need to worry about me."

"My partner got all the information we needed."

And you won't tell me. "So, has there been any word about the real Laurel Pardo? Daniel said he reported her missing once you let us disembark in Puerto Baquerizo Moreno." *Couldn't he share that?*

Zuniga folded his hands on his desk and looked at me. "I'm afraid not. We've dispatched messages to all the boats known to be in the area that day, but no one reports seeing her. Another cruise ship was in Gardner Bay the next day and sent some passengers for a wet landing on the beach. If Laurel Pardo had swum to shore, they would have spotted her."

I saw a glimmer of hope. "I think Laurel was a good swimmer. The land wasn't that far away from where we were snorkeling."

"The current might have been against her." Zuniga's voice softened. "We might never find her."

His words dashed my hopes.

"I'm sorry," said Zuniga. "She was your friend?"

"We'd just met on the cruise, but she was someone I could see becoming a friend." Laurel had been so funny and easy to talk to; I'd been on the verge of feeling comfortable enough to confide in her about my humiliating business failure at the hands of Jerome Haddad.

"We haven't given up," Zuniga assured me. "Two reporters from the local newspaper were near Espanola that day, and we haven't heard from them yet. But there's so much water, and the currents are unpredictable. Some divers disappeared a few years ago, and we never found their bodies."

I shut my eyes. I'd sensed right away that neither of the boats from the *Archipelago Explorer* had picked up Laurel, but I'd wanted to believe Fernando when he insisted she was safe. Why didn't I demand we go back and look for Laurel right then?

"You were courageous to insist something was wrong." Zuniga smiled. "A good friend."

"Maybe not good enough."

"You're too hard on yourself."

There was something trustworthy in Zuniga's chocolate eyes, something about the way he looked at me, something that made me feel I'd known him much longer than a few days. The feeling was not unlike what I'd sensed with Laurel. I hoped I wasn't making a mistake; my track record for judging character had been abysmal. I reached into my pocket. "We found Laurel's flash drive." I held up the tiny device. "Another passenger picked it up in the infirmary, where my grandmother dropped it."

Zuniga nodded, waiting.

I extended my hand to Zuniga, the flash drive still clutched in my fingers. "Under the circumstances, shouldn't the police keep this? Property of a missing person?" Even though I now knew Michelle's accident was unrelated, it felt safer to relinquish possession of the flash drive containing Laurel's research. I remembered the disarray in Laurel's cabin right after her disappearance. Someone might have been looking for those files. Someone might have wanted Laurel gone.

Zuniga took the flash drive. "I thought you said there were just vacation pictures on it."

"There's more."

"You've read what's on it?"

A shiver crept down my spine, despite the sweltering heat of the room. *What have I done?* The police could be corrupt. Or Zuniga could be a rogue corrupt officer, in on the conspiracy to silence Laurel. There were no witnesses to our conversation. No witnesses to the fate of the flash drive. No copies, except for one document in Michelle's email. And Laurel's computer, which housed the originals, was missing.

Zuniga studied the flash drive as if he were not sure what to do with it.

"Most of the documents are in Spanish," I said.

"You don't understand Spanish?"

"I'm sorry." I wasn't sure why I was apologizing. For being the ugly American with no desire to learn the language of the country I was visiting? To protect myself from being harmed for knowing too much, since I wasn't able to read the secret documents? "I never studied it in school. I'm not good at foreign languages." *Foreign.* I winced. I was in his country, and I was calling his native language foreign.

Zuniga tapped the flash drive on his desk. "Then I guess I have some reading to do."

I fidgeted in my chair, longing to breathe some cooler air.

"Do you think documents on this flash drive made Laurel a target? That they deliberately left her behind in Gardner Bay?" Zuniga studied the device in his hand. "And perhaps Fernando was involved?"

"It's possible," I replied. "I leave that conclusion to you. You're the detective, and your office doesn't have any openings." With a wink, I stood. This time, he didn't stop me.

A dimple appeared under Zuniga's mole as he rose to show me out. "Wise decision."

"Will you let me know what you find out?" *The cruise will end, and I'll go home, perhaps never knowing what happened to Laurel.*

With his hand on the doorknob, Zuniga ignored my question and switched to pleasantries. "What does the cruise line have planned for you here in Puerto Ayora?"

Music to my ears. I had permission to rejoin the cruise ship. "Tomorrow, we'll visit the Darwin Research Station."

"You'll enjoy it." Zuniga's eyes scanned my frame from head to toe as if assessing me as a regular person instead of a suspect.

"We were all hoping to see Tio Armando."

Zuniga's hand froze on the knob. The door's opening was too small for me to squeeze through and bid *adiós*. "Tio Armando? Didn't you see him on San Cristóbal?"

Why did I bring up Tio Armando? He's about to read the tortoise's whole story. All of Laurel's research. "He wasn't at the Beagle Galapaguera. Someone moved him."

"Moved? Where?" Zuniga frowned. "Tio Armando is a celebrity here in the islands. He's been at the Beagle Galapaguera since he was discovered. How do you move a famous animal that huge without everyone knowing about it?"

I slinked between Zuniga and the office door. "Another mystery for you to solve, Detective. The reading material I gave you might help."

Zuniga gaped as I scooted past him and broke free, back into the lobby. Without turning around, I knew he was still watching me.

Janice and Jessy went into Detective Zuniga's office together, faint smiles on their faces as they exchanged places with me.

I decided there must be a law requiring a parent to be present during the questioning of a minor, and I found that protocol reassuring. Like maybe Ecuador wasn't a barbaric country where the authorities would throw someone in jail and detain them without due process.

Elena and the two deckhands lingered in the lobby, but Daniel had left.

I addressed one of the deckhands, who'd looked up when I came out of Zuniga's office. "Can we leave if he's already talked to us?"

The deckhand's face was a blank.

Elena said something to him in Spanish.

Translating for the ugly American, I thought, as the deckhand shook his head in response to Elena.

Elena looked at me. "No one has told us anything. Daniel said he'd be at the store across the street if anyone is looking for him."

I wanted to go outside for some fresher air, even though I knew it was just as hot. I sat down next to Elena. "What do you recommend doing here in Puerto Ayora?"

Elena thought for a moment. "We'll visit the Darwin Research Station tomorrow, so don't miss that. It's right outside town."

I found comfort in Elena's statement about the planned visit to the Darwin Research Station as if life would return to normal and we'd be back on our cruise agenda by morning. That we'd move past the nightmare of Fernando's death and the police interrogations.

"If you have some time this afternoon," Elena continued, "it's pleasant to walk along the waterfront. You'll see some interesting hand-painted murals. And there are several nice beaches not far away."

"What are you planning to do?"

"I hope to go home tonight. I live in a nearby town, Bellavista."

"With your family?"

"I have my own place," said Elena. "But some of my relatives live nearby. My sister checks on things when I'm gone."

Since reading Laurel's findings about Tio Armando, I'd taken more interest in Elena's tortoise research. "You said you worked at a tortoise reserve when you were younger. Was it on this island?"

Elena brightened. "El Chato. It's in the highlands. One of the best places to observe Galapagos tortoises in their natural habitat."

"Didn't you say you'd worked at the Darwin Research Station, too?"

"I did. That was later."

"Did you meet Lonesome George?"

Elena smiled. "He was a favorite of the tourists. Staff, too."

"How does Tio Armando compare?" I watched Elena's smile lose some of its brightness.

Elena swallowed. "Tio Armando is popular. But he's not as well known yet."

"How did you know he's the last of his species?"

"Sub-species. We can breed him with similar animals and perhaps save his line."

"Sub-species." I lifted the wet hair off my neck and fanned myself with it. The pedestal fan in the lobby whirred at top speed, but it could barely stir the humid air. "I mean, did someone do DNA testing or something?"

Elena's lips tightened. "Scientists have done their due diligence."

"Did Laurel Pardo ever talk to you about her research on Tio Armando?"

"Laurel?" Elena flinched.

"Why were you so surprised when Daniel said he'd reported her missing?" I focused on Elena's face. "You said she didn't get on your boat that day to ride back to the ship."

Elena's face paled. The smile had gone.

The door to Detective Zuniga's office opened, and Janice and Jessy hurried out. Jessy was crying.

CHAPTER EIGHTEEN

Elena and I exchanged questioning glances as mother and daughter brushed past us and bolted out the front door. A rush of warm wind filled the room in their wake.

Detective Zuniga beckoned Elena to his office. She rose. Head down, she did not make eye contact with me again.

The office door closed behind them.

I eyed the exit. *Why am I still hanging around here?*

With a nod at the two deckhands, I got up and walked out.

The sun beat down on the concrete sidewalk, but a gentle breeze blew in from the bay to dissipate the heat. I took a deep breath and turned toward the water.

Squawking pelicans and gulls hovered around an open market where fishermen unloaded their catch from the boats into slatted wooden boxes whisked away as soon as they were filled. The smell of fresh fish permeated the salty air. Dockworkers called to one another in Spanish as they guided small boats to the quay, tied them up so they could unload, and made room for more arrivals.

Vendors gutted their fish and laid out the specimens on long concrete tables for locals and tourists to purchase. As they worked, their helpers shooed away begging sea lions and pelicans.

One worker tossed a scrap of fish innards at a flock of waiting birds. Three pelicans dived at it, squabbling in a free-for-all until another worker tossed more scraps their way. The competitors scattered, grabbing for the new offering of smelly treats.

When a worker turned his head, a young sea lion catapulted itself from the ground and slid onto the concrete table, its maw open and ready to devour a newly-laid-out fish. Just in the nick of time, the aproned worker spun around and swatted the animal back down to the brick floor.

I spotted Janice and Jessy entering a souvenir shop across the street from the fish market. *Nothing like a little retail therapy to calm a pouty teenager.* I wanted to catch up with the pair and continue my conversation with Janice about charities, but I wasn't in the mood for browsing in a tourist shop.

Across from the shop, I found a sun-bleached bench covered in bird droppings and a darker substance even thicker. Before I could find a clean place to sit, a low bark stopped me. A black, bulky object rolled from underneath the bench: a young sea lion. It raised its head to study me as if deciding whether I was fit to share its bench. "Sorry to interrupt your nap." I shook my head, amused at how talking to a sea lion seemed normal. I opted to stand.

In less than fifteen minutes, Janice and Jessy came out of the shop, each carrying a large plastic bag. Janice waved, so I walked over to speak to them.

"Find anything interesting?" I observed their bulging bags.

"Not a lot of selection, but I bought presents for most of the people on my list." Jessy peered into her bag. "I wonder if these T-shirts fall apart after you wash them."

I strode alongside the Roberts pair. "How many people can say they have a T-shirt imported from the Galapagos? You'll be the envy of your class when it's time to tell about where you went on your summer vacation."

"Naw," said Jessy. "It's a private school, and most of the families take exotic vacations. Some of my friends think nothing of jetting off to Paris or London for the weekend."

Michelle and Roberto had jetted off to Paris or London for the weekend more than a few times in all the years they worked for the airlines. Yet they were middle class. Somehow, that thought narrowed the class gap between me and the Roberts family. And here we all were, cruising the Galapagos, one of the most exotic locations I could imagine.

We walked a few steps in silence. I couldn't tell if my company was welcome, or if it would be best for me to excuse myself and explore the streets of Puerto Ayora on my own.

"But how many of your friends can say they've been suspects in a homicide investigation?" The shocked look that passed between mother and daughter made me wish I could stuff the words back into my mouth and swallow them.

The silence that followed was longer and even more awkward than before. I should have revisited the subject of charities.

"What happened to Fernando was an unfortunate accident," said Janice, through clenched teeth. "It was his own fault."

His own fault? The thought formed, but the words did not leave my lips.

Jessy's eyes watered. The retail therapy had lost its effect. "I'm sorry, Mommy."

Janice pulled Jessy into a hug, stroking her back with the shopping bag still in hand. "You didn't do anything wrong, honey."

I cleared my throat. "I didn't mean—"

Janice looked at me. "Of course, you didn't. She's just upset about this whole situation."

Jessy sobbed harder. "I should have—" Her words dissolved into a muffle as she buried her face in her mother's shoulder.

"What happened?" I asked. Like me, the Roberts women—or at least Jessy—must have had some contact with Fernando close to the time he died.

"Let's sit." Janice motioned toward the bench where I'd seen the sea lion.

I pointed to the dried excrement coating the surface.

"Oh." Janice wrinkled her dainty nose.

"Gross." Jessy made a disgusted face.

We spotted another bench closer to the waterfront and walked to it.

"Better." Janice pulled a new Galapagos-themed beach towel from her bag. She spread the towel over the surface of the bench, then sat down and eased Jessy beside her. I joined them on the edge of their towel.

Jessy sniffled. "I thought he liked me."

"I'm sure he did," I reassured her. Fernando liked females of all ages. I remembered how he had fondled me on the deck, minutes before he had met Jessy. *What a sleaze.* "What did he do?"

The rims of Jessy's wet blue eyes had become red and swollen. Her sobs came out in spasms.

Janice's mouth hardened. "He had no right."

I turned away, trying to piece together Fernando's movements after we'd parted. It had to have been Jessy peering around the corner at us. "Did he ask you to meet him by the pool?"

Jessy nodded.

Janice sighed.

"And you met?" I prompted.

Jessy nodded again. Fresh tears trickled from her eyes.

Janice rubbed her daughter's shoulders.

"What did he do?" I asked again.

More tears.

"Why did you think he wanted to meet you?"

Jessy shrugged through more tears. "I thought he liked me."

Janice looked at me. "You forget the girls are only sixteen. They haven't dated much. And Jessy has some . . . " She pressed her lips together as if they were about to reveal too much. "Some medical issues."

"You and your sister are very attractive," I said to Jessy, not wanting to delve into any private medical issues. "You have to be careful not to invite the wrong kind of attention." As soon as I heard the words exit my mouth, I knew they sounded trite and preachy. I winced. I'd heard advice like that when I was Jessy's age, and I didn't always heed it. It just annoyed me.

Jessy wiped tears from her cheeks with the back of her hand.

Her mother handed her a tissue.

"I'm sorry, Mommy."

I wondered what it had been like for Detective Zuniga, trying to get this mother-daughter pair to recount their story, a rambling tale peppered with tears and apologies and false starts. It sounded like one of them might have witnessed Fernando's last dive into the pool. But whatever happened, their encounter with Fernando had taken place after mine, and thus Detective Zuniga must believe me to be innocent. What a relief. I looked at Janice. "You interrupted them?"

Janice massaged Jessy's back, and her blue eyes strayed to the bay. Her head started to nod in agreement.

Then her hand froze in place.

Janice straightened and craned her head toward the pier. "Oh, my god! I know that man."

Back on the *Archipelago Explorer*, Michelle took a luxurious hot shower and then put on fresh clothes. Giovanna had not yet returned from her second interview with the police.

Michelle blow-dried her short hair and then applied her magenta lipstick and a smattering of translucent face powder. It was hard to shake the unnerving feeling that haunted her when she thought of Giovanna and Fernando on the open deck, and then Fernando dead in the pool. *Did Giovanna tell me the whole story?* Michelle knew her granddaughter couldn't have had anything to do with Fernando's accident but were the police convinced? If Fernando's death was an accident, why were the police still interrogating people? Why were they questioning Giovanna?

She checked the time as she fastened her gold Seiko watch around her wrist. *Five-thirty already. How long should this interview take?*

Giovanna had her smartphone with her. Her cell service did not work outside the United States, but perhaps she'd found a Wi-Fi connection.

Michelle opened her laptop to check her email. She'd send Giovanna a message in case she was somewhere she could receive it and reply that she was okay.

After she pressed "Send," she crossed her fingers that the Wi-Fi connection would hold long enough to deliver her message to her granddaughter.

The message went through, and a new message had just arrived from Roberto.

She was about to read Roberto's message when there was a knock at the door.

With a groan, she opened the door to find Deborah and Sue standing in the hallway.

"Cocktail time," said Deborah. "Let's go watch the sunset."

Despite some cloud cover, the sunset resembled a painting, with bold streaks of purple and orange coloring the sky. The clouds, outlined in the sun's fading glow, enhanced the drama of the spectacle.

While Michelle, Deborah, and Sue sipped iced beverages, Deborah encouraged Michelle's participation in her recounting of their close sighting of the manta ray during the snorkel trip that afternoon.

Sue's eyes grew large as Michelle and Deborah took turns telling how the giant animal had breached right next to their inflatable boat.

"I asked that American girl, Jenny, for some pictures," said Deborah. "I was too amazed to do anything but watch, but she snapped that camera like a pro. She said she's posting a video to YouTube."

"I'd love to see the pictures." Sue sounded wistful.

"Silly, if you'd gone snorkeling with us, you wouldn't have missed so much of this fantastic wildlife."

Sue wrinkled her broad nose. "Can you see me squeezed into one of those skintight wetsuits? And with my luck, I'd get attacked by a shark."

"They say the sharks around here aren't dangerous if you don't provoke them," said Michelle. But she concurred that

Sue's plus-size body would not fit into a ship-supplied wetsuit, even though the material stretched.

"Never have been a big fan of the water." Sue cast a glance at the churning sea below.

"Not sure how I persuaded her to come on this cruise," agreed Deborah.

"It's worth it without getting wet." Sue tipped her margarita glass toward the others in a toast. "Look at that sunset."

"And I'm sure you'll join us for the trip to the Darwin Research Station tomorrow?" Michelle touched her glass against Sue's. "Maybe we'll see Tio Armando."

Deborah's eyes widened. Sue averted hers.

Michelle sipped her daiquiri, savoring the taste of fresh-squeezed lime. "You must have read Laurel's research about that tortoise when you had her flash drive."

Sue stirred her drink with her straw and avoided looking at Michelle.

Michelle continued, "It contradicts the hype we've heard from Elena."

"A lot of rubbish, if you ask me." Sue let out a slurp with her straw.

Laurel's research, or Elena's hype about Tio Armando's sole-survivor status? Michelle wondered.

"Did you see those DNA tests," Michelle said, "comparing Tio Armando with animals from that tortoise colony on Isabela Island? I don't think anyone else wants to hear about it."

"Why would Laurel hand over a flash drive with such sensitive information on it to a relative stranger?" asked Deborah. "Did she not think you would see it?"

Laurel had not struck Michelle as a careless person. "Insurance?" she guessed. "Safekeeping, in case something happened to her?"

"And you think something has," said Sue.

"Giovanna does."

A waiter came by with another tray. Deborah and Sue exchanged their empties for fresh drinks, but Michelle shook her head and held up her half-full glass.

"I think we all agree that no one has seen Laurel since we left Gardner Bay," Michelle continued when the waiter had left. "Deborah, you and I have talked about this. With Giovanna." *Giovanna might have been the last person to see Laurel alive, just as she might have been the last to see Fernando alive.* The thought gnawed at Michelle. *An unlucky coincidence.*

Sue looked at Deborah. "But didn't Laurel ring us that afternoon, after we set sail? You're the one who talked to her."

Deborah crunched a piece of ice. "I thought it was her. I mean, she said, 'It's Laurel.' What reason did I have to think otherwise?" She swallowed. "But now, I'm not so sure. Nobody has seen her. And she didn't sound like herself on the phone."

"You've said that several times," Sue reminded Deborah.

"Could it have been a man who called?" asked Michelle. "Or was it a woman's voice?"

"Could have been either," conceded Deborah. "The voice was husky, muffled even. I assumed she was coming down with a cold."

"Have you stopped by her cabin again to see if she might be in there?" Michelle sipped her drink.

"I go by there a couple times a day," replied Deborah. "But there's never any answer when I knock on her door."

"Giovanna and I went by that afternoon while the cabin steward was cleaning." Michelle eyed the darkening sky. "And the door was open."

"Let me guess." Sue took another big slurp of her margarita. "Laurel wasn't in there."

"Neither was her computer." Michelle finished her drink and set her empty glass on a nearby table. "It looked like someone ransacked the place."

"Crikey." Sue pressed a hand against her plump cheek.

Michelle looked at her watch. It was almost six-thirty. "We still have a briefing tonight, don't we?"

I turned in the direction Janice was pointing. "I know that man," she repeated, bristling like a mother cat confronting a ferocious pit bull.

A swarthy middle-aged man, several days unshaven, baggy shirt untucked, was being led along the pier, handcuffed, from a boat to a waiting police car. I squinted. *No! Could it be?*

"Jerry Haddad. Son of a—" Janice spat the words. She put the emphasis on the first syllable of his last name, instead of the second, so I almost didn't recognize it.

Jerry? Even Connie didn't call him that.

An overzealous officer tried to hurry the prisoner into the car, which earned him a violent elbow jab. The officer jumped back as if struck by a snake, but his partner closed in, and the captive complied.

"What the hell is he doing here?" grumbled Janice.

A flood of emotions hit me. I'd known Jerome Haddad was coming to the Galapagos. I'd been tracking the progress of his journey on the *Second Wind* through the social media postings and clues left by his wife, my former friend Connie, who had never unfriended me on Facebook.

And here he was. What now? I wanted to see him punished for his crimes, and most of all, to stop him from preying on anyone else. All my energy had gone into the quest—to gathering evidence of his web of financial crimes, spying on his movements, pestering various agencies to charge him with something illegal, any offense to warrant punishment. *I never thought I'd find him. What a divine coincidence. What an opportunity...*

Jerome Haddad, in police custody. I only wished I'd been the reason for his arrest. However it had happened, though, I hoped they'd detain him for a long time—accused of a violation serious enough to stick. *And if he experiences a little rogue police brutality . . .*

The police car drove away. Janice stared after it.
Jessy had stopped crying.
I turned to Janice. "How do you know Jerome Haddad?"

CHAPTER NINETEEN

s the police car disappeared around a corner, Janice turned away and spat, "Jerry Haddad is the most dreadful, disgusting, despicable human being I've ever met." She rolled her tongue along her teeth as if to wipe away a bitter taste. "If you could call him a human being. *Monster* is more fitting."

I closed my gaping mouth.

"Whatever they got him for, I hope they throw away the key." Janice glared at the spot where the officers had forced Jerome into the police car.

"What did he do to you?" I asked.

Jessy rested her chin in her hands as if ready for a story she'd heard before.

Janice looked at her daughter, and I sensed Janice was toning down her language for Jessy's sake.

"That S.O.B. almost destroyed Big D Children's Literacy Foundation," Janice began.

"What?" My eyes grew wide. "How?"

"He came to me when we were just taking off. Said he admired my work, and he wanted to open a chapter in Florida." Janice shook her head. "What a charmer he was. Showed me pictures of sad little inner-city kids in Miami. Cuban refugees. Talked about how my program could benefit them. How it would help them learn to read English."

"Let me guess," I said. "He brought financing. He told you what you wanted to hear." I gazed up at the sky as a flock of sea birds passed overhead.

"Yes!" Janice raised her eyebrows in disbelief. "He set up a huge fundraising drive for the Miami branch. All my big donors opened their wallets. I cheered them on and encouraged them—shamed them—into giving more, pressuring all their contacts. One business owner even set up a donor challenge, matching all contributions dollar for dollar."

I touched my forehead with a clairvoyant flourish. "And I bet all the money went into Jerome Haddad's pocket?"

"Did you read about it? It was front-page news for weeks."

"I wish I had." I gazed at the bay, still full of fishing boats coming in. "Then I wouldn't have trusted him with the financing for my spay/neuter clinic in Georgia."

Now Janice's jaw dropped. "You, too? Oh, no! When did this happen?"

I clenched my fist. "He sailed here in a yacht financed with my building as collateral. His last big purchase before he declared bankruptcy this spring." I shifted my gaze to the empty road where the police car carrying Jerome Haddad had passed. "Not sure where that fancy toy is now. I was half-expecting to see it tied up at the dock here. I bet he sold it before it could be repossessed."

"He's slippery as an eel," Janice agreed. "Left me naked to face the angry mob. And then got scary abusive when I questioned him about what he'd done."

"Wow! I'm so sorry."

"I thought I was going to jail." Janice stroked her daughter's ponytail. "He shattered my dream."

It was as if I was hearing my own story being told by someone else.

"By then I'd met Jim and we'd gotten engaged," Janice continued. "Jim and his father had connections. Lawyers who unraveled the mess, proved I'd been swindled. I still had to pay back a lot of the donors, but Jim's family helped."

"That was fortunate." My respect for Jim Roberts jumped up a notch.

"And the best part was, Big D Children's Literacy Foundation survived." Janice smiled for the first time since we'd spotted Jerome Haddad on the pier. She had perfect white teeth like her husband and daughters. "We floundered for a few years, trying to overcome the negative publicity and rebuild trust, but now we're strong. I owe a lot of that success to Jim. He and his team of lawyers made the Haddad fiasco go away."

I wished Tim had been half as sympathetic to my situation as Jim was with Janice. Instead of blaming me for trusting Jerome. Calling off the wedding. So much for the part about "for richer or poorer, for better or worse." Good riddance to him. Janice's story had a happier ending than mine.

"The experience brought Jim and me closer together." Janice's eyes moistened. "That was a long time ago."

"Mommy." Jessy reached for her mother's hand.

"These hotshot lawyers of Jim's," I said. "Why weren't they able to pin anything on Jerome? He committed fraud! He stole tens of thousands of dollars! Why isn't he rotting in prison?"

"They focused on clearing my name and saving my charity instead of going after Jerry. The paper trail was sketchy. So convoluted. That man is smart. He's a lawyer, too, you know, and he's a master at covering his tracks."

"Tell me about it. So many shadow companies, all owned by him or his wife, incorporated under various names, using different nonexistent P.O. boxes. Changing names, addresses, and phone numbers every few months."

"And then he vanished." Janice's blue eyes stared at nothing. "He has family in Lebanon. We thought he might have gone there. I didn't know he'd slithered back to the States." Her eyes returned to my face. "Sounds like he picked up where he left off."

"You don't know how many letters I've written, phone calls I've made." I sighed. "There's a government agency for everything, but no one seems to have jurisdiction over the dealings of Jerome Haddad. Everyone refers me somewhere else and wishes me luck."

"I wish I'd known he'd returned." Janice shook her head. "I hate that he did the same thing to someone else. And got away with it once more."

I gazed down the empty road again. "He hasn't gotten away with it yet."

The evening briefing on the *Archipelago Explorer* had few attendees, as many of the guests were still ashore. Michelle searched the auditorium for Giovanna but did not find her.

Daniel talked more about the Charles Darwin Research Station they'd visit in the morning. Pictures of the modest, seventies-era buildings of the interpretive center were projected on the screen as he spoke. He repeated some of the information from his lecture the day before.

"The Puerto Ayora station, the main location, was established in 1959 to promote conservation and education about the ecosystems in the Galapagos." Daniel pushed his glasses up his nose. "The Charles Darwin Foundation helped create Galapagos National Park and thus establish protected status for so many unique species."

He pressed the remote. A picture of smiling scientists filled the screen. *One of those women resembles Laurel,* Michelle thought. *Could it be her? I wonder when that photo was taken.*

"The Darwin station boasts a team of over one hundred scientists, educators, students, researchers, and volunteers from all over the world, all with a common goal—to learn more about this archipelago's natural resources so we can better manage and preserve them." Daniel pressed the remote again and the screen changed to a picture of a large land iguana. "Since 1976, the Darwin Foundation has sponsored a land iguana breeding program."

Michelle noticed Janice and Jessy slip into the darkened room and take seats near the door instead of making their way to the empty chairs next to Jim and Jenny.

"And we all remember Lonesome George," Daniel was saying to the image of the famous tortoise now on the screen. "A biologist named Joseph Vagvolgyi found him in 1971, the last survivor of the Pinta Island giant tortoises."

"What about Tio Armando?" called a voice.

"We're still trying to learn his whereabouts," Daniel replied and moved to the next slide.

"How could such a national treasure disappear?" insisted the male voice in a strong Latin accent. "An animal so big."

The picture on the screen had changed again to pens of young tortoises.

"In 1965, the Darwin Foundation established its giant tortoise repatriation program, and it's still going strong." Daniel's firm tone suggested he had nothing more to say about Tio Armando. "You'll get a good glimpse of how it works tomorrow."

Helga and Dieter had plans for dinner ashore, so they were not in the briefing. Otherwise, Michelle suspected they would have kept pressing Daniel for more information regarding Tio Armando's whereabouts. The other guests took Daniel's hint and dropped the subject.

Michelle's eyes strayed again to the doorway. She knew Janice, Jessy, and Daniel had all gone ashore with Giovanna for a second interview with the police. *Why isn't Giovanna back with the others?*

"We've arranged for a bus from the pier to take you to the research station tomorrow morning around eight," Daniel said. "And buses back as well. But some of you may enjoy the walk. You'll have a few hours of free time to explore the town of Puerto Ayora before we set sail for North Seymour Island tomorrow afternoon."

"Walk? Ha." Sue wiggled her swollen feet. "Thanks, but I think I'll take the bus."

The briefing ended, and the auditorium began to empty. Some people rushed out, others lingered and chatted among themselves, a few stopped Daniel with questions as he put away the audiovisual equipment.

Michelle stood within earshot of the Roberts family as they reunited. The twins hugged each other, and Jenny showed Jessy pictures from the snorkeling trip that afternoon. Jenny thumbed through the wildlife shots on her digital camera as Jessy oohed and aahed.

Janice and Jim faced each other, and Michelle could almost feel the arctic blast. "So, were you able to convince the cops you didn't kill your boyfriend?" Jim's jaw stiffened like concrete.

Boyfriend? Michelle stepped back, feeling like a voyeur. But a cluster of chattering Japanese women and a row of chairs blocked her egress. Deborah and Sue had taken a different aisle down the maze and had already escaped the room.

"It won't be a problem for your precious resort," retorted Janice, her voice frosty.

The twins looked at each other, and Jessy's eyes watered. Jenny touched her sister's hand, and they both averted their eyes from their parents.

"Thank God for that." Jim turned his back on Janice. "But I can't believe you dragged our daughter into it."

"You weren't there," Janice argued. "Maybe if you'd stopped working for five minutes—"

"You're unbelievable, woman." Jim squeezed into an opening in the crowd and disappeared.

Michelle turned her head to spare Janice from embarrassment.

"Come on, girls," said Janice. They moved toward the exit, which cleared the path for Michelle.

Giovanna had not returned to the ship. After checking the cabin, Michelle made her way to the upstairs restaurant. The tantalizing aroma of grilled fish aroused her appetite.

With a glance around the terrace for a familiar face who might want company, she settled into a seat at an empty table near the rail so she could watch the waves and relax in the warm night air. *Deborah and Sue must have gone to the dining room. I've had enough of their company for one night anyway.* Michelle had eaten alone at restaurants many times during her flight attendant career, and the prospect did not bother her, but this was the first time she had dined by herself on this cruise.

The waiter brought her a menu and a glass of chilled Chardonnay. "Thanks." She opened the menu. "What's the special tonight?"

He pointed to the chalkboard. "Grilled tuna steak."

"Is that what I smell?" Michelle craned her neck toward the kitchen and took a whiff of the charcoal-broiled fish.

Lifting his nose to the air, the waiter nodded.

"Then that's what I'll have, please." She closed her menu and handed it back to him. "Thank you."

"Mind if I join you?"

Michelle looked up to see Jim Roberts seat himself in the chair across from her. He turned to the waiter, who was walking away, and held up a bar glass. "I'll have what she's having, and another scotch-on-the-rocks. Please."

Michelle smiled. "I guess you were confident in my answer."

"I was in the mood for a healthy discussion about global warming." The Ultra Brite smile flashed, although Jim's eyes did not smile.

"What kind of discussion can I have with someone who disregards science?"

"Oh, but not all scientists agree."

"You're right." Michelle sipped her wine. "Some studies are funded by people with an agenda."

"Everyone has an agenda."

The waiter brought Jim's drink and set it on the table. Jim picked up the glass and took a gulp.

Michelle watched. "I thought you'd be out visiting your resort property."

"You mean like, having dinner there?"

"Maybe."

"It's not finished yet. No one here is in a hurry to do anything." His eyes made a quick scan of the outdoor dining area.

"I always have to remind myself that these off-shore projects take three times as long."

"You were expecting more? Maybe people on the golf course already?"

Jim laughed. "We're taking a tour of the site tomorrow after the visit to that turtle place."

"You mean the Darwin Research Station?"

"Whatever." Jim drained the rest of his scotch. "The place where they'll feed us all that evolution propaganda."

"Propaganda?"

"Oh, I forgot. You buy it." Jim rattled his ice cubes. "Anyway, would you like to join us for the site visit tomorrow? It might help you see my project in a different light."

The invitation took Michelle aback.

"Your daughter's welcome to come along, too. If you two don't have other plans."

"I can't speak for Giovanna." Michelle took another sip of wine. "But I'd like to see your property. Thanks for inviting us."

Jim hailed a passing waiter for another drink and winked. "We Americans have to stick together."

The waiter arrived with their meals. The grilled tuna steaks sizzled on the plates. Michelle's mouth watered as she inhaled the aroma of seared rosemary with a hint of dill.

Another waiter followed with the scotch Jim had requested and a bottle of Chardonnay. He topped off Michelle's glass.

Michelle unrolled her flatware and placed the linen napkin in her lap. "I guess you didn't know, but Giovanna is my granddaughter. I don't have a daughter."

"Granddaughter?" Jim sat up straight in his chair. "You must have been a child bride."

"Not a bride."

Jim pounded his hands against his forehead. "I don't want to hear it. I have two sixteen-year-old daughters."

Michelle cut a piece of tuna with her fork and lifted it to her mouth. The fish was moist, and the blend of herbs, chili, and citrus delighted her senses. She chewed slowly to savor it.

"What was it like to be a single mom?" Jim asked, between mouthfuls.

"I wouldn't know." Michelle took another sip of wine.

He raised his eyebrows.

Oh dear, I've opened a can of worms, she thought. *It's got to be the wine.* "I gave the baby up for adoption."

"What?"

"My boyfriend was struggling to stay in college to keep from being drafted and sent to Vietnam, and neither of us was ready to get married. Best decision we ever made because it would have been a disaster."

"But . . ."

Michelle sipped more wine, aware she had exceeded her usual allotment tonight. *How did I get started down this path? The story is too complex for a casual conversation.* "My parents wanted me to go to college, and college was my dream too, which would have never happened if I'd kept the baby. It was a traumatic year of my life, but after it was over, it was like I'd pressed the undo button and gone on with my plans."

Jim attacked his tuna steak like he had not eaten all day. "You never thought about the baby you gave up?"

"I did. But I'd made my decision. I took the other fork in the road." She picked up her fork again as if to illustrate her point.

"Then what about . . .?"

"Giovanna's mother found me fifteen years ago. My son—Giovanna's father—was killed in the first Gulf War, so I never got to meet him."

Jim swallowed a mouthful of mixed vegetables. "Oh, no."

"He died around the time Giovanna was born." It still hurt to think about the baby she never got to see grow up.

"I'm sorry."

"Giovanna and I are connected by a man neither of us ever knew. Giovanna's mother was our link to him, but now she's gone, too."

Jim gave her a sympathetic grimace.

"*Voilà*, that's how I became a grandmother. And now you know my life story." Michelle stabbed a piece of roast potato with her fork. "I'm not sure why I told you."

"Well, you know a lot of my business, too." Jim pushed some vegetables onto his fork with his knife.

"And I'm sorry about—"

The waiter came to remove their plates and asked if they wanted dessert.

Michelle declined. Over the waiter's shoulder, she noticed Janice and the twins walk onto the terrace.

"Nothing else for me." Jim rattled the ice cubes against his glass and took a last swig of scotch.

"Will your wife be joining us tomorrow?" Michelle asked. Janice and the twins stood at the entrance to the restaurant area as if deciding whether to bother with dinner. They must have seen Jim, but they did not move toward the table.

"I don't know." Jim set down his glass.

"Look, I don't know what happened, and I don't expect you to tell me."

"My wife has a problem staying faithful." Jim traced a droplet of water down the side of his glass with his thumb.

"What?"

"I should have realized it when we met. She was dating someone else, and she kept seeing both of us for a while." He stared into the ice cubes, sparkling under the artificial light of the outdoor restaurant. "Until he screwed her over big time, left me to clean up the mess."

"But wasn't that a long time ago?"

"She hasn't stopped." Jim rubbed the condensation on the side of his glass. "She's bipolar—takes meds for that—and if the dosage gets off a little, she turns into a wild woman."

"Really?"

"Even on this ship. Our family vacation. Nice."

"What? Who?" Despite overhearing Jim's earlier accusation, Michelle had a hard time picturing that polished socialite, mother of twins, in the throes of passion with a womanizer like Fernando.

Jim shook his head. "It's over now."

Michelle touched her hand to her mouth. "Fernando? Was that why the police wanted to question Janice again?"

Jim's face reddened.

"But you still love her? After all this time, you must have faith in the relationship, or you would have left." Michelle rested her chin on her hand, studying the paradox of Jim. *Confident corporate mogul, cuckolded—repeatedly—by a woman he worships.* "Why do you stay?"

Jim's face reminded Michelle of a confused puppy.

Michelle's eyes swept from Jim to Janice, who still lingered at the entrance. "Your wife and daughters walked in a few minutes ago. Why don't you go ask her about tomorrow?"

Jim followed Michelle's gaze. He removed his napkin from his lap, set it on the table, and then rose. "Excuse me."

Michelle waited for a few moments, and then she, too, folded her napkin and rose from the table.

To give Jim and Janice a wide berth, Michelle approached the twins, who had moved several feet away from where their parents were talking. They looked over the rail at the ocean and pointed out sea birds to each other as the birds dove into the dark water to ambush unsuspecting fish. "Excuse me, Jessy."

Jessy turned. "Yes, ma'am?"

"This afternoon, you and your mother were with my granddaughter, Giovanna, weren't you? At the police station?"

Jessy nodded.

"Have you seen her since then?"

Jessy pushed a wind-blown strand of blond hair out of her face. "She hung out with us for a while after we finished talking to the policeman."

At least he didn't arrest her. "But Giovanna didn't come back to the ship with you?"

"She said she wanted to look around town a little longer. There was someone she had to see."

Michelle's heartbeat quickened. "Who?"

Jessy shrugged.

"Did she say where she was going?"

Jessy's hand covered her mouth. "Giovanna's not back yet?"

Jenny turned away from the rail to face Michelle. She frowned at her sister.

Michelle studied the puzzled expressions of the twins. *Where's Giovanna?*

CHAPTER TWENTY

Inside the musty Puerto Ayora Tavern, Detective Victor Zuniga perched on a bar stool, an almost untouched draft beer on the counter in front of him. There was only one other customer in the room, seated at the far end of the bar—a dive instructor acquaintance, lost in alcohol-numbed thoughts.

Zuniga studied the rough diagram he'd sketched of the *Archipelago Explorer*. Along the side of the paper, he had jotted time coordinates. For each person of interest, he'd sketched caricatures and then cut out a paper avatar. He erased and re-drew small details in his timeline and map of the ship, referred to his notes, and then moved the avatars around his map, like chess pieces, plotting the last evening of Fernando Ferrar's life.

He picked up the "Daniel" avatar. The eloquent cruise director had been Fernando's boss. After the story Giovanna and Michelle had told him about a missing passenger on Fernando's watch, Daniel had good reason to be angry with Fernando. *Daniel had wanted to confront him.*

Zuniga wrote the time "2300" and circled it. Daniel had scheduled a meeting with all the guides for eleven p.m., and its purpose had been to gather information about Laurel Pardo's disappearance. *The cruise line had to get its story straight before reporting the incident to the authorities. But why wait four hours from the time Giovanna and Michelle had told him Laurel was missing? So much for any sense of urgency.* Zuniga touched his lip with the eraser end of his pencil. *Wouldn't Daniel consider a missing passenger an emergency? The longer they waited to search for her, the less chance for a rescue.*

With a little digging, Zuniga had discovered that Laurel Pardo was not just any passenger. Her father, Hector Pardo, the next-of-kin emergency contact listed with the cruise line, was a wealthy, award-winning producer of nature documentaries. Attempts to reach him had been unsuccessful because he was shooting a film on a remote island in the South Pacific. Zuniga hoped he would have answers available by the time Señor Pardo found out his only daughter had vanished in the Galapagos. He could only imagine the disruption an irate father and an insatiable media could bring to his quiet community.

Zuniga looked back at his diagram. Earlier in the evening, Daniel claimed he'd been in the kitchen, dealing with another crisis—a stowaway situation. Laurel Perillo, sister of one of the kitchen workers. *Daniel concerned himself with a live, healthy stowaway instead of a marooned guest?* Zuniga sighed. *Maybe Daniel thought the stowaway posed a security threat. And the next morning, Daniel used the situation to avoid complicating my investigation into Fernando's death by admitting he had not reported a missing passenger. Very convenient. Even more convenient that their names are so similar. Blame it on a misunderstanding or clerical error if he got caught.*

Zuniga tapped his forehead. There were problems with Daniel's timeline. The attack on Michelle DePalma by the stowaway in the library had happened between nine and nine-thirty. If Daniel had discovered Laurel Perillo's presence earlier in the evening, why was she still trying to elude him? *Maybe she was doing something else in the library.*

Regardless of his other transgressions, all Daniel's movements that evening were accounted for and corroborated by staff and passengers. *Daniel had no reason to kill Fernando. He had the power to fire him if he'd wanted him gone.* Zuniga set down Daniel's avatar.

Zuniga had already eliminated the two deckhands who had found Fernando, dragged him out of the pool, and tried in vain to revive him. Both had been in bed before nine p.m.; other crewmembers had verified their alibis. According to the autopsy report, Fernando had been dead for hours by the time they pulled him out of the water at five a.m. Fernando had not attended Daniel's eleven p.m. staff meeting, so Zuniga figured the time of death must have been around ten or ten-thirty. He set aside the avatars of both deckhands.

He picked up the "Elena" avatar. When Fernando missed the staff meeting, Elena claimed she'd gone to search for him. She had walked by the pool and called his name, but the lights were out, and she had not looked into the dark water. *The lights were out. Was that usual? Was it safe?* Zuniga made a note to ask. *Was it even true?*

Elena seemed distressed because she had missed that detail. "What if Fernando was still alive?" Elena had wondered aloud to Zuniga. "Could I have saved him?"

Or maybe when Elena passed by the pool, the incident had not yet happened? That would put the time of death after eleven. *But then why had Fernando skipped Daniel's meeting? Had he found female company after all? And who, then?*

Zuniga consulted his notes again. Elena and Fernando had been friends and had worked on many ships together. *She doesn't seem to have a motive for murder; there's no history of arguments that escalated into violence.* Zuniga had not detected any romantic entanglement, which might have erupted into jealousy if Elena had caught Fernando wooing female passengers. *Which he did often, with Elena's knowledge.* Other than the few minutes of her search on the upper deck, Elena's account of her movements that evening was supported by passengers and crew.

But Elena is hiding something. Zuniga stroked his lips with her avatar. *What is it?*

Michelle returned to her cabin after dinner. She found everything as she had left it—no evidence that Giovanna had returned. She checked her watch against the travel alarm on her nightstand. Ship-to-shore shuttle service was operating all night, and many cruise passengers had opted to sample the Puerto Ayora nightlife. But Giovanna was not a fan of bars and nightclubs.

With a sigh, Michelle opened her laptop. *Giovanna's almost twenty-five years old, and she's been self-sufficient for years. There's nothing I can do now except make myself sick with worry.*

The internet was working, so she logged into her email account. There was no response yet from Giovanna. Michelle opened the message from Roberto that had arrived right before she left for the evening briefing.

The cats were fine. After several weeks of drought, it had rained. And Tim had called.

Tim Edwards, Giovanna's ex-fiancé. Tim said Giovanna had not answered his calls and texts.

She's angry because you broke up with her, Tim, Michelle thought. *Because you didn't stand by her when she needed you, when her dream business collapsed. It wasn't her fault; it happened because of that unscrupulous partner she got mixed up with. But you blamed her. I thought you were better than that.*

Roberto had told Tim that Giovanna and Michelle had gone on a trip together. "I hope that was okay," Roberto wrote. "I didn't tell Tim where you went."

Michelle smiled. Roberto had always been afraid to overstep with Giovanna because he wasn't her blood relative. She reread the email. It didn't matter if Tim knew where they'd gone. The Galapagos islands were hard to get to. She doubted he'd come looking for Giovanna here, and even if he did, it would not be a bad thing.

Michelle dashed off a quick reply to Roberto, assuring him he had not violated Giovanna's privacy with his disclosure. She told him about the snorkeling trip and the manta ray, the hike on Plaza Sur, and their upcoming visit to the Darwin Research Station. Tio Armando...*no need to bring up that.* She also left out Laurel's disappearance, Fernando's death, and that it was almost ten o'clock at night and Giovanna was not back from shore yet.

At the bar, Detective Victor Zuniga studied his makeshift map of the *Archipelago Explorer*. He picked up the "Elena" avatar again.

Elena's responses this afternoon had been troubling. Zuniga had only asked her to come back for additional questioning to pinpoint the time of her search for Fernando, to get a firmer idea of his time of death. And he also hoped to find out if Elena had noticed anything in the pool area or near the Roberts suite that she had omitted in her first interview.

Zuniga reviewed his notes. When Fernando missed the eleven o'clock staff meeting and Elena could not locate him, everyone assumed he'd charmed his way into the bed of one of the female passengers, which further enraged Daniel. The meeting had been brief, since Fernando was the main person Daniel wanted to question about Laurel Pardo's disappearance. According to Daniel, none of the other guides claimed any knowledge of the incident, nor could they confirm or deny the young researcher's presence on board.

But Elena had guided the other boat full of deep-water snorkelers on that fateful outing. When Zuniga asked her about it, she admitted she had not picked up Laurel.

When Zuniga asked Elena why Fernando might have thought Laurel got on Elena's boat after speaking with her on the radio, Elena's face had paled.

But she had recovered, saying, "Rafael was bringing another boatload of passengers back from the beach around the same time. Maybe Fernando talked to Rafael on the radio."

Elena insisted she'd known nothing about Laurel's disappearance until Daniel mentioned it at the staff meeting.

Daniel might have believed her, but I don't, Zuniga thought.

Michelle read more email and was about to sign out when a new message appeared. It was from Tim Edwards. Tim was the son of a childhood friend of hers, and she had known him most of his life, but he was not a usual correspondent. Most likely, his decision to contact her had something to do with Giovanna.

She opened the message.

Polite as always, Tim apologized for bothering her but said he'd been unsuccessful in his attempts to reach Giovanna. He had some news she might want to hear. News about Jerome Haddad.

Michelle scrolled down. Tim had included a link to an online article from a newspaper in Florida.

She clicked on the link and waited for the article to open.

A grainy photograph of Giovanna's ex-partner accompanied the article. Even in black and white, those cold, piercing eyes gave her the creeps.

The story was about a group of senior citizens who had contributed to a donor-advised fund set up by JerCo Investments, LLC. A sidebar defined a donor-advised fund as a wealth management product that enabled investors to maximize their tax deductions at once and then direct contributions to various charitable organizations over a longer period.

The IRS had audited several of the seniors, and it turned out the charities in the fund set up by JerCo Investments were all bogus. The seniors owed thousands of dollars in additional income taxes and penalties because of the disallowed deductions.

Shell organizations for Jerome Haddad, Michelle suspected as she read. A lawyer had taken up the cause on behalf of the seniors and filed a class-action suit against the Haddads.

But then Jerome Haddad had declared bankruptcy and left the country.

Detective Zuniga sipped his beer, which had grown warm. He continued to study his drawings.

From what he'd gathered from the interviews, none of the cruise passengers had known Fernando long enough to develop a hatred strong enough to kill him. Zuniga had not turned up previous relationships between the victim and any of the guests—apart from Laurel Pardo, who had most likely been off the ship already at the time of Fernando's death. Laurel and Fernando had both worked at the Darwin Research Station during overlapping time periods. As had Elena.

Janice Roberts was tough to read. There were holes in her story that deepened each time Zuniga questioned her. *And of all the suspects, Janice seems least sorry Fernando is dead.*

Jessy Roberts had cried enough for herself and her mother. Between the tears and Janice's admonishing looks, it had been hard for Zuniga to get a straight answer from Jessy about anything. But he knew Jessy had seen Fernando close to his time of death.

Zuniga's superiors had warned him to exercise care around the Roberts family. Jim Roberts was CEO of a major resort chain that had purchased property outside Puerto Ayora. Construction of a first-class resort represented a huge influx of cash to the local economy. Angering the CEO with accusations about his family might jeopardize the project. *And I'd be the pariah responsible,* thought Zuniga.

He took another sip of beer and set aside the mother and daughter avatars.

Michelle stared at the message from Tim. *Should I reply?* Politeness dictated she must at least acknowledge receipt.

What to say? *I can't speak for Giovanna, and I might give Tim false hope if I let him think Giovanna would be glad to hear from him. Should I tell Tim where we are? Would Giovanna mind?*

The information should interest Giovanna, and she might be pleased Tim had cared enough to bring it to her attention. Perhaps, because of her obsession with her former partner, this story was old news; Michelle had not perused the reams of data about Jerome Haddad her granddaughter had collected.

Michelle shivered. *I haven't seen Giovanna show so much rage since the tantrums she threw as a child. What will Giovanna do if she confronts Haddad? And here's more fuel for the fire.*

Michelle knew Giovanna wouldn't want her to keep this information from her. *Perhaps this class action suit will satisfy her quest for justice. Others Jerome Haddad harmed are uniting. Maybe this lawyer can be the one to stop him.*

Michelle hit the forward button and typed in Giovanna's email address. "Thought you might be interested in this article about Jerome," she wrote, omitting the subject of the verb, which could have been "Tim," "I," or "we."

Message on its way, Michelle went back to the original email from Tim. She hit reply. "Dear Tim, what a nice surprise to hear from you. I hope you're doing well. I forwarded the information you sent to Giovanna. Please tell your mother 'hello' for me when you see her. Best regards, Michelle."

She paused. Did "Best regards" sound too businesslike? She backspaced and typed, "Love," then changed her mind. "Love" seemed too intimate since Tim and Giovanna were no longer engaged. It was almost a betrayal of Giovanna. "Sincerely"? *No, too businesslike again.* She took a deep breath. *What does it matter?* She settled on, "Take care" and hit send.

Michelle looked at her watch. She should go to bed. But she knew she wouldn't sleep until Giovanna had returned to the ship.

Detective Victor Zuniga picked up the "Giovanna" avatar. *The name "Giovanna" sounds almost musical. Not a usual name for an American. Could it be Italian, maybe? Portuguese? Greek?*

He closed his eyes and pictured her. Such an earnest face. A smile that hinted at vulnerability under a veneer of worldliness. Such stunning, penetrating eyes. What color were they anyway? Kind of a greenish-gray? Almost blue in certain lighting.

According to the timeline he'd put together, Giovanna had thwarted a *rendezvous* between Fernando and Jessy. *Wrong place, wrong time.*

And Fernando had become distracted. *Any man would be. Giovanna Rogers is much more intriguing than a moonstruck teenager.*

Zuniga stared at his papers. Juggling trysts, Fernando was bound to find trouble. *A jealous woman? An angry parent? It would have almost served him right. Almost.*

But no one deserves to die. And it's my job to ensure the victim gets justice.

He picked up his glass and took another sip of beer. He gazed around the dim room, filling with more customers: the usual fishermen, local tour guides, and a few tipsy tourists. Two locals had started a game of pool. Someone sauntered over to the jukebox and selected a song from the eighties.

Zuniga was about to resume work on his puzzle when Giovanna walked into the bar.

CHAPTER TWENTY-ONE

I spotted Detective Victor Zuniga bent over the counter and almost turned around to leave the Puerto Ayora Tavern.

Too late. Zuniga had seen me and waved me over. *What now?* I remembered afternoons of binge-watching Columbo reruns with Michelle. How the frumpy, bumbling detective gained the trust of his prime suspects and then kept needling them until they backed themselves into a corner. *Just one more thing, Ma'am.*

No longer in uniform, Zuniga looked like a regular guy hanging out in a bar. A *hot* guy. Every shiny, dark hair in place, jeans and Polo shirt tight enough to showcase his muscular body without looking vulgar.

With a deep breath I walked toward the counter, an insect lured into a spider's web.

Zuniga's calloused hand guided me by my bare elbow onto the stool beside him. His touch felt strong but gentle.

"I don't suppose you've had a chance yet to look at the flash drive I gave you?" I steadied myself on the high stool.

Zuniga twitched an eyebrow. "Not yet."

"Don't wait too long."

"I'll read it when I get home."

His chocolate-brown eyes sparkled under the pendant light hanging over the counter. I hadn't noticed before how long and thick his lashes were—a trait, many women would lament, wasted on a man. "They won't ever find Laurel, will they?"

"I'm sorry." He touched my bare shoulder. "Probably not." He moved his hand from my shoulder, took a sip of beer, and then asked, "Want something to drink?"

"Are you buying?"

"As long as you're reasonable." A drop of foam clung to his upper lip, and he wiped it away with the back of his hand.

"No frozen piña colada with a fancy umbrella?"

He chuckled. "This is not that kind of place." He signaled the bartender. "Maybe when Leisure Dreams opens."

"A beer is fine." I looked at the bartender, who had come over to take my order. "Do you have an IPA?"

"A what?" Zuniga exchanged an amused look with the bartender.

"You know, an India Pale Ale."

"How about a draft Pilsner?" Zuniga suggested. "That's the only beer they serve."

I caught their mocking exchange. "Fine."

There were papers strewn across the counter next to Zuniga. It looked like a map and some cut-outs. "Playing paper dolls?"

Zuniga grinned. His crooked front tooth gave his smile an impish quality. He leaned across his work. "Official police business."

"Is one of those paper dolls me?" I craned my neck to see around his protective arm and almost lost my balance on the barstool. I sobered as I recognized his diagram of the *Archipelago Explorer's* decks. "Sorry, I shouldn't . . ."

He gathered up his papers.

The bartender set a tall glass of foamy, golden beer in front of me.

Zuniga raised his glass. "*Salud.*"

To not being in jail, I thought, returning his toast with a smile. I was thirstier than I'd thought, and I downed half my beer. It was refreshing and more bitter than American lagers.

Our eyes met.

"Am I still a suspect?" Was it the long, crazy afternoon and evening or the strong beer that made me feel so reckless in front of an attractive man who had the power to arrest me?

There was that arched eyebrow again, offset by the lopsided smile.

I held my gaze. *Why am I teasing this police officer? So, I can end up in the jail cell next to Jerome Haddad? Taunt my nemesis from the inside?*

I'd felt so vindicated this afternoon, seeing my former business partner hauled off that boat in police custody. After I left Janice and Jessy Roberts, I couldn't resist returning to the police station to glimpse Jerome Haddad behind bars. Zuniga had already gone off duty, and his colleague, who spoke very little English, had guffawed once he'd figured out I'd come to the station to gloat, not to bail out the prisoner.

Jerome's temporary confusion over the purpose of my visit had been *so* worth it, too. *The audacity of that jerk believing I'd bail him out!* The look on his face—changing before my eyes from a smug but hopeful smirk to a disappointed and surly scowl—had been priceless.

Zuniga caught one of the paper avatars slipping out of his folded-up deck plan, and the motion brought me back to the present. I could not identify the likeness, but its label read, "Daniel." Zuniga stuffed the avatar back inside the paper and pulled out another one. "I know what happened."

I almost dropped my beer. The golden liquid sloshed against my glass.

"She did it." Zuniga stared at the wall of bottles behind the bar as he held up another avatar.

Who is that? My eyes widened as I spotted the label on the cut-out in his hands.

"But we'll never make a case for murder." Zuniga must have given the bartender a subtle signal because fresh beers appeared in front of us.

I searched his brooding face.

"Fernando Ferrar has no family. No advocate." Zuniga sipped his beer.

I felt sad for Fernando. And for Zuniga, for not being able to get him justice. I drained my first beer, pushed aside my glass, and laid claim to the new one.

"The Leisure Dreams resort will be a big deal. A huge boon for the local economy."

I touched my glass, but my hand shook too much to pick it up without spilling.

"Things would get ugly. Especially for me." He looked at his folded deck plan.

Even though I'd had my suspicions, I was still having trouble processing his accusation. Yes, Fernando had come on to Jessy. But did that have something to do with his death? "What are you saying happened? I'm not following. Can you tell me?"

He continued to stare at his deck plan on the counter.

"Why did she do it? I'm missing something." I started to touch his shoulder but then withdrew my hand mid-air. The gesture was too familiar, too much of an overstep. We'd just met. He was a cop, and I was a suspect. Or former suspect.

Zuniga turned to face me. "It was an unfortunate accident."

"You said that two days ago, on the cruise ship. Yet, you dragged us all into the police station this afternoon, still talking about it. You don't think Fernando's death was an accident."

"I can't prove otherwise."

"You were hoping for a confession?"

"People don't confess unless they feel remorse." Zuniga shook his head.

"So, tell me what you think happened." I traced droplets of water on the outside of my glass. "I mean, if you can."

"Maybe it *was* an accident. Maybe it was self-defense." Zuniga took another sip of beer. "She didn't mean to shove him so hard. A lioness defending her cub, she didn't know her own strength."

Eyeing the paper avatar in his hand, I thought about my attempts at conversation with Janice and Jessy Roberts after we'd all left the police station. Those two had known more than anyone about Fernando's last moves.

Zuniga stared at the wall of bottles.

"How did it happen?" I whispered. He looked so distraught, so childlike, that I gathered the courage to put my hand on his shoulder as if we were friends. "Talk to me."

He unfolded his drawing and spread it on the counter. "After Fernando left you, he went to the pool to meet Jessy Roberts. Pre-arranged." He moved the Fernando and Jessy avatars next to the spot on the map marking the pool.

Zuniga and I looked at each other, shaking our heads and clucking like two disapproving parents.

"It was Jessy I saw peeking around the corner while I was talking to Fernando." I leaned over the plan and showed him the location where Jessy had appeared. Our shoulders touched.

"Stargazing?" With a chuckle, Zuniga winked.

"Stargazing." I smiled, remembering Zuniga's skepticism during our first interview.

He pointed to the ship's pool on the diagram. "Fernando became amorous, and Jessy sent mixed signals."

I felt a pang of guilt for rejecting Fernando that night, or rather, driving him away with my mention of Laurel. *The lecher.* "Jessy is only sixteen. He was playing with fire."

"Exactly. And then here comes Momma Bear." Zuniga made a swooshing noise through his teeth as he moved the Janice Roberts avatar toward the spot by the pool.

"Then what? She tells them to stop?"

"They don't listen at first, so she gets physical. Drags Jessy away, shoves Fernando off her. When Fernando lets go of Jessy, he loses his balance. Falls into the pool. Hits his head on the way in."

"So, it was an accident."

Zuniga shook his head. I couldn't tell if he was agreeing or disagreeing with my statement. "Why didn't they call for help?"

I swallowed. "Maybe Janice didn't realize Fernando hit his head?"

Zuniga stifled a sarcastic humph.

"Maybe all she could think of was pushing him away from her daughter."

"That's what Señora Roberts claims," said Zuniga. "She's sticking to her story."

I touched his arm again. "You don't think justice has been served?"

His eyes registered defeat and he repeated into his beer, "Why didn't they call for help?"

"Too embarrassing. Too hard to explain." I grabbed my beer and took a slug. Its bitter taste did not compete with the bitterness of the words I held back. *Left the mess for someone else to find and clean up.*

"My superiors have warned me to lay off. Close the case. I thought if I talked to them one more time, interviewed more witnesses, someone would spill the truth." He gathered up his work again.

We drank in silence for a few minutes.

"So, it's over?" I set down my glass.

"Death by accidental fall." Victor turned to me with a resigned smile. "It's not like on TV. Not every crime gets solved. Not every victim gets justice."

I thought about Jerome Haddad locked up in the local jail. *An inkling of justice.* "You had a prisoner brought in late this afternoon. Jerome Haddad?"

Victor put down his beer and eyed my face. "How did you know about that?"

"I know the man. He's a scoundrel. I hope you never let him go."

Victor laughed. "The man from the yacht?"

"Is that where he came from?" *The yacht he financed by bankrupting my business?*

"His yacht ran aground last night near Caamaño Island. Careless accident. There's a large fuel leak polluting the water, and the impact may have damaged a reef. Haddad was arrogant and uncooperative when the park service went out to question him today, so we arrested him." Victor took another sip of beer. "We'll have to let him go."

"You can't!"

Again, Victor did the one-eyebrow arch I found so charming.

I felt for my smartphone, which had been threatening to slide from my pocket as I twisted on the barstool to make myself comfortable. "Let me show you some examples. Do they have Wi-Fi here?"

Zuniga said something to the bartender in Spanish, and he babbled an unintelligible response. I looked at my phone but could not find a strong signal.

"He says the router has been down for a couple of days," Zuniga explained.

"What's wrong with it?" *How do these people live without communications?*

The bartender shrugged.

"Can I look at it?"

Zuniga and the bartender exchanged confused glances.

"You think you can fix it?" Zuniga eyed me with a newfound curiosity.

"I won't know until I try."

The bartender gestured for me to follow. I slipped off my barstool and walked behind the counter. The bartender led me through a swinging door to a tiny dark storeroom. He pointed to a box perched on top of a storage shelf. Something out of the last century, or at least a decade old.

"Do you have a stepladder or a chair I can stand on?"

Victor had joined us in the musty storeroom, and he moved a straight chair from a cluttered desk next to the shelf. "I'll hold it, so you don't fall."

I climbed onto the chair and clung to the shelf to balance myself. At least the backing was bolted to the wall; I would have hated to pull the whole storage shelf and its contents down on top of us. Victor kept one hand on the chair back and the other on my waist.

The chair wobbled as I leaned forward to inspect the device, and Victor tightened his grip on my waist. His touch made my spine tingle.

My fingers passed through a cobweb draped around the box. I cringed but found the power button. Depressed it for a few seconds. Then let it go.

Nothing happened. I tried again. And again. One more time. Green lights blinked on. Like Christmas.

I beamed. "Let's see if that works."

Victor took my hand and helped me down. Our faces passed within inches of each other. Our eyes met, and our hands clasped together longer than necessary after I'd planted my feet on the tile floor.

Back at the bar, I picked up my smartphone. Now there was a strong signal for a nearby locked network. "What's the code?"

The bartender handed me a slip of paper. "Another beer? On the house."

I typed in the numbers for the Wi-Fi code and shook my head. "All I did was reboot the thing."

Victor and the bartender smiled at each other.

Messages were waiting and I accessed my email first, out of habit. There were new ones from Tim, which I deleted unread. There was nothing more he could say. We were done.

But here was a recent message from Michelle. The second one sent this evening. *Michelle.* I looked at my watch. My grandmother would be wondering where I was. I opened the most recent message so I could send a quick reply, let Michelle know I was still alive and free.

The message I opened contained another message Michelle had forwarded from Tim. Tim had sent an article about the class action suit in Florida against Jerome. I'd read a lot about that case, and I hoped those seniors succeeded where Jerome's other victims had failed. *Why did Tim send me this story? Does this mean he's sorry he accused me of being naïve, since others have also fallen victim to Jerome's swindle?*

I displayed the article about the senior citizens and thrust my smartphone in front of Victor. "Here's one case. This is the man you have locked in your jail cell."

Victor squinted at the tiny print.

"Here." I leaned close to him and zoomed in on the document, enlarging the font.

"Thanks." He glanced at me, took the phone, and then skimmed the article.

I watched him read, impatient for him to finish and digest the essence of Jerome's malevolent character. "Still want to let him go?"

"I don't want to, but I don't have a choice."

"Don't you have any connections with the U.S. government to get him extradited?"

Victor handed the phone back to me. Again, our hands seized an opportunity to touch. "This looks like a civil case."

"He's a criminal."

"Is he wanted by the F.B.I.?"

"He should be."

Victor smiled. "Here in the Galapagos, the main crimes we prosecute are wildlife trafficking and other environmental destruction. And narcotics."

"Environmental destruction. What about the reef he damaged?" I put my phone back into my pocket.

"If we're lucky, he'll pay a fine."

I put my chin in my hands.

Victor touched my shoulder. "I'm sorry he hurt you."

"Jerome Haddad is an evil man. You'd understand if you saw the dossier I've compiled on him." I straightened. "Will you be around tomorrow?"

Victor smiled. "I live on this island."

I looked into his eyes and speculated about Victor Zuniga as a person. *Does he have a wife and kids? A live-in girlfriend? A pet?*

"With your family?" I let myself ask.

"Alone."

Not married, then. Maybe. "We have free time here in Puerto Ayora built into our schedule tomorrow, after the visit to the Darwin Research Station," I said. "Can we meet? Maybe you'll have looked at Laurel's flash drive by then, and we can figure out what happened to her."

"We?" But his eyes showed kindness.

"You're the detective, I know. But I might have been the last person to see Laurel alive, and I feel some responsibility. I should have made sure we didn't leave her behind."

He nodded, his eyes still on my face. "I can't change what happened."

"But maybe you could at least figure out why? Find out if someone left her out there. Shouldn't that person, or those people, face justice?"

"You mean, if it wasn't an accident." His mouth twitched, revealing the crooked tooth.

"If it wasn't an accident."

He tilted his beer glass and took a long drink. "To make up for not getting justice for Fernando Ferrar?" He set down the empty glass.

I touched his hand. His eyes traveled from my face to my fingers.

"Also, if you'll be around, I want to bring you the documents I've collected on Jerome Haddad. Maybe you can find something in them that will give you a reason to hold him until he can be extradited."

He smiled. "I'm not going anywhere."

"Shall I come to the police station after our tour?"

Victor gave me an amused smile; my face must have appeared over-eager, like a puppy determined to go for a walk. "It's a long way to the police station from the Darwin Research Station. Why don't we meet somewhere closer? Perhaps by Darwin's statue in town?"

"Where's that?"

"On Charles Darwin Avenue, the main street. Next to a large blue mosaic in the shape of a rainbow. A little park. You can't miss it." He stroked his smooth chin. "My favorite restaurant is just around the corner. I'll buy you lunch if you like. The cuisine doesn't compare with the ship's, but—"

"I'd like that." I could feel my face light up.

We exchanged smiles like a couple who had just set their first date. Only it wasn't a date. It was police business.

My phone was again escaping my pocket, and I shoved it back. "Promise me you won't let Jerome Haddad go until you've seen my documents?"

Zuniga smiled again. "I'll do my best."

"His wife will try to bail him out. Stall her."

"His wife?" Zuniga's brow furrowed.

"Yes, Connie. She and I were friends in college. That's how I got mixed up with Jerome. She's traveling on the yacht with him. She's been posting pictures to Facebook and Instagram. Sending out Tweets whenever they set sail for a new location. Even posted some YouTube videos of them living the high life."

"We didn't find anyone else on the yacht."

My mouth fell open. "What do you mean?"

"With today's technology, it's not unusual for a yacht that size to sail around the world with a single operator. Of course, this guy wasn't as skillful as he thought he was since he ran aground." Zuniga gathered his paperwork from the counter.

"But I know Connie was with him." My stomach churned. *Where's Connie?*

CHAPTER TWENTY-TWO

Victor insisted on walking me to the pier where the shuttle boat waited to take guests back to the *Archipelago Explorer.* "Our streets are safe, but I want to make sure you're not stranded here alone all night." He touched my elbow as he guided me out the tavern door. Again, my spine tingled.

Being stranded here with him wouldn't be so bad. I wondered what his place was like. A house? Apartment? Tidy? Messy? What kind of furniture? A comfortable bed? Someone to share it with?

Music boomed from a nearby nightclub. The streets, although not crowded, didn't feel deserted. The aroma of smoked meat wafted from a restaurant we passed, reminding me I hadn't eaten dinner.

As I contemplated the stone sidewalk beneath my sandals, I launched into my account of my business-venture-gone-bad with Jerome Haddad. I hadn't meant to share so many details, but once I started talking, the words flowed like lava down the slopes of a volcano. I searched Victor's face for signs of boredom, but the kindness in his brown eyes never wavered. So, I kept talking.

I confessed I'd at first been skeptical of Jerome's interest in my nonprofit venture. I'd made my living as a corporate auditor, and I liked to think I was a good one. But Connie had reassured me, vouched for Jerome's character, his good heart, his love of animals, his vast experience with nonprofits. His legal expertise, connections, and phenomenal fundraising successes added to his value as a partner. The prospect of an accelerated timeline tempted me. What an advantage to have a clinic ready to go, ready to start helping. Pet overpopulation was rampant in our rural Georgia county, and the longer we waited to offer affordable spay/neuter services, the more unwanted kittens and puppies would be born. And adoptable companion animals would continue to be killed in shelters at alarming rates. Even Tim had seemed convinced we should move forward with Jerome as a partner.

For a few months, I'd been on top of the world. We were doing great work, helping pet owners who wanted to do the right thing but didn't have the money to take their animals to a full-service veterinarian.

And then it had all unraveled. Tears sprang to my eyes as I described the nightmare when I realized all the money was gone. How we couldn't pay our bills. Suppliers had trusted us, and we let them down.

Victor reached into his pocket and produced a bar napkin. With an apologetic smile, he handed it to me.

I dabbed my eyes with an amused sniff at the makeshift handkerchief and continued my story.

Tim had been livid. It was all my fault.

Victor's forehead creased. His mouth started to open.

Before Victor could say anything, pass judgment like Tim had done, I explained how I'd put it all together. Jerome. He'd taken it all, weaving a convoluted web of lies, funneling donations into fake accounts to secure fake services, for which we paid real money. I hadn't seen it coming. But as an experienced auditor, I should have. Maybe Tim was right. He was only the veterinarian. I was the accounting expert. It *was* my fault. I was the failure.

Victor listened without interrupting. Without trying to dole out advice or tell me where I went wrong. Talking to my grandmother about my misfortune had helped but baring my soul to an unbiased stranger felt different, therapeutic.

When I'd finished my tale, Victor gave my shoulder a tender squeeze. "I'm so sorry he did that to you."

"But like I said, my ex-fiancé insists I should have known better."

Victor shook his head. "The man's a professional con artist. It's not your fault."

I grinned, and Victor's warm smile made me glad I'd confided in him. As we passed a seafood restaurant and inhaled new cooking smells, I glimpsed our reflections in the window and imagined us as friends.

"Your English is very good for a local," I remarked. I wondered if "for a local" diminished my compliment. *I should have left that part off.* At least I hadn't called him a foreigner. Except for a slight Latin accent, his English was as good as mine, and it wasn't even his mother tongue. "Did you learn it in school?"

"After my parents divorced, my father married an American woman and moved to California." He touched my elbow and steered me away from a loose cobblestone. "I spent almost every summer with them."

My bare elbow felt warm where he'd touched it. "I guess living in another country is the best way to learn the language."

"Definitely," Victor agreed.

We strolled in comfortable silence for a few more minutes. Like a couple, out for the evening, blending in with other locals and tourists on the street. "How did you end up in the Galapagos?"

"Got lucky. Drew a temporary rotation," he replied.

"Is the Galapagos a plum assignment?"

"Like a vacation." He smiled, and his white teeth shone under the streetlights. "Usually."

"Then you'll go back to the mainland someday?" I watched him survey our surroundings as we chatted. "If you want to advance in your career?"

He sighed. "I don't think about that now."

A familiar black Zodiac was tied to the well-lit pier. Gentle waves lapped against the boat's sturdy rubber sides. Its operator dozed on a nearby bench. A pungent odor pierced the salty air and I soon spied the source: a large sea lion sleeping on the bench next to him.

The boat operator stirred as we approached.

"What time does the next shuttle leave for the *Archipelago Explorer*?" I asked.

The boat operator sat up and shook himself awake. "Is anyone else coming?"

I looked over my shoulder, out to the street. Victor was still beside me. "Just me."

"You are ready?" The man stood and stretched. He handed me a life vest.

I looked at Victor, almost reluctant to bid him goodnight. I wouldn't have minded if the boat operator had told me there'd be a wait, as long as Victor waited with me. In fact, I'd hoped there would be a wait so we could continue our conversation.

The boat operator climbed into the Zodiac and began preparations to cast off.

Victor held one side of the life vest as I slipped my arm inside.

Our hands touched again when we each reached for the straps to fasten the vest around my torso.

"Nice and tight." Victor's eyes met mine.

The boat operator extended his hand to help me aboard.

I turned to Victor.

His lips parted as if the thought of kissing me had crossed his mind, and I'd have welcomed the gesture had he made it. I thought about planting a kiss on him. But maybe he'd consider kissing me unprofessional, and my gesture would backfire.

Instead, he took my hand and helped me into the Zodiac. I felt another spark as his strong arms guided me over the rubber edge and he handed me off to the boat operator.

Our eyes met at the moment our touch disengaged. The opportunity for a kiss had passed.

Footsteps sounded against the wooden boards of the pier. "Wait for us!" cried a nasal voice.

Joseph was supporting Peter, his fellow flight attendant, who did not appear to be in as much of a hurry. Neither was walking a straight enough line to pass a field sobriety test.

Victor and the Zodiac operator exchanged amused smiles.

When Peter and Joseph reached the edge of the dock, Victor and the boat operator helped them don life vests and board the small craft where I waited inside. The inflatable boat dipped to one side under the young men's weight as they scrambled aboard.

"*Cuidado*," warned the boat operator. *Careful.*

Once Peter and Joseph had settled into the boat next to me, Victor scanned the pier for more late arrivals. He shook his head.

The operator nodded and cast off.

I waved good-bye to Victor and watched him grow smaller and smaller until he dropped his hand and headed back toward the town.

"Oh, Giovanna, he's cute," slurred Peter. "Good for you, girl."

I felt myself blush.

"And the way he looks at you," said Joseph. "He's got it bad, dear."

Joseph and Peter must not have recognized my escort as Detective Zuniga from the onboard interrogations, nor had they remembered me being singled out for additional police questioning. Seeing no need to remind them, I smiled like the Mona Lisa.

The wind picked up as we traveled farther from shore. I rubbed my bare arms, wishing for the wool cardigan that still lay in my suitcase. "Did you have fun in Puerto Ayora?" I asked my boat mates.

"Cool town." Joseph nodded. "I'm glad we had this extra time here."

"And we found Tio Armando!" blurted Peter.

"Tio Armando?" I asked. "Where?"

"We didn't find Tio Armando," Joseph corrected his friend.

"We met the guy who has him." Peter pushed a lock of sandy hair off his forehead.

"He said he did," agreed Joseph. "Or he was supposed to get him. Something like that."

"He was buying everyone shots." Peter expelled a loud hic-cup.

"Shots? Of what?"

"Something strong." Joseph giggled.

"Wait a minute." I turned toward Joseph. "Who was this guy?"

Joseph shrugged.

"He said he was building a new resort," said Peter. "With an inter . . . interpet . . ."

"Interpret... interpretive," Joseph supplied.

"Interpretive." Peter still struggled with the word, but I fig-ured out what he was trying to say. "With an interpretive center attached."

"No, maybe it was just an interpretive center," Joseph amended.

"What was his name?" My heartbeat quickened. "Not Jim Roberts, from our ship?"

"No, it was some Ecuadorian guy." Peter drummed his chin. "I guess he was Ecuadorian. Seemed like a local. The Galapagos are part of Ecuador, right?"

I nodded.

"He had some Arabs with him," added Joseph. "I think they were the ones with all the money, eh, Peter?"

"Where is his resort?" I asked. "In Puerto Ayora?"

A wave slapped the side of the Zodiac, causing it to pitch to one side. A spray of saltwater wet our faces. I leaned in the op-posite direction.

"Whoa," said Joseph to the boat operator. "Can't you control this thing?"

Peter clutched his throat. "Make it stop."

An even bigger wave tossed us aside like a rubber toy in a bathtub. We got soaked. Joseph fell against me, and I helped him right himself.

Peter leaned over the side of the boat. "I'm gonna be sick."

As another wave struck, Peter vomited into the ocean. Even in the dark, I could see partially digested food particles sticking to the side of the Zodiac.

The seas calmed as we approached the lee side of the *Archipelago Explorer*, enough to allow us to transfer from the inflatable boat to the ship without mishap.

We climbed the steep steel stairs to the main deck and flipped over our tags on the locator board, the last ones to turn green.

Jerome Haddad stared through the iron bars of his filthy cell. *An ocean view*, he mused. *How charming.*

Where was Felipe? Did his business partner not understand the word *urgent? He must be out drinking and carousing and talking too much. Has he set up the meeting with the team from Dubai yet?*

Things were not going as planned. Connie had seemed so loyal for so long. But she was cunning. *Did she think she could get away with betraying me? Did she think her past devotion gave her a free pass?*

And then there was Janice. *The ultimate Jezebel.* For eighteen years, Jerome had yearned to reunite with her. He had fantasized her apologizing, begging, promising never to betray him again. He had never expected to see her standing on the shore of Santa Cruz Island this afternoon, a vision in the breeze, accompanied by a beautiful daughter who should have been his.

Lovely Janice, the author of my destiny. As soon as Jerome had traveled to Miami to expand Big D Literacy's operations, Janice had married that cocky, entitled Jim Roberts. She had expected Jerome to remain her faithful servant, to ply the fruits of his labor into her precious charity, taking nothing in return. *That was not the way it worked, not the way I'd planned our future.*

It had been so easy to divert the funds, to finance the lifestyle he deserved—a life like Janice wanted with Jim Roberts. People loved to donate to worthy causes. Everyone felt good about themselves. And if all the money didn't go where he claimed it was going, no one got hurt. It was tax-deductible, disposable income for the donors, and he could help them dispose of it.

Most charities struggled to make ends meet. Most had noble visions they seldom fulfilled. In fact, many of them floundered, not having any idea how to execute those mission statements when donations arrived. A shortfall of funds was normal and expected for a new venture. A good sob story often persuaded donors to open their wallets and purses again. And if one of his businesses offered a matching challenge, even more donations poured in.

Janice thought he'd hurt her. But she had brought that ruin on herself. She hadn't waited for him to explain. She didn't understand the economics of running a tax-exempt foundation. It was the story that sold, not the actual grinding work. She didn't realize the potential her operation had, didn't understand how it was possible to create wealth out of a bit of seed money, what she had entrusted to Jerome when she put him in charge of the Miami branch of Big D Literacy. *Like the loaves and the fishes.*

Janice. Even after all his time with Connie, all the satisfaction she had brought him, their marriage vows, he still pined for Janice. Seeing her on the shore today stirred bittersweet memories. Starry blue eyes hanging on his words in adoration. Her long, golden tresses brushing his chest. Peach-soft skin against his. His first true love.

And yet Janice's glare today had been full of hatred. Even after all these years.

Jerome eyed a carpenter bee flitting against the plaster ceiling, looking for an escape. *Hold the door open for me, buddy, when you find it,* he thought.

He'd read somewhere that there's a fine line between hatred and love. It had to be true. Janice's hatred might only be a mask for the smoldering love she still harbored for him.

And then there was Gio. If Hell had a goddess, it was Gio. Giovanna Rogers and Janice Roberts together? What was that about? Had his eyes deceived him? *What a nightmare.*

Giovanna Rogers was all Connie's fault. "The perfect seed," Connie had assured him after she had introduced the two. Idealistic, passionate, irrational. Someone who could articulate her vision well and rake in tens of thousands of dollars in donations. And then lose interest before she'd accomplished anything. *Ha!*

Connie had never told him what a pain and a nag Gio could be. How driven she was when she set her mind on something. How she'd try to meddle in the books, ask him to account for the income and expenditures, try to keep track of donations and dictate how to allocate the funds. The books were his sacred territory. It was always part of the agreement.

He had sensed trouble when Connie mentioned Giovanna's accounting career. An auditor who pored over the finances of large corporations? *Talk about asking for trouble.* But Connie had assured him Gio had finished that phase of her life; she'd grown tired of looking at numbers. She wanted to be a philanthropist, save the cats and dogs.

And Connie had never guessed Gio would take the money they'd accumulated and buy a clinic. All those hard-earned donations they had worked together to collect. She and that wimpy veterinarian boyfriend of hers. Whose idea had that been? Giovanna had liquidated her personal savings and added them to the business, and without authorization from Jerome, she'd found a move-in ready building. From slick drawings on a PowerPoint used to wow potential donors, good for years of fundraising toward a dream, the promised clinic had sprung into a brick-and-mortar edifice open for business. A money pit. And every time Jerome turned around, Giovanna or Tim was ordering supplies and equipment. *Spending my money.*

At least he'd persuaded her to use his loan company to finance the building, to pull her cash investment out to meet operating expenses. To put the money back under his control where it belonged, "invested" so it would grow. If Giovanna had listened to him, she would not have lost all her money. It was her own fault. A charitable foundation was supposed to bring in money, not spend it. Why couldn't she get that? Each venture had to be structured and managed so the whole empire wouldn't crumble like a cut-rate construction project.

Jerome could sense from Gio's body language when she stood on the shore glaring at him that she was still angry about the lost funds. She blamed him. It had been hard to decipher who had projected the most hatred—Gio or Janice.

If he'd had any doubts about her feelings, Giovanna had cleared them up earlier this evening, when she'd paid him a visit at the jail.

At first, he'd thought she was his salvation. She was giving him a chance to explain. "Gio," he'd called to her. "Thank goodness." He would be out of jail tonight. They might go out to dinner, have some laughs, and then he'd invite her into his latest venture so she could recoup her losses. Maybe she could help him charm the team from Dubai.

But Gio's eyes had turned a steely gray. She'd puckered her mouth as if she wanted to spit. Or hiss, like one of her stupid cats. She'd pressed her pert little nose between the bars. "You're right where you belong, Jerome Haddad. I hope they lose the key."

The officer on duty didn't understand much English, but he could read body language. And he'd laughed.

Giovanna Rogers would not get away with humiliating Jerome Haddad like that.

Michelle tossed and turned. First, she was too hot, and she kicked the covers off. Then she was cold, so she wrapped herself into a cocoon of blankets, unable to warm up. She drifted off to sleep but then a dream jolted her awake. A huge manta ray with a long, pointed tail and an evil grin like the devil sprang from the ocean.

Even in the darkened room, she could tell Giovanna had not slept in her bed.

Michelle switched on her bedside lamp. A thought had been buzzing at her like a no-see-um since this afternoon when they'd glimpsed that shipwreck off Isolete Caamaño.

She climbed out of bed and padded to the desk. She flipped open her laptop and turned it on.

The internet was still working. She typed in a Google search for *Second Wind*. In a moment, images of a familiar yacht popped onto her screen.

The cabin door opened. Michelle looked up.

Giovanna had returned.

Jerome Haddad stared at the dark waters beyond the walls of his jail cell. His nose had become almost desensitized to the stench of mildew and urine.

Tomorrow morning, he would demand a phone call to the American Embassy. He would turn this travesty into an international incident. The Puerto Ayora police and the Galapagos National Park Service would owe him an apology.

He heard voices speaking rapid Spanish. One of them sounded familiar.

Footsteps.

A key turned in the iron door and moments later, it swung open.

The guard who had laughed at him earlier stepped aside and grunted for him to come out.

A thick shape stood in the waiting room. Felipe Santore, his business partner.

"It's about time," said Jerome.

CHAPTER TWENTY-THREE

Michelle looked up from her computer as I opened the cabin door. I'd expected her to be asleep in bed, not sitting at the desk. "Giovanna! Thank goodness. I worried when you didn't come back to the ship with the others."

I strode to my grandmother's side and put my hand on the back of her chair. "Sorry, I sent you an email about an hour ago."

"I've been lying in bed for the past two hours." Michelle gestured toward the rumpled covers of her bed across the room. "I kept wondering what had happened to you, and I couldn't sleep."

The image on her computer screen stared back at me. "Why were you looking at Jerome's yacht?"

Over a cup of tea, Michelle told me about her snorkeling expedition that afternoon, and how they had come across a shipwrecked yacht. "I knew that name, *Second Wind*, sounded familiar," Michelle said.

"Jerome Haddad is in the Puerto Ayora jail," I told her, snuggling against the back of the upholstered couch and warming my hands with my teacup. "I saw the police bring him in." I didn't mention I'd paid him a visit. That I'd taunted him. And I'd enjoyed it.

Michelle sipped her tea. "Rafael said the boat owner might be in trouble if his accident caused environmental damage."

"Connie will try to bail him out." I picked up the china teapot and poured myself more tea, then added a spoonful of raw sugar. "If she didn't already wise up and leave him." *Please, let that have happened.* Ever since Victor told me the authorities had found no one else on the yacht, I couldn't shake the sensation that something was wrong. Where was Connie? In her last Facebook post, which looked like a selfie, she was standing on the yacht.

"Speaking of the police station, how did it go?" Michelle set her empty cup on the glass coffee table. "Everyone else came back before dinner."

I looked at my grandmother over the rim of my teacup and took a long sip. *She won't come out and say it, but she thought they'd arrested me. I should have let her know sooner I was okay.*

"Did you give the detective Laurel's flash drive?"

I nodded as I set down my cup. "And he believes me: Laurel is missing. Daniel admitted he sent an imposter for the police interview about Fernando's death."

Michelle dropped the spoon she had been lining up on the tray. "We thought that might have happened, but—"

"We were right."

"But my gosh! How can Daniel get away with such deliberate interference in an investigation? Two investigations."

I shook my head and stifled a yawn.

Michelle looked at the clock. "Let's try to get some sleep. We can't figure it all out tonight."

Dreams of Jerome, Connie, Laurel, and Fernando, plagued my sleep, punctuated by visions of Victor Zuniga's lopsided smile and chocolate eyes. I still woke up at seven, before the alarm buzzed. While Michelle showered and dressed, I gathered my paperwork on Jerome Haddad and stuffed it into my backpack.

"Are you going to take a shower before breakfast?" Michelle towel-dried her short hair as she emerged from the bathroom.

I zipped my backpack. "I'll be quick."

"We have time." Peering into the mirror on the wall, Michelle ran a comb through her wet hair. "I forgot to tell you last night, but Jim Roberts invited us to visit the site of the new Leisure Dreams resort today."

I stopped in the bathroom doorway. Before yesterday's revelations about the role Janice and Jessy had played in Fernando's death, I'd have loved the opportunity to visit the Leisure Dreams property. Now, I wasn't sure I could spend an afternoon with the Roberts family. *Michelle doesn't know. We talked so much last night about Jerome and the police station, and Laurel's imposter.* I swallowed. "When?"

"After we finish with the Darwin Research Station. We'll have a couple hours of free time in Puerto Ayora before we have to be back on the ship."

"I have to see Victor."

"Victor?" Michelle turned to face me, her eyebrows raised.

"Detective Zuniga. Victor Zuniga." My face grew warm. I hadn't told Michelle about my encounter at the bar last night with the sexy detective, nor any of his revelations about Fernando's death investigation.

"You call him Victor now?"

"That's his name."

Michelle glanced at my backpack beside the door. "Oh, Giovanna, they don't have jurisdiction."

"I'm sure Victor can find a reason to keep Jerome in jail." I cast a glance toward my backpack. "Besides, I hope he's looked at Laurel's flash drive by now. Maybe the information on it will help us find out what happened to her."

"Us?"

"Well, the police."

Michelle nudged me toward the bathroom. "Go on, take your shower. We should eat a good breakfast before we head out."

As I closed the bathroom door, I heard Michelle murmur, "You'll need it."

The Roberts family sat together in the bustling dining room. The family members appeared almost as chipper as they had the first day of the cruise.

I found it hard to look at Janice. *So fresh and cheery, as if she hadn't ended a man's life a few days earlier. She must know she's off the hook now.* Victor Zuniga's startling disclosure about what Janice had done overshadowed the solidarity I'd felt with her after we'd shared experiences of founding charities and being duped by Jerome Haddad.

I started toward an empty table on the opposite side of the dining room, but Jim raised a glass of orange juice and caught Michelle's eye. *What is that? He's her new best friend?* He beckoned us over to his family's large table, and Michelle pivoted in their direction.

Dragging my feet like a reluctant toddler, I followed.

I nodded at the Roberts family, set my backpack on a chair, and then proceeded to the buffet table.

An artistic arrangement of colorful fruit dominated the buffet. As I heaped lush slices of amber papaya onto my plate, I felt a soft hand brush my elbow. I looked over my shoulder.

"Glad you made it back to the ship okay," Jessy said. "Your grandmother was worried about you last night."

I handed Jessy the tongs for the fruit tray. "I ran into Vic— uh, Detective Zuniga in town."

Jessy gasped. "What did he want? I thought we were done."

"We are." I turned and moved toward the hot entrée items. *I'm done with you, done with your mother, done with people who don't answer for their crimes.*

When I returned to the large table, my grandmother was sipping coffee and nibbling a flaky pastry plucked from a plate Janice had passed around. Michelle chatted with the Roberts family as if they were old friends. Deborah, Sue, Helga, and Dieter had crowded into the cozy little group, having pulled up chairs from nearby tables.

"Giovanna," Jim greeted me. It was the first time I'd heard him call me by name, and he pronounced it correctly. "A group of us plan to have a look at the new Leisure Dreams property after our Darwin tour this morning. Would you like to join us?"

I looked him in the eye. "Will we see Tio Armando?"

A hush fell over the table. Jim's magnanimous smile lost some of its dazzle.

Deborah set down her coffee cup. "That would be something, eh Jim? We've heard how you Texans like to go big."

"Tio Armando is still missing." Jim stabbed a sausage with his fork. When he looked up, his public-relations smile was pasted back on. "But I think everyone will enjoy our visit."

A modest sixties-style building on the outskirts of Puerto Ayora housed the Darwin Research Station Visitor Center. A rustic wooden "Welcome" sign marked the entrance. Minibuses dropped us near the sign, where Elena waited.

Peter tapped my shoulder as we stepped off the bus. "Giovanna, dear, would you mind taking a photo of the two of us next to the sign?" Apart from bloodshot eyes, he seemed almost recovered from his night on the town.

Joseph handed me his camera and went to stand by the sign, on the opposite side from Peter.

I centered the iconic sign in the viewfinder, flanked on either side by the two flight attendants. Peter and Joseph posed with arms outstretched like Vanna White turning letters on *Wheel of Fortune*.

"That's an interesting drawing," I remarked. "I wonder if it has any special significance."

Joseph tilted his head to the right to look at the drawing carved into the wooden Welcome sign. "It's a tortoise."

"Two tortoises," giggled Peter. "I guess the little animal is a tortoise, too. And goodness, what are they doing?"

"What do you think, Silly? This is a tortoise breeding center." Joseph tossed his head and grinned wickedly for the camera.

I pressed the shutter. "Want me to take another?"

As soon as I finished the second shot with both Peter's and Joseph's approval, an Asian gentleman from our bus, with a slight bow, asked me to take his photo. He posed beside the sign.

The camera clicked, and then, before I could hand it back to him, his wife joined him for another photo. When the shot was complete, using sign language, the wife begged me to take a picture of her alone.

Elena waited at the entrance for those of us taking photos. Rafael escorted another group toward the grounds.

I was the last from our group to reach the entrance. I strolled to Elena. "Was it nice being home for the night?"

"Very relaxing," Elena replied.

"What can you tell us about the logo on the Welcome sign? Is there some particular significance?"

"I don't know." Elena signaled for the rest of the group to join her. When she had gathered a dozen of us, she began, "The other group has left to look at the tortoises, but I'd like to show you something special first."

Michelle had gone on with Rafael's group and her new best friends, the Roberts family. She was unaware of their culpability, but I couldn't abide hanging around with them. Janice seemed so confident that the police had exonerated her and Jessy from any wrongdoing connected with Fernando's death. And what did Jim know? He must have pulled strings. Victor Zuniga had hinted as much. *Privileged aristocrats, all of them.*

I turned my attention to Elena.

Elena snapped into tour guide mode. "Last year, the Darwin Foundation started an exciting program in cooperation with the San Diego Zoo to save mangrove finches from extinction." She walked toward one of the smaller buildings and gestured for us to follow. "A good friend of mine works on the project and has agreed to show us his laboratory, if you're interested."

"Sort of a behind-the-scenes tour?" I asked.

Several tourists wandered off toward the tortoise exhibits, but a small group of us stayed with Elena.

"The mangrove finch is the rarest of Darwin's finches and only lives on the island of Isabela," Elena explained. "We estimate there are fewer than eighty of the birds left."

She knocked on the door of the small building. "An invasive species of parasitic fly lays its eggs in the finches' nests and then its larvae suck the blood from the nestlings. Chick mortality is almost one hundred percent."

A tall Ecuadorian scientist wearing a white lab coat and thick, black-rimmed glasses opened the door. He ushered in Elena with our group.

The cramped work area smelled like over-ripe fruit. We struggled to squeeze into the small room without disrupting the white-coated scientists bent over microscopes.

The man spoke in Spanish and Elena translated. "A team from the Charles Darwin Research Station traveled to Isabela Island, the largest in the Galapagos archipelago. They collected nests with unhatched or newly-hatched eggs and brought them back here in portable incubators." She nodded at a row of small incubators lined up on a table against the wall.

The man spoke again, and Elena added, "Scientists and volunteers kept the eggs incubated until they hatched, and then fed the chicks up to fifteen times a day until they fledged."

"Fledged?" asked one of the elderly Japanese men, a perplexed look on his face.

"Until they could fly. And could feed themselves."

Elena's friend gestured toward a young woman who was feeding a gray chick, using tweezers to stuff bits of food into its gaping mouth. The chick had nestled in a tiny ramekin lined with tissue.

We all emitted appreciative ahs and sighs.

"What do you feed them?" asked a woman.

"Wasp larvae, moths, bits of ground chicken and papaya." Elena pointed at a plastic container where the scientist was dipping her tweezers for another mouthful.

"Will you release these birds into the wild someday?" I asked.

"We've already released the first batch of fledglings," Elena replied. "We take them back to Isabela, to their natural environment, and monitor them for a month before they go off on their own."

Elena's friend said something else, and she translated, "So far, the project has shown every sign of success, and we're confident we'll be able to save this rare species from extinction." She shook her friend's hand and then waved us toward the door.

Elena waited until our entire group had exited the building and the door was closed again. "Ladies and Gentlemen, we will now head over to the Fausto Llerena Tortoise Breeding Center."

"What's it called again?" asked a woman.

"The tortoise breeding center is named after Fausto Llerena, who was the primary caretaker for Lonesome George," Elena explained, as our group began walking. "It was a sad day for us all when George died in 2012, without leaving a descendant."

"How old was Lonesome George?" asked another woman.

"No one knows for sure, but we estimate he was over one hundred years old. He was found on Pinta Island and brought here in 1972."

I walked alongside Elena as we strolled toward the tortoise breeding center. "Did you learn anything more about Tio Armando's whereabouts while you were away from the ship?"

Elena shook her head. "Rumor has it, there's a private sale pending, but no one I've talked to has any information about it. I hope the buyer doesn't take him away from the islands."

"Could someone do that?"

"Money can be persuasive."

"Peter and Joseph," I began. "You know, those two flight attendants from our cruise?"

Elena furrowed her brow for a moment and then recognition dawned.

"They met someone in town last night who talked about the sale."

"Who?"

"I don't think they got his name. Sounded like he was a local, though."

We'd come to a sign depicting the history of Lonesome George, with R.I.P. carved onto a wooden plaque. Peter and Joseph stood by the sign, reading.

"Speak of the devil," I said to Elena.

"Hey, Giovanna, there you are," said Peter. "Can we trouble you to take another photo?" He spread his arms. "Joseph and me next to George. Or what's left of the poor guy."

"Sure." I held out my hand for the camera.

"Hey, Elena," said Joseph. "We heard they shipped George to a taxidermist in the United States to be stuffed. Is that true, eh?"

I snapped the photo and handed the camera back to Peter as Elena launched into her history of Lonesome George again for the benefit of Peter and Joseph.

I glanced at the public restrooms we'd just passed, feeling the effects of the two cups of coffee and a large glass of juice I'd consumed at breakfast. "Please excuse me."

There was only one other woman in the ladies' room, so I didn't have to wait in line.

When I came out of the stall, I took a better look at the dark-haired woman standing at the sink. Her head had turned away, but I glimpsed her reflection in the bathroom mirror. Long bangs, long nose, large brown eyes.

I felt my breath catch in my throat. "Laurel?"

CHAPTER TWENTY-FOUR

s I studied our faces side by side in the restroom mirror, I wondered which of us looked more stunned.

The woman turned to confront me. A flicker of recognition crossed her bronzed visage.

"Giovanna Rogers... remember?" I stammered, wondering if I were talking to a ghost. Or maybe an evil twin. "From the *Archipelago Explorer.* Aren't you Laurel Pardo?"

The woman moved closer and extended her hand. It was Laurel. Alive. "I forgot it's Friday, and you have a stop here."

"What are you doing here?" I blinked, still trying to come to terms with her reappearance. "I thought you'd drowned! What happened at Gardner Bay? We were snorkeling and then . . ."

"Didn't Fernando tell you?"

"Fernando?" His name escaped my lips as a squeak. I could still hear his voice. *The other boat already picked her up. Don't worry.* I looked at Laurel. "There was another boat? What other boat?"

"Yes, Fernando was supposed to—"

"Fernando is dead."

"What?" A fresh layer of shock covered Laurel's face. "That can't be true."

Grim-faced, I nodded.

The lilt of Midwestern accents preceded the entry of three American tourists into the ladies' room.

Laurel signaled me toward the exit with her eyes. I followed her outside.

She clutched my arm and led me down a path behind the restrooms, to an area closed to the public. The worn vegetation, a dilapidated wooden bench, and a few cigarette butts on the ground betrayed an employee smoking hangout.

"Tell me what happened to Fernando." Laurel sat on the bench, looked at me, and patted the space beside her. "He can't be dead!"

"I may have made a mess of things for you." I dusted off the surface of the bench before I sat.

"What do you mean?"

With a sigh, I told Laurel how worried I'd been when we'd become separated in the water and I had not seen anyone pick her up. When I watched Fernando turn Laurel's tag over, I needed to find out for myself whether she was back on board. And then I never saw her on the ship again, and her cabin appeared ransacked. "I told Daniel something might have happened to you in Gardner Bay."

"Daniel?"

I nodded.

Laurel wrung her hands. "I didn't tell him I was leaving. I wasn't sure who I could trust."

"But Fernando knew?"

"Fernando didn't agree with me, but he went along with my plan to slip away. He's . . ." Laurel bit her lip. "He was a good friend." Tears welled in her dark eyes. "Fernando is dead?"

"I'm sorry." I wanted to ask her where she'd been, how she'd left without anyone noticing, why she'd left, but I had to wait for her to get past her shock about Fernando's death.

Laurel wiped her eyes with her sleeve.

I reached into my backpack and handed her a tissue.

Laurel took it and blew her nose.

"Sorry, but I did something stupid." I shuddered. "I gave your flash drive to the local police."

"My what?"

"Remember, you gave my grandmother Michelle a thumb drive with some photos on it?"

Laurel wiped her nose again with my tissue. "Those were copies. I have all the original photos on my computer. It's still on the ship, I guess. Fernando was going to—"

"There were also some research documents and other correspondence on your flash drive." I lowered my voice, although I saw no one nearby. "Did you even know? Research about Tio Armando."

Laurel's brown eyes widened. "You read my research?"

"We didn't mean to pry. But you had disappeared." A black fly buzzed around us, and I swatted it away. "I thought there might have been a connection." I wiped perspiration from my brow. "We didn't know what to do."

"I'm sorry. I didn't realize."

"And then yesterday, I gave your flash drive to Victor."

"Victor? Victor who?"

I blushed. "Victor Zuniga. One of the local police detectives."

"The police?"

When Laurel's perplexed expression did not relax, I continued, "He was investigating Fernando's, uh, death."

"And what happened to Fernando? You still haven't told me."

I explained that when the police came on board the cruise ship to investigate the death, they didn't tell most of the passengers who was dead, and I'd assumed Laurel was the victim, that perhaps they'd found her body in the ocean. My assumption was how Detective Victor Zuniga first realized Laurel was missing.

"You thought I was dead?"

"Or marooned somewhere. I hadn't seen you since we were in the water. I imagined something sinister had happened to you." My voice had become shriller, and I toned it down an octave. "After I read your research, I thought there might be a conspiracy to shut you up. Jim Roberts wants Tio Armando for his new resort. Fernando told me not to stick my nose where it didn't belong." Michelle had warned me not to let my over-active imagination cook up a crazy conspiracy theory, and once again, I'd proved her right. My suspicions had been silly.

"But what happened to Fernando? Tell me, please." Laurel's face creased.

I cringed. "Some deckhands found him at the bottom of the pool the morning after you disappeared. The police have ruled it an accident." I omitted the part about Janice and Jessy Roberts being present at the scene. And that they were most likely responsible for Fernando's accident, although Victor had admitted he couldn't prove it. Innocent until proven guilty. "They think Fernando slipped and hit his head when he fell."

Laurel buried her face in her hands. "Poor Fernando. I'm shocked."

"Everyone was."

"He was such a good friend, so full of life. Wow, how could that have happened?"

I blinked. *I can't tell her. Let someone else, if the truth ever comes out. According to Victor, it might not. What good would it do to tell her?*

"We volunteered together here at the Darwin Research Station last summer, working with baby tortoises." With her index finger, she wiped away another tear that had seeped from the corner of her eye, smearing her mascara. I hadn't realized she'd been wearing any. "He made me laugh all the time. I can't believe he's gone!"

I watched Laurel process her grief for a moment, and then placed a tentative hand on her shoulder. "The police think you may be dead, too. At least missing. Daniel reported you missing."

Laurel looked up. The rims of her eyelids were red. "Maybe that's a good thing."

"What do you mean? Are you in danger? Tell the police. The Galapagos National Park Service is wasting resources looking for your body."

Laurel sighed. She squeezed the tissue I'd given her, which had become limp and smeared with mascara.

I handed her another tissue. "Why did you leave the way you did? I didn't even see another boat. I assumed Fernando was talking about one of the ship's Zodiacs."

"My friends from the newspaper were waiting on the other side of the rock. I found out some things the night before, and it was urgent that we get this story out before the end of the cruise. I had to talk to some scientists here."

"A story. About Tio Armando?"

Her eyes widened, but she nodded. "I'm sorry I worried you, sorry to drag you into all the drama. I thought Fernando would explain."

"So, you planned all along to leave? And Fernando knew?"

Laurel grimaced and dipped her head.

"And you couldn't tell me beforehand? We were snorkeling buddies!"

"The fewer people who knew, and the less they knew, the better."

"But why? And why leave then? Why not wait until we were on dry land?" I scratched my head. "For a story?"

Footsteps approached. We heard Elena's voice, "Giovanna? Are you okay?"

The guided part of their tour was winding down and fellow cruise passengers were scattering. Those who were planning to visit the new Leisure Dreams property with Jim Roberts formed a cluster around the Roberts clan.

Michelle had not seen Giovanna since they left the buses at the entrance to the visitor center. Giovanna had been playing designated photographer for fellow cruise passengers in front of the famous Welcome sign.

Lots of tourists visited the Darwin Research Station without a guide, unlike in most other areas in the Galapagos. Plenty of detailed labels in both English and Spanish marked the trails, so many visitors preferred to explore on their own, lingering over the exhibits or rushing through them at the pace set by their schedules and interests. Michelle understood the tight quarters of the cruise ship and the closely-supervised, activity-filled days sometimes infringed on Giovanna's need for space and solitude, so the self-guided route might have suited her today.

I hope she's enjoying the park and hasn't skipped out to meet that detective, to pester him about detaining Jerome Haddad. She must know there's nothing he can do. Ever since she'd seen the mountain of research Giovanna had compiled, the time and energy her granddaughter had invested in tracking her former business partner, Michelle could not dismiss the uneasy feeling that something awful was about to happen.

"Where did Giovanna go?" asked Jenny. "Isn't she coming with us?"

"I thought she'd enjoy seeing your property." Michelle scanned the crowd of tourists for Giovanna. "But there's something else she's determined to do today."

"What would that be?" Janice moved closer to Michelle.

"It's a long saga." Michelle sighed.

"Tell me."

Michelle looked at Janice, whose blue eyes had focused on her face, ready to listen, with more curiosity than she would have expected from a new acquaintance. *Do I have a right to share my granddaughter's story?* "Giovanna was in business with a man who cheated her, and she's very bitter about it. Turns out he's here in Puerto Ayora. In jail."

Janice's expression did not change, as if the news was not a revelation.

"Giovanna thinks she has evidence that will persuade the local police to extradite this man to the United States, or put him away for good," Michelle continued, unable to stop once she'd started telling Giovanna's tale. She needed someone else to weigh in, to assess the danger Giovanna was courting with her obsession. "I don't know what she's thinking. She's known all along he was sailing here, in a yacht he bought with what she claims are funds he stole from her."

"Jerry Haddad." Janice's eyes narrowed.

Michelle touched her hand to her lips. "Yes."

"Good. I hope that evidence is solid. He needs to stay locked up."

"She told you?" Michelle remembered that Giovanna and Janice had spent yesterday afternoon together at the police station, and Jessy said they'd hung out for a while afterward. Giovanna must have talked about Jerome.

"Not the whole story, but enough," Janice said. "We watched the police bring him ashore."

Michelle touched her forehead. Giovanna must have visited Jerome in jail last night instead of heading back to the ship with the others, to see for herself that he was behind bars. *She didn't tell me that part when she got back. What was she thinking? She's playing with fire.*

"I know the scumbag, too," said Janice.

"You know him, too? Jerome Haddad? But how—?" *Another tidbit Giovanna didn't reveal.*

Jim strolled over in time to catch the last of their conversation. "Who are you talking about?"

Janice blinked.

"Not that scoundrel, Haddad?" He gave Janice a sharp look. "Why ever would you bring him up now? Can't we leave that sordid affair in ancient history?"

Janice kicked a pebble and refused to meet her husband's eyes. "He followed us here."

Jim grabbed her arm. "And when were you planning to tell me this?"

Michelle looked from one Roberts spouse to the other and then held up her hand. "Wait. He followed *you* here? How do you two know Jerome Haddad?"

Elena stared at Laurel. "What are you doing here?" A light breeze rippled through the trees surrounding the employee smoking area. The black fly had left us alone.

Laurel lifted her head toward Elena, her long nose pointed into the air. "This is one of the most successful giant tortoise breeding centers in the Galapagos."

"That doesn't answer my question." Elena stepped closer. "No one here believes your lies."

My jaw dropped. Elena did not seem astonished to find Laurel alive.

"Unlike you, the scientists here are interested in keeping a sub-species from going extinct, not treating its last member like a carnival act," Laurel huffed. "And even worse: *pretending* he's the last member when evidence shows he isn't."

"You don't know what you're talking about." Elena's dark eyes glowed like hot charcoal. "He had the best care at the Beagle Galapaguera, on San Cristóbal."

"You know that was going to change."

Elena muttered something in Spanish.

Laurel countered, her voice raised.

Elena lashed back. I couldn't understand the words, but they sounded threatening.

Laurel's face grew hot and she clenched her hand into a fist.

"Excuse me," I said. "What's going on?"

The two women looked at me like I was one of the island's iguanas who had wandered up.

"She's read my research," Laurel explained to Elena, back in English.

Elena studied me. "So, Giovanna, what did you think?"

I looked down, watching a battalion of ants march toward a discarded fruit pit. "Most of it was in Spanish."

"And most of it was fiction," Elena sneered.

Laurel puffed her cheeks. "Money over truth."

"Money keeps our research going. *No escupas dentro del vaso del que has bebido.*"

Laurel must have noticed my confused expression at Elena's lapse back into Spanish. "Don't bite the hand that feeds you," she translated.

"I still don't understand." I pointed at Laurel. "You were missing, but now you're not. Tio Armando is still missing. Or is he?"

Janice jerked her arm away from Jim. "Let's not do this now." Her eyes strayed to the group gathering at the entrance of the Darwin Research Station for the visit to Leisure Dreams.

"How did you know Haddad was here?" Jim lowered his voice, which made it only audible to Janice and Michelle.

Janice expelled a sigh. "I saw him on the pier yesterday afternoon. In police custody. I don't know what he did, but he's where he belongs."

Michelle turned to Jim. "The *Second Wind.*"

"The *Second Wind?*" Jim's face was a puzzle, then lit up as the pieces fell into place. "The yacht we saw run aground yesterday? That's Haddad's yacht?"

It was Janice's turn to look puzzled.

"Yesterday, when we were snorkeling near Isolete Caamaño, we came across a yacht that had run aground," Michelle explained. "It belongs to Jerome Haddad."

"Why would they take him to jail for running aground?" asked Janice.

"He damaged a reef and polluted the water with a fuel spill," said Michelle. "Remember, Jim, what Rafael heard on the radio? How they were evacuating the area?"

"They're such environmentalists here." Jim gestured at his surroundings, the institution that was a true tribute to conservation. "They won't be able to hold him for long, though. Unfortunately."

"That's why Giovanna wants to talk to the police today," said Michelle. "She believes her evidence of Jerome's financial crimes will provide a reason to hold him longer, or perhaps extradite him to the United States."

Jim pivoted to Michelle. "Haddad ripped off Giovanna, too?" His eyes glinted and his lips tightened into a scowl. "That man is pure evil. We should have hunted him down and destroyed him eighteen years ago, after what he pulled with Big D Literacy. That was my first instinct! The cover-up was a mistake because it let him off the hook." He shot Michelle a desperate look and then hung his head. "I am so sorry."

"Tio Armando is missing?" Laurel stared at me as if I'd fabricated the whole story. Like Michelle might have reacted. "How can he be missing? He's a huge animal."

"You tell me," said Elena, kicking a stone across the sandy clearing.

"Wait. You think I took him?" Laurel scoffed. "How would I do that? He weighs over five hundred pounds."

"It's no secret Jim Roberts wants to move him to Leisure Dreams," I said. "But I'm not sure he even knows where Tio Armando is. When we got to the Beagle Galapaguera, Jim seemed as shocked as the rest of us that someone moved the tortoise."

Laurel brushed her long bangs out of her eyes. "Oh, no. I thought we had more time."

"You're talking in riddles." Elena waved her arms. "More time for what?"

"To get the truth out." Laurel paced. "Stop the bidding wars. Get the animal somewhere safe. Keep him here in the islands."

"Someone is plotting to take him away from the Galapagos?" I looked at Elena, remembering how she had expressed that fear to me just before I went to the ladies' room.

"They must be here already." Laurel stopped her pacing and put a hand over her mouth.

"Who? A buyer for Tio Armando?" I cocked my head at Laurel. First, she'd seemed surprised the giant tortoise was missing, but now I suspected she knew more than she'd let on.

"You've talked to Felipe," Elena wagged an accusing finger at Laurel.

"Who's Felipe?" Even though the conversation had switched back to English, I was having trouble following.

"Felipe is the researcher who discovered Tio Armando, on Floreana," Elena explained.

"So the story goes," said Laurel. "Or maybe Felipe took Tio Armando from his clan on Isla Isabela and planted him on Floreana. And then 'discovered' him."

Elena glared at Laurel. "Felipe would never do that. He cares about science. Tio Armando is from Floreana."

"Felipe also cares about money. And power. And attention."

"People who don't have money want it." Elena sniffed. "People like you who have plenty of it don't understand."

Laurel rolled her eyes and made a sour face at Elena.

"So, does Felipe *own* Tio Armando?" My head hurt. "Doesn't all the wildlife belong to the Galapagos National Park Service?"

"Theoretically," said Laurel. "I told Felipe we should publish the truth, get a breeding program going, and save the sub-species. Tio Armando is still an endangered animal, just not the last one standing."

"Tio Armando has become too valuable as a loner," scoffed Elena. "Too many tourist dollars at risk. Provided your research is even true."

I turned to Elena. "Earlier, you said something about a private sale pending. Someone other than Jim Roberts? Is this Felipe person involved? And how can he sell an animal the National Park Service owns?" As I spoke, I realized how naïve I was to believe most people played by the rules. I'd seen firsthand, from my dealings with Jerome Haddad, how a scammer could collect money with no intention of delivering the promised goods. *This Felipe character can profit from brokering a sale without even owning Tio Armando.*

"Anything for a buck," said Laurel. "Felipe has an American partner who's helping him finance a new reserve here, and now Felipe has outbid Jim Roberts for Tio Armando. Felipe will get to run his own place and take care of Tio Armando. He didn't relish taking orders from Jim Roberts."

"But what's this about Tio Armando being taken away from the islands?" I was so confused. Jim Roberts, Felipe, someone from out of the country? "Isn't Felipe's reserve here? Who's taking him away?"

Laurel waved her hand in front of her face. "Felipe would never let someone take Tio Armando away from the Galapagos. When the buyers see tomorrow's paper, the sale will be off. They'll go back to Saudi Arabia or Dubai, or wherever it is they're from. And Tio Armando will stay in the Galapagos."

Elena's eyes widened. "You didn't convince the new editor to print that garbage?"

Laurel's smile was a gloat.

Elena shook her head. "You don't know what you're doing to the tourist industry. We warned you."

"Saving Tio Armando is more important. He needs to be in a breeding program, not shipped off to the Middle East or paraded around like a circus animal."

"What will Felipe say?" Elena sighed. "What about the reserve he's building with that American investor? Tio Armando will be the star attraction. What's the American's name?"

"Something Haddad. I've never heard of him, but he's well versed in fundraising and setting up nonprofit projects like this."

My mouth dropped. "Haddad? Not Jerome Haddad?"

"Jerome," replied Laurel. "I think that's it. Jerome Haddad."

I threw back my head and laughed until tears streamed down my face.

CHAPTER TWENTY-FIVE

The first thing Detective Victor Zuniga did when he arrived at the police station was to check on the American prisoner. To his dismay, the jail cell was empty, cleaned out. When he walked into his office, he found Jerome Haddad's release papers on his desk.

Zuniga sank into his chair and picked up the papers.

Jerome's business partner, a tortoise handler named Felipe Santore, had paid the fine; there was no reason to hold Jerome Haddad any longer. Zuniga examined the paperwork, searching for an irregularity. Everything appeared to be in order. Victor could not be angry with the night officer.

Jerome Haddad was free.

I've failed Giovanna, Victor thought. He ran his fingers through his hair. He could not get her story out of his head. *The nerve of that swindler Haddad. The nerve of her fiancé for blaming Giovanna!*

Giovanna. Her hypnotic, intelligent eyes. Her contagious smile. He could still feel the warmth of her soft hand when he'd helped her from the chair in the back room of the bar, and again when he'd said good-bye to her at the dock. How tempted he'd been to beg her to not to leave.

Such irrational thoughts. Not only was she too close to his investigation, she was an affluent American who sailed on luxury cruises, a businesswoman, way out of his league. They were from different worlds. Giovanna would leave the Galapagos in a few days to return to her world, and he would most likely never see her again.

He stared at the grimy walls of his tiny office. This was the life he had chosen.

She expected him to meet her later today, to take her to lunch, so she could show him more evidence of Jerome Haddad's financial misdeeds. Victor fumed at the thought of what Haddad had done to Giovanna's dream. She cared so much about helping animals, and she'd given up her career, invested all her savings, to pursue that mission. Should he look over the data she had compiled, waste her time, knowing he could do nothing to help her? Knowing it was only an excuse to see her one last time? Was it fair?

He couldn't stand her up, leave her with only the memory of his betrayal, his failure to do what she had asked. *Don't let Haddad go.* That was all she'd wanted, and he couldn't deliver. Perhaps he could explain, make her realize how the law limited his power, and provide a sympathetic shoulder she would need.

He drummed his fingers on the desk. And then he would have to purge her image from his mind. Life would resume as if he had never met her. Was that even possible?

Another reason to see her was to deliver good news, news that might ease her disappointment at the release of Jerome Haddad. Out of his pocket, he pulled the flash drive Giovanna had given him yesterday. He smiled to think she had trusted him with it.

After reading the documents on the device last night, Zuniga learned that her missing friend Laurel Pardo had once volunteered at the Darwin Research Station. This morning, he'd placed a phone call to the Darwin Station and confirmed Laurel Pardo had stopped by their office yesterday. Regardless of whatever happened in Gardner Bay, Laurel had not drowned at sea. They had called off the search. Attempts to reach Laurel's family had been unsuccessful and were now no longer necessary. *Giovanna will rejoice that her friend is alive.*

Setting aside Jerome's release papers, Zuniga contemplated the allegations Laurel had made in her research. Tio Armando related to a colony of giant tortoises on Isabela Island? Not the last of his sub-species, not the Lonesome George replacement tourists flocked to see? Zuniga understood why people in the tourism industry, including the cruise line, might not welcome the news, and why Laurel might have found herself in an environment hostile enough to cause her to leave the voyage. What if she'd talked to someone about her findings? Shattered the myth.

And then there were the emails, rumors buzzing about a sale. An entrepreneur who was building a theme park in Dubai wanted to buy Tio Armando as the star attraction of a special Galapagos exhibit. But who could sell the giant tortoise and allow his removal from the islands? Who would want to? Tio Armando was a national treasure, a source of local pride.

With a glance at the stack of files from the *Archipelago Explorer* investigation still on his desk, Zuniga thought back to his interviews with Elena. How she'd bristled when he'd tried to probe Fernando's cover-up of Laurel's disappearance. How she had danced around answering his questions about her own actions on the snorkeling trip. Elena had seemed unconcerned that a passenger might have died on her watch; Zuniga had even suspected she'd had something to do with Laurel's demise. Now her demeanor made sense to Zuniga. Elena had known nothing tragic had happened to Laurel, that Laurel had left the snorkeling group of her own volition and sworn her to secrecy.

And yet she had done nothing to stop Daniel from launching a fruitless search.

Zuniga shook his head. The authorities had expended a lot of effort on the hunt for an individual who was not missing. All because of a misunderstanding. Or perhaps a conspiracy. Should he file charges?

The police radio on his desk crackled. "We've finished searching the *Second Wind* again."

After his conversation with Giovanna last night, Zuniga had felt uneasy, thinking they might have missed something at the scene of the wrecked yacht. So, he'd asked the investigating officers to conduct another search. Early this morning, a team had set out for the *Second Wind*, which was still bobbing near Isolete Caamaño, awaiting clearance by park authorities.

"Find anything?" Zuniga held his breath.

"Come meet us at the dock. We should be there in about fifteen minutes."

Back at the Darwin Research Station, both Laurel and Elena stared open-mouthed as I recounted my story about Jerome Haddad. I described his pyramid of fake charities and supporting businesses that fed off the income stream from unwitting philanthropists.

"Oh my gosh." Laurel's long bangs had grown wet from perspiration, and she pushed them off her forehead. "We have to tell Felipe."

"Are you sure?" Elena pressed her temples. "All this talk is giving me a headache. I'm not following the scheme. How can one person keep it all straight?"

I unzipped my backpack and produced the paperwork I had organized to show to Detective Zuniga. I glanced at my watch. It was almost time to meet him.

Elena waved me away, but Laurel studied the documents. "So, you're saying this is another scam?"

"I'm willing to bet whatever funds your friend Felipe raises for his tortoise reserve are going straight into that scumbag's pocket." I could feel my blood pressure elevating. "Jerome will find a fancy way to divert them, and Felipe won't know what happened until his business crumbles."

Laurel picked up sheet after sheet and skimmed. "Unbelievable."

"He has no conscience," I said.

Laurel showed one document to Elena, which depicted the house of dominoes I'd drawn to summarize Jerome's money trail. "Look at this."

Elena stared at the paper. Her mouth opened, but no words came out.

Laurel took a cell phone out of her pocket. "I'm calling Felipe right now."

Detective Zuniga stood on the pier as the police boat cut through the water. An ambulance and a National Park Service van waited at the head of the dock.

"Four land iguanas, five juvenile tortoises, and a woman," the officer commanding the boat had said on the radio. "All locked in a secret hold."

"And?" Zuniga had asked, afraid to breathe.

"The animals appear to be in good shape. The woman, not so much."

Zuniga winced, remembering the radio conversation he'd had before he left the police station. That was the reason for the ambulance and the National Park Service van.

The police boat bumped the pier, and Zuniga caught a thrown line. He wrapped it around a bollard as others rushed down the dock.

As soon as the officers had tied up the boat, the paramedics leaped into action. They loaded the unconscious woman onto a stretcher. Her skin tone was ashen blue.

"I alerted the air ambulance service," said Zuniga. "The Puerto Ayora hospital doesn't have the equipment to treat her, so they're ready to fly her to the mainland."

A paramedic felt the woman's throat for a pulse and shook his head. He looked at Zuniga. "The air ambulance won't be necessary."

Jerome Haddad's disdainful blue eyes scanned the interior of Felipe's compact bungalow. His back ached from sleeping on the lumpy couch, but at least it was better than the jail cell cot where he had almost spent the night. Tonight, he'd need to find a good hotel. A comfortable king-size bed. A private bathroom with a big soaking tub. He'd bill the Tio Armando Foundation account.

Too bad Leisure Dreams - Galapagos isn't open yet, he thought. That resort promised to be more to his liking than anything he could find today in Puerto Ayora. And what irony, what poetic justice. A serpentine smile crept over his lips as he relished sticking it to that arrogant Jim Roberts.

Felipe emerged from the small bathroom, a towel wrapped around his thick waist and a toothbrush dangling from his mouth. Droplets of water clung to his hairy barrel chest.

Jerome took a deep breath. The sluggish island life annoyed him. "When are you going to show me this famous turtle I'm investing in?" He wondered how long he could hold off his buyer from Dubai before he had to produce the animal or return the agent's deposit. Felipe was still raising a lot of donations for the reserve he thought he'd be building here, and Jerome would need some of that money to transport the huge beast out of the country.

Felipe removed the toothbrush from his mouth and started to speak when the cell phone on his coffee table vibrated. He walked to the table and grabbed it.

He listened for a long time without replying. A white trickle of toothpaste leaked down his chin. His dark eyes swept to Jerome.

Jerome fidgeted. *What could be so important? Felipe is too much of a scatterbrain to be a reliable partner. I'll be glad when we finish this deal, and I can get away from these desolate islands.*

Felipe's facial features tightened. He glared at Jerome.

Michelle had not realized how big of a deal the visit to the Leisure Dreams site was turning out to be. Jim Roberts had chartered a minibus to transport all his guests. During their tour of the Darwin Research Station, the group had expanded as word circulated about the outing. Even Rafael had wangled an invitation.

The bus met them at the entrance to the visitor center, by the Welcome sign where Michelle had last seen her granddaughter snapping posed photos for fellow cruise passengers. She wished Giovanna had joined them for the visit to the Leisure Dreams site. But Giovanna was determined to meet that police officer and present her evidence of Jerome Haddad's financial crimes, as if the poor officer had the power to make Jerome pay for what he had done to her.

As she boarded the bus and found a seat in the back row next to Deborah and Sue, Michelle hoped Giovanna would not be foolish enough to confront Jerome Haddad, to take the law into her own hands. *At least he's behind bars, for now,* she thought.

Michelle vowed to be understanding and supportive when her granddaughter returned, disillusioned, to the ship this afternoon.

Jerome Haddad's hands shook as he turned the key in the ignition of Felipe's Honda Civic. *You were a foolish man, Felipe. One conversation with a crazy woman made you question the deal we've been planning for months. One crazy woman brainwashed by the ranting of that traitor, Giovanna Rogers.*

Gio will pay. How dare she sabotage my business deal?

The engine would not turn over. Jerome banged the wheel and tried again to start the car.

Et tu, Felipe? You should have known better than to double-cross me. Playing me against Jim Roberts, driving up the bid for that stupid turtle, Tio What's His Name. Did you think hiding the beast from me was funny? What gall!

The engine rumbled to life on the third try.

Felipe deserved whatever he got. Jerome gripped the steering wheel with sticky hands and maneuvered the vehicle down the gravel driveway. He backed onto the two-lane asphalt street and turned toward town.

With one eye on the road, he searched the cluttered interior until he found a semi-clean rag. He used the rag to wipe his hands, one at a time, and then the steering wheel and the gear shift.

It would be smart to get rid of the knife, but he might need it again; he had no other weapon. Most everything he owned was still on board the *Second Wind*. He wiped the knife with the rag and then tossed the rag out the window.

Zuniga leaned over the woman's body. She was so pale and still. *Thank God, she's not Giovanna.*

"Here's the stab wound," a paramedic said, pointing to a spot on the woman's neck. "Not fatal, as it missed the carotid artery. It took several hours, but she bled out."

Zuniga closed his eyes, trying to shut out the image of the woman's painful, lonely death. *Could we have saved this poor soul if only the team had searched the yacht more thoroughly the first time?*

"It's not an iguana bite, then?" asked an officer.

The paramedic shook his head. "Definitely a knife. But the iguanas might have licked up some of her blood."

"Do we have any identification?" asked Zuniga.

"Nothing found at the scene," replied another officer from the police boat. "He might have thrown her documents overboard. I bet he planned to do the same with the body. Most likely, it's the wife."

"The boat owner is still in jail, isn't he?" asked the first officer. "Now it makes sense why he was so belligerent when we tried to board and question him about the accident."

"Unfortunately, no," said Zuniga. "We released him last night, after his business partner paid the fine. But he can't have gone too far. I've alerted the airport. And we have contact information for the man who bailed him out."

"We'll find him." The officer touched the gun in his holster as the paramedics loaded the stretcher into the ambulance.

The park service employees, clad in thick leather gloves, set about caging the animals and transferring them from the boat to the waiting van.

Giovanna. Zuniga looked at his watch. *I hope she understands.*

He prayed she'd still be waiting for him at their appointed spot, that she would not assume he had stood her up. Although he could no longer spare the time to take her to lunch or to even review her documents, at least he could drive by and let her know he wouldn't be able to meet with her. And she needed to know Jerome Haddad was much more dangerous than she realized.

CHAPTER TWENTY-SIX

Back at the employee hang-out behind the Darwin Research Station, Laurel held the cell phone against her ear. "Felipe?" she repeated, pacing. She stopped and looked at Elena and me, still seated on the bench. "The line went dead."

"He's in shock after what you told him about Jerome Haddad," I suggested. "I feel sorry for him. Do you have any good therapists on Santa Cruz island?"

"No. Something's wrong." Laurel stared at the phone in her hand. "After I told him all that stuff about his partner, Haddad, I think he put the phone down because he started yelling at someone in the room. And then I heard a scuffle."

"Did he say who was there?" asked Elena.

"No." Laurel ran her fingers through her bangs. "I did most of the talking."

I felt the blood rush from my face. *He couldn't have been talking to that scam artist. Jerome is in jail.*

"Maybe Felipe didn't believe you," said Elena. "And he hung up in disgust." She waved a finger at Laurel. "I'm surprised he even let you talk, after the rumors you've been spreading about Tio Armando."

"If only these fools would listen. You build up the hype about an animal, make him seem rarer and more valuable, and then you risk losing him." Laurel looked at me. "Come with me to Felipe's house. Bring your papers."

"Where?" I gripped my dossier of Jerome Haddad. Was she talking about trying to convince Felipe of Tio Armando's DNA results, which I didn't have, or Jerome's treachery, evidence of which I had plenty?

"Felipe doesn't live far from here," Laurel assured me. "Just down the road."

"I promised to meet Vic– Detective Zuniga." I glanced at my watch. "And I'm late."

"Laurel, why don't you go with her to meet her detective friend?" Elena flared her nostrils. "Then all three of you can head over to Felipe's house. If something's happened to him, you'll have the police with you for protection."

"No." Laurel looked at me. "No offense if he's your friend, but the police will want to ask me too many questions. I don't have time for that right now."

"Sorry," I said. "I thought you'd met some tragic fate. You should have trusted me enough to tell me you were leaving the ship. You didn't even have to tell me why."

"Everything is a crisis with Laurel," Elena explained. "She couldn't wait a few days to meddle with the sale and spout off about her crazy tortoise theory, so she had to sneak away from the cruise in a wetsuit. Now she's sure something terrible has happened to Felipe because he hung up on her."

"You weren't on the line." Laurel's face tensed. "Something happened."

"You go meet your Detective Zuniga," Elena said to me. Her tone was mocking as if to imply there was something between us, and I blushed because I hoped there was. "I'll even give you a lift, so you won't be late."

"Thanks." I stashed the papers in my backpack and slung it over my shoulder. "That will help."

"No problem. Come on, I'm parked around back."

We all rose and started down a footpath.

"And you don't have to tell the good detective I said hello." Elena smiled. "Laurel and I will go check on Felipe."

After Elena dropped me off, I stood next to the greenish-colored bust of Charles Darwin on a triangular traffic island at an intersection in central Puerto Ayora. The noon sun blazed. I'd already read the plaque on the stone pedestal beneath the sculpture. A giant sea-blue arch behind me depicted a three-dimensional mural of the beloved wildlife species Darwin had studied. This had to be the correct meeting place. I checked my watch again. *Have I missed him? Yes, I arrived late, but couldn't he have waited more than a few minutes?*

Did he decide not to bother coming? Did he forget?

I patted the bulge in my backpack containing the paperwork I'd compiled about my former partner's accounting misdeeds. *I've already accomplished more than I expected,* I thought. *Laurel warned his current partner; that's huge.* Perhaps I could save someone else from financial ruin and misery at the hand of Jerome Haddad.

I knew Victor and his colleagues in local law enforcement did not have the power to prosecute Jerome for what he'd done to me, to my business, to my dream. Or to have him extradited to the United States. That was just a fantasy, I knew. But sharing my story with Victor last night, feeling his sympathetic eyes on me as I poured it out, had seemed somehow liberating, a catharsis. I remembered the way Victor gazed at me without judging, without telling me what I'd done wrong, what I should have done to prevent becoming a victim. He hadn't tried to fix me. Unlike the way Tim reacted to the whole debacle. Tim had been my fiancé; he was supposed to love me, to trust me. Yet Victor Zuniga, a relative stranger, had been more supportive.

Maybe I'd treated Tim unfairly. He'd had utter faith in my judgment, and I'd disappointed him. Victor had no such expectations for me to dash.

I wanted to see Victor again. Look into those kind, brown eyes. Watch that rakish smile form on his luscious lips.

Peter's advice about immersing myself in another culture to learn a foreign language made me giggle. "Get a lover," he'd said. I felt my cheeks redden as I pictured myself in Victor's arms, his lips brushing mine, his hands caressing my body . . .

I stole another glance at my watch. *How much longer should I wait? Who am I kidding? He's forgotten all about me.*

It was getting hotter. I wiped my brow. *How stupid is this, standing on a corner like an idiot, waiting for a man who isn't coming? Maybe I should head back to the ship, where I can get some air conditioning and a cold drink. Lunch.*

Or should I go by the police station? It's not that far from the pier. Victor has no way to contact me if he had to delay or cancel our meeting. And if Jerome is committing fraud in the Galapagos, that should be reason enough for the police to keep him behind bars where he belongs. Yes! They can't let him go now.

I hoisted my backpack and began walking.

Felipe's car shimmied like the alignment was off. *The moron can't maintain his vehicle*, thought Jerome. *What else is wrong with his operation?*

He slowed the Honda Civic as he approached downtown Puerto Ayora. He couldn't remember the name of the bank, but there must be only a few financial institutions in this backward town. *The sooner I can withdraw the funds and get out of here, the better.*

Tourists meandered in the streets, either oblivious to moving vehicles or trusting that no one would run them down. *Imbeciles*, thought Jerome. As he reached a traffic island containing the bust of some famous forefather, he glimpsed a familiar figure sauntering across the boulevard.

Suntanned limbs, confident gait, fly-away brown hair. *Could it be?* She was here; he'd seen her near the pier with Janice yesterday.

He slowed down, not caring if he annoyed the driver behind him.

It is.

Giovanna Rogers.

A sitting duck.

So easy.

He entered the traffic circle and pressed the accelerator to the floorboard.

Michelle looked out the window of the minibus as they rolled into the central part of Puerto Ayora. Kumiko snapped a photo of the bust of Charles Darwin.

Someone commented on the famous blue arch, and the bus driver slowed down so passengers could take pictures.

Michelle's eyes followed the camera's sights. *Is that Giovanna?*

They rounded the traffic island, which enabled Michelle to get a confirming view of her granddaughter walking away from the statue, starting across the main street.

"Jim!" called Michelle.

Like a mother hen, Jim strolled the aisle, tending to his guests. He turned around.

"There's Giovanna. Do we have room for one more?"

As the bus changed lanes to pull alongside Giovanna, a black, four-door Honda Civic sped by in a blur, tires squealing.

Laurel pounded on Felipe's paint-chipped door. The doorbell button dangled from wires coming out of the wall plate.

When there was no response, she pounded harder.

"Careful," warned Elena. "Don't break it down."

"Felipe?" called Laurel. "Are you in there?"

"His car is gone," said Elena. "He must have left." She looked at her watch. "I need to get back to work. We're sailing this afternoon. One of those tourists will complain that I didn't escort them back to the ship."

Laurel glanced at the driveway, empty except for Elena's old Volkswagen Beetle. "You might be right. Maybe he went to talk to his so-called partner. Giovanna said this Jerome guy is in jail."

"Are you coming back to the ship? Fernando and I packed up your cabin the day you left, but your things are still on board."

"I don't know yet. Daniel must be furious with me." As Laurel moved away from Felipe's door, she almost lost her balance on a loose step. "I still think something's off here."

Elena spotted the open window. "Let's see if anyone is inside."

Laurel stood on tiptoe to peer through the window; the sill was about five feet above the ground. She gasped.

"What?"

"I think I see him. Help me up."

Elena leaned against the stucco wall and made a stirrup with her hands for Laurel to step into. She groaned. "You're heavy."

"At least I'm not the one trying to boost *you* up." Laurel hoisted herself onto the sill, pushed aside the hanging screen, and lifted the window frame. In a moment, she tumbled inside.

She picked herself up from the linoleum floor. "Felipe!"

Felipe lay sprawled on the kitchen floor, naked except for a towel draped over his body. Blood trickled from a gash in his side.

Laurel bent over her friend, checked for a pulse and listened for breath. His vital signs were faint. She picked up the towel and pressed it against his wound.

She sprang to the door and flung it open. "Elena! He's hurt. It looks like he was stabbed."

"Stabbed?" Elena shrieked as she rushed inside. "Should we give him CPR?"

"He's still breathing, but we need to stop the bleeding." Laurel dashed back to Felipe and resumed pressure on his wound. "Call for an ambulance!"

Elena's face whitened as she looked closer at Felipe. She fumbled for the cell phone in her pocket. Her hands shook as she retrieved it, and her fingers struck the numbers.

As she spoke into the phone, neither she nor Laurel heard the car pull into the driveway, nor the footsteps plodding up the walkway.

CHAPTER TWENTY-SEVEN

'd given up on the prospect of a *rendezvous* with Victor. Something must have come up and he couldn't wait for me. I tried not to feel disappointed. But if I'd missed our meeting because I was busy learning about Jerome's latest scam, it was worthwhile. I was on my way to the police station to report it. They couldn't release Jerome now.

"Giovanna!"

As I stepped into the street, I looked up to see a minibus pull alongside me.

The doors of the bus opened. It was the tour Jim Roberts had orchestrated to show off his new Leisure Dreams property. *Jim Roberts.* He had a stake in seeing Jerome's fraud spree end. I should tell him what I'd learned about his competition for Tío Armando. And once Laurel's research surfaced, he might even withdraw his bid.

Familiar faces smiled. Arms beckoned. *Michelle.*

I climbed aboard.

"Glad you could join us, Giovanna." Jim stepped aside so I could squeeze by with my backpack.

"Jim, I..." The expectant faces of my fellow cruise passengers urged me to take a seat so they could resume their journey.

I avoided eye contact with Janice and the twins as I moved down the narrow aisle toward my grandmother.

Helga stared out the window. "Did you see that car almost hit us?" she said to Dieter while I was passing within earshot. "He's driving way too fast."

My eyes swept to the window where Helga pointed. A dust-covered black Honda Civic zigzagged through traffic and sped down the main street.

"Maniac," said Dieter. "He could have killed someone."

Deborah edged closer to Sue to make room for me on the last row next to Michelle.

"Go ahead and say it," I challenged Michelle as I plopped onto the seat.

"What?"

"'I told you so'."

"I didn't say anything." She twisted in the seat to face me.

"But you're thinking it."

"How do you know what I'm thinking?" Michelle stifled an amused smile.

I unstrapped my backpack and shifted it to my lap. "Victor . . . Detective Zuniga never showed up."

"Maybe he had more pressing police business."

"Right. So much happens in this town. Last month they caught a pickpocket on the beach."

"There was a death on a cruise ship." The amusement had left her voice.

"Ruled an accident. Case closed." I stole a glance at Janice and Jessy, sitting at the front of the bus. *They've forgotten all about poor Fernando. An accident. Right. If your husband is a big corporate mogul.*

"And Jerome Haddad." Michelle's eyes bored into mine.

I wiped my heat-flushed face with the back of my hand. "About Jerome Haddad..."

"I'm sorry, Giovanna." She put her hand on my shoulder.

"I'm not." I was ecstatic that I might have foiled Jerome's plans for a new scam in the Galapagos. Even if the authorities couldn't hold him, maybe I'd saved another person from being cheated. Donors who'd contributed to the care of an endangered tortoise might not have their money diverted to fund luxury toys for a crook. Feeling superior, I stole another glance at Janice. *Unlike you, Janice. You only cared about undoing the damage Jerome did to you and your charity, not about stopping him from hurting anyone else.*

I took a deep breath and looked at Michelle. "I have so much to tell you. About Jerome. And about Laurel. She's alive!"

Detective Zuniga double-checked Felipe Santore's address. An old Volkswagen Beetle was parked in the gravel driveway, and the front door to the small stucco house stood open. He pulled his police car behind the Beetle, then jumped out and hurried up the walkway, hand on his holster.

A dark-haired woman in khaki shorts rushed outside, hands covered in blood.

Zuniga drew his gun.

Eyes bugging like a goldfish, the woman held up her bloody hands.

Zuniga blinked. "Elena?"

What was she doing here? Didn't she still have a job as a guide on the *Archipelago Explorer*? The cruise ship would sail for North Seymour in a few hours.

"Where's the ambulance?" Elena cried, hands still in the air, eyes darting past him. "We need help!"

"What happened?" Zuniga lowered his gun. "I'm looking for Felipe Santore."

"You might be too late." Elena gestured toward the house and waved for Zuniga to follow her inside. "He's in bad shape."

Another dark-haired woman bent over the supine body of a naked man, pressing a towel against his side. Blood had seeped onto the floor around him.

She moved aside to make room for the detective. "We found him like this. I'd been talking to him on the phone, and then I heard a struggle. The line went dead, and he didn't pick up when I called back. So, we came to check on him."

Zuniga spotted the stab wound in Felipe's side. Blood still trickled out, although the woman had been applying pressure on the area with the towel.

"Was anyone else here? Did you see anyone leaving?"

"No, but Felipe's car is gone," said Elena.

"The Volkswagen is yours?"

Elena nodded.

Zuniga leaned toward Felipe's face. "Señor? Can you hear me? Can you tell me who did this?"

Felipe remained unresponsive. His breathing was shallow, his pulse still weak.

While Elena described Felipe's Honda Civic to Zuniga, the paramedics arrived.

Our bus filled with chattering *Archipelago Explorer* passengers traveled through the dusty streets of Puerto Ayora. Not focused on the scenery nor our traveling companions, I told Michelle about running into Laurel and foiling Jerome's latest scam.

"Slow down," begged Michelle. "Laurel is alive?"

I nodded.

"But how? What happened? Where did she go?" Michelle's face was a question mark.

"You wouldn't believe it, but I think Jerome—"

"Wait! Why did Laurel leave the cruise? Where has she been? How did she get here?" Michelle cast a glance at Deborah and Sue, engrossed in conversation, not listening to us. "Does she know she's a missing person?"

"I don't have all the details, but she said some friends from the local newspaper picked her up in Gardner Bay. She'd found out some buyers from Dubai were planning to take Tio Armando to the Middle East and show him off like a circus animal. She figured once the story came out about him not being the lone survivor, the buyers would renege on the deal and Tio Armando would stay here in the Galapagos where he belongs, as part of a breeding program to revive the species." Michelle's eyes widened as I spoke, and her lips moved as if repeating my words to herself would make them more comprehensible. "Fernando and Elena knew all about Laurel's plan, and they covered for her."

"Elena knew? Why didn't she say anything?" Michelle blinked as if trying to compute the information I was rattling off.

"She didn't agree with Laurel's decision to spill the beans about Tio Armando. But she could have saved everybody a lot of anxiety. The police are still searching for Laurel at sea." I sighed. "If only Detective Zuniga had shown up, I could have told him they can stop looking for Laurel. And they have another reason to keep Jerome in jail."

Our bus rounded a lagoon and then turned onto a narrow gravel road. Heavy construction equipment parked along the shoulder suggested paving in progress.

"This is a new road, private access to Leisure Dreams," said Jim. He looked at his watch and then at the silent equipment. "And the construction crew should be at work by now."

"Welcome to South America," said Dieter.

"Siesta time," advised Rafael.

"Already?" Jim scowled.

Rafael shrugged. "It's a hot day."

Now that the pavement had ended, the ride grew bumpy. The driver slowed to a tortoise's pace as he steered the bus around enormous potholes. The vehicle dipped and lurched over the uneven ground.

Out the windows, we viewed a wall of green. Vegetation was so thick that branches scraped and thumped against the sides of the bus as it passed.

Helga cracked her window for fresh air, and a butterfly fluttered in, causing excitement inside the cabin until someone coaxed the insect outside again. I thought its wings were beautiful—a rusty brown with an orange stripe and a black spot that looked like a big eye.

"Where is this place, Jim?" called Deborah. "Are you sure you're not getting us lost in the jungle?"

"I hope the ship doesn't sail without us." Sue held her hand next to her face as another leaf-laden branch slapped the window beside her.

"They can't. We have Rafael as a hostage." Deborah chuckled.

After a few more minutes of bouncing and jiggling, the bus arrived at a clearing. We could see the deep blue ocean beyond a stand of mangroves.

Remembering my visit to the Maui property, I recognized the peach and teal Leisure Dreams logo affixed to a grand but unfinished stucco structure. It looked like the Galapagos property was being built on a much smaller scale than its sister resorts, but it fit the environment. The main building's design resembled other Leisure Dreams hotels: a multi-level crescent tailored to the landscape, giving almost every guest room an ocean view.

Gravel crunched under the tires as our bus pulled into a carved-out circular drive and then stopped.

Playing the tour guide, Jim hopped out and stood beside the bus steps with the driver to help us descend. "I've asked some of our staff to come out here today to welcome you," Jim said. "Please go inside and have some refreshments."

Kumiko held up her large handbag as she started down the step.

Jim looked at the driver and nodded. "Please leave anything you want on the bus. It'll be safe out here."

I left my backpack in my seat. No reason to drag it around the resort. *Jim's right; there should be no danger of it being stolen out here in the middle of nowhere.*

We disembarked, taking in our surroundings. A refreshing ocean breeze rustled the mangroves.

Michelle smiled as Jim took her hand. "So, where's the golf course?"

I nudged my grandmother, playing along. "Jim, you're not thinking of building a golf course here in the Galapagos?"

He indicated a stand of thick brush and cactus. "We'll put it over there if we can ever get the permit."

I looked where he was pointing. Michelle's eyes followed.

"What's that?" asked Helga, who had just stepped down from the bus. She stopped behind Michelle and me.

"The golf course." Michelle made a sour face.

Helga harrumphed.

"You can't tell from here, but there will be spectacular ocean views from many of the holes," Jim bragged. "And the lava outcroppings will serve as some great natural obstacles."

Michelle spread her arms. "Why do you need a golf course? This site is beautiful like it is. Why not leave the land unspoiled and make a nature trail?"

Jim frowned.

"People visit the Galapagos for the ecological experience," Michelle continued. "Not to play golf."

"But now they'll be able to do both." Jim led us toward the building.

Helga hung back with Michelle and me. "Maybe we can still talk him out of destroying this land for a golf course. I will make it my mission."

The entrance and the lobby of the hotel promised to be as grand as any other Leisure Dreams property. A revolving door flanked by two glass side doors led to the marble-tiled reception area. A curving, double staircase led from the lobby to the second-floor landing where the guest rooms were located. Soft classical music began to play, and the aroma of fresh flowers filled the air.

"Very nice." Dieter nodded his approval to Jim. "Good sound system, too."

"Thanks," said Jim. "They just got it installed, so I'm glad it's working."

Several staff members appeared, bearing trays of ice water and fruit juice. My throat felt parched, and I joined the thirsty guests clustering around the trays. The bus driver came inside and soon we were all sipping cool beverages.

"Can we go upstairs?" asked Deborah.

"I wouldn't yet," replied Jim. "There's a lot of finishing needed up there, and I wouldn't want anyone to fall through a floor or step on a nail. I have a display here to show you what the rooms will look like."

On a table in the lobby sat a mock-up of one of the guest rooms. I presumed the marketing team had created it for potential investors to visualize the final product. There were murmurs and sighs of appreciation as my fellow cruise passengers pored over the model.

"Where's the pool, Daddy?" asked Jenny. "Is it finished?"

"Not ready for a dip yet, honey." Jim nodded toward the rear exit. "It's out here on the terrace."

Some of the visitors followed Jim and Jenny outside. The rest of us lingered in the lobby, admiring the splendor peeking through the construction chaos like a spring bulb.

I stood next to Janice as I examined the intricate pattern in the marble tile floor. Our eyes met, and I averted mine. I moved away and joined Jim, Jenny, and others out on the veranda. I needed to talk to Jim, enlist his help with making sure Jerome stayed in jail, but the timing had to be right.

The empty pool was almost finished, and its clover-leaf shape fit into the landscape. Mosaic tiles lined the bottom and sides. A lava outcropping had been plumbed as a "natural" fountain set to re-circulate water into the swimming area.

A lava lizard scampered across the water fixture and dove into a crevice.

"I wish we could go swimming, Daddy." Jessy tugged her father's sleeve.

He patted her small hand. "Next time, honey. We'll all come down for the grand opening."

More cruise passengers joined us poolside, making complimentary remarks about the pristine setting. A sweet smell emanated from the tropical vegetation. I didn't know enough about flowers to identify which of the colorful blossoms produced that scent.

Darwin's finches fluttered and chirped in the stand of Scalesia trees that shaded one side of the terrace. And yet the trees did not block the hotel's splendid view of the boat-dotted harbor and the sprawling town of Puerto Ayora across Academy Bay. Despite the arduous journey over the primitive road to reach the Leisure Dreams site, we were close to civilization.

Down an incline, steps led to a new wooden pier that extended into the bay. Beside it, several slips lay waiting for guests' boats.

I heard a rustling in the bushes near where I stood. I turned toward the shrubbery in time to see an enormous tortoise emerge from the brush, like a monster rising from the sea. One of its front feet was missing a toe.

Rafael strolled onto the veranda and stopped in his tracks. His cup slipped from his hands. Droplets of water doused his shoes as the cup rolled across the terrazzo. He gawked at the pony-size tortoise. "Tio Armando!"

xcited murmurs and cries rippled through the crowd of cruise passengers gathered around the Leisure Dreams hotel's empty pool. Heads turned and jaws dropped. I couldn't believe my eyes.

"Tio Armando?" came a gasp.

"It can't be," said someone else.

"But how does Rafael know it's him? These tortoises all look alike."

Another voice answered, "It's the toe. Remember, he's missing a toe on his front foot."

"The right one or the left one? Are they sure it's the same animal?"

We all stared at the shelled behemoth whose beady black eyes blinked as if Tio Armando was just as startled to find an audience.

Then the giant tortoise bit off a newly planted geranium from a flower bed lining the pool terrace and chewed. Green leaves and orange petals hung from his beak.

Rafael glared at Jim. "Sir? Did you know this animal was here? Loose on your property?"

Jim looked as stunned as everyone else. His incredulous expression reminded me of the one he'd worn after our visit to the Beagle Galapaguera on San Cristóbal two days earlier when the staff told him Tio Armando had been moved. "The enclosure . . ." Jim stammered. "We haven't finished the enclosure. I don't know..."

"He's not in an approved pen." Rafael watched the tortoise as the last of the geranium snack disappeared into his mouth. "How did this happen?"

Grounds workers materialized and Jim conferred with them, his voice anxious and his face reddening. Heads nodded and shoulders shrugged. More people scurried about.

In the meantime, the rest of us gathered around Tio Armando in awe.

"Don't touch him." Rafael took command.

Dieter gave Rafael a cold look. "What would you have us do then? Your cruise line promised we would see Tio Armando. And until now, you have not delivered."

"You can take photos," Rafael conceded. "But don't sit on him, and don't feed him." He took his cell phone out of his pocket. Staring at the screen, he shook the device and then moved to the edge of the veranda to pick up a signal.

I stepped back as more people gathered around the giant tortoise to admire and photograph him. I wondered who had transported Tio Armando from San Cristóbal, and how long he'd been roaming the Leisure Dreams site. Was someone caring for him, or had his captor dumped him here to fend for himself?

I strained to remember what Laurel had said about the reserve her friend Felipe was building. Was it near here? Felipe had outbid Leisure Dreams for the privilege of housing Tio Armando. If Jerome was in charge of construction, that reserve might be nothing more than slick, doctored photos and diagrams on a PowerPoint for presentation to potential donors. *But wouldn't Felipe know? If he loved Tio Armando so much, wouldn't he want to oversee the project, watch the reserve come to life?*

Is Felipe working with Jerome? Or Jim? And what about the Dubai buyers? Where do they come in? Should I even tell Jim what I found out about Jerome and Felipe?

Perhaps Felipe was playing everyone against each other.

Never motivated to learn a foreign language, I now wished I understood Spanish, so I'd have caught what Laurel and Elena had bickered about when we were back at the Darwin Research Station. Those two must have known more about the battle for Tio Armando than they told me.

I sighed. How Tio Armando got to Leisure Dreams was not my concern. I was glad to see him safe. It didn't matter to me if he wasn't the last of his species, or whether the world knew it. No one had killed Laurel because of her research. I hoped, for the sake of the locals, that Tio Armando would stay in the Galapagos, but where he lived was not my problem. Maybe Jim Roberts was part of a conspiracy or a pawn among competing interests. The whole intrigue had distracted me from my goal of bringing Jerome to justice.

While deliberating the mystery of Tio Armando's journey, I was missing a private audience with the most famous attraction in the Galapagos. And I'd left my camera in my backpack, which was still on the bus. It would be a shame not to get a photo of Tio Armando at Leisure Dreams, although others were taking plenty of shots and would share. Jenny was capturing some great close-ups.

But I wanted my camera. I caught sight of the bus driver, who sat on the edge of the empty pool, sipping a glass of fruit punch. "Is the bus unlocked?" I asked him.

He took another swig of punch and nodded.

I slipped back inside the building and crossed the now-deserted lobby toward the front entrance. I pushed open the glass door and let myself out.

Janice Roberts sat on a large boulder outside the building, filing her polished nails.

I had to walk right past her.

"Giovanna," said Janice.

I pretended not to hear and continued toward the bus.

"Giovanna," Janice called louder.

I turned to give a cursory wave and a look I hoped would not invite conversation.

Janice ignored the rebuff. "Giovanna, I'm sorry about Jerome Haddad."

"Jerome?" I stopped walking. "Why?"

"I should have made sure he didn't hurt anyone else. But I didn't do that. I washed my hands of him, got him out of my life." She set down the nail file. "I can't stop thinking about what he did to you—and countless other people—and that I could have prevented it. Jim and I put our energy into repairing the damage he did to my charity instead of keeping Jerry from running the same scam again and again."

I took a step toward Janice. "Jerome Haddad is not your fault." I looked her in the eye. "But Fernando is."

"Fernando?"

I gave Janice my auditor stare until she averted her eyes. Did I detect a flinch?

Janice pressed her lips together. "You weren't there."

I took a step closer. "But you pushed him, didn't you? And then left him to die."

"You don't have a daughter." She flipped blond hair into her face.

"Okay, I get it. He was coming on to Jessy. That's disgusting. But is it a reason to kill someone?"

"It was an accident." Janice smoothed the hair off her forehead.

"Yes, that's what the police have decided."

"She didn't mean . . . " Janice clasped a hand over her mouth. "Uh, I . . . I didn't mean to push him that hard."

I watched Janice's face. "She? *Jessy* pushed him?"

Janice looked away. "*I* pushed him. But it was an accident."

"You were protecting Jessy."

"Yes!"

"From the police. Not from Fernando."

Janice bit her lip. "It was me. I pushed him. My daughter did nothing wrong." Tears welled in her deep blue eyes.

"I get that you needed to stop him. But I don't understand how you could have left him there to drown." I sat down on the rock next to Janice. "Why didn't you call for help?"

"He was probably already dead."

"But we'll never know for sure, will we?"

"Jessy went into hysterics." Janice shook her head. "I was thinking about my daughter, not that animal." She put the nail file back in her handbag. "He had so little respect for me, he came after my daughter the very next night. As if nothing had ever happened between us."

"What do you mean?" I tilted my head. I must have misunderstood. *Janice and Fernando?*

"I think you can guess." Janice's tear-filled eyes focused on my face. "You know how Fernando was. I saw him flirting with you, too."

"But you and Jim—"

Janice put her head in her hands. "I made a mistake. A terrible, terrible mistake. Jim may never forgive me."

I gazed at the ground, nauseated. *How could she?* A lava lizard darted by. Janice and Jim were the perfect couple. They had a perfect family, a perfect life. Jim stood by Janice when Jerome Haddad almost destroyed her charity. How could Fernando have tempted Janice to stray?

And Fernando was such a sleaze.

I shivered, ashamed of the lusty feelings I'd harbored when Fernando had kissed me on the upper deck. I'd almost succumbed to his charms. If his role in Laurel's disappearance hadn't preoccupied my thoughts . . . I no longer felt as sorry for Fernando, the victim.

Janice broke the silence. "I know he didn't deserve to die that way—no one does—but I hope you can understand why I didn't rush to help him."

I tried to banish the image of Janice and Fernando coupling, tried to visualize the scene at the pool. Fernando coming on to Jessy after I'd rebuffed his advances. Janice intervening. A struggle. A fatal fall. "But it was over. He wouldn't come after Jessy again."

"It was an accident! What do you want me to do? I made another mistake. I can't bring Fernando back." Janice wiped her brow. "And like I said, I don't think there was anything we could have done. The way his head cracked against the side of the pool when he went down . . . " She winced. "He landed in the deep end and wasn't moving."

I covered my face with my hands. "So, you just walked away? Back to your suite? Went to bed like nothing happened?"

Janice sighed.

How could she? I looked at Janice. "And when the police came on board, wanted to question everyone about a death . . . Didn't you have some idea about what was going on?"

Janice just stared at the ground.

What is wrong with you, Janice? "Why didn't you come clean then? Save everyone a lot of time and grief? You said it was an accident."

"I'm sorry. I should have handled it differently. But we have to move on now."

Sure. You're back with your cozy little family like nothing ever happened; you're no better than Jerome. I shook my head. "If anyone else had done this . . . I'm so tired of seeing people commit crimes and get away with them. Where's the justice?"

"And what would be justice?"

Before I could reply, a dusty, black, four-door Honda Civic roared up the circular driveway, flicking gravel with its tires.

CHAPTER TWENTY-NINE

The paramedics laid the unconscious Felipe on a stretcher and carried him outside to the ambulance waiting in his driveway.

Zuniga turned to the two women who had found the bleeding man.

"I have to ask you more questions." He looked at Elena. "You can confirm the victim is Felipe Santore, the homeowner?"

Elena pushed a strand of dark hair away from her face. "Yes, I told you already."

Zuniga stroked his smooth chin. *So, this is the man who bailed Jerome Haddad out of jail. Where's Haddad now?* "Do you know if Señor Santore lives alone?"

"As far as I know." Elena's eyes darted around the room. "It's not like we're best friends or anything. Felipe is just an acquaintance. Someone I once worked with."

"Does he have any enemies? Anyone who would hurt him?"

Elena shrugged. "Felipe has pulled some questionable deals in the past. But I don't know of anyone who hates him enough to . . ." She shuddered.

Zuniga noticed the other woman slinking toward the door while he was talking to Elena. "*Señora? Momentito, por favor.*"

Laurel stopped.

Zuniga turned to Laurel. "And your name, Señora?"

Laurel gulped. "Laurel Pardo," she whispered.

Detective Zuniga raised an eyebrow. "Laurel Pardo... missing from the *Archipelago Explorer.* A possible drowning at sea."

"I'm sorry." Laurel tossed her bangs out of her eyes. "I just found out they reported me missing. I didn't mean for that to happen." She swallowed. "I didn't mean to cause trouble."

Zuniga eyed her. "You didn't think people on that ship would worry when you didn't come back from a snorkeling expedition?"

"Fernando was supposed to . . . " Laurel hung her head.

"And you." Zuniga pointed at Elena. "You knew there was no drowning at sea."

Elena held up her hand. "I knew Laurel planned to leave, yes, but I only found out today where she had gone."

"We invested a lot of manpower in the search," said Zuniga. "Boats, divers."

"Wait . . . you didn't call my father, did you?" Laurel's brown eyes blazed.

"No one has reached him yet."

"Thank God."

Zuniga pictured Giovanna's concerned face, how she had fretted about her failure to sound the alarm sooner. "Your friend will be relieved."

Laurel met his eyes. "She already knows."

Zuniga blinked. "You've talked to Giovanna Rogers?"

Laurel nodded. "Today, at the Darwin Research Station."

"She was surprised to see you?"

Laurel smiled. "Quite."

"I thought Giovanna had gone to meet you, Detective," said Elena. "I dropped her off in town."

"I was late, and she must have already left." Zuniga gazed at the crime scene. "Last night, Felipe Santore bailed a man named Jerome Haddad out of jail. We now have more questions for Señor Haddad. I came here because I thought Señor Santore might know where Haddad is." He looked from Laurel to Elena. "Do either of you know Jerome Haddad?"

Both women shook their heads.

"And I still need to talk to Giovanna Rogers. When I drove by our meeting place, she wasn't there."

"I bet she went back to the ship," said Elena. "We're sailing this afternoon."

"At least we warned Felipe," said Laurel. "Thanks to Giovanna." She stared at the spot where Felipe had fallen. "I hope it still matters."

"Warn Felipe?" Zuniga asked. "Warn him about what?"

"That he's in business with a con man," said Laurel. "This Haddad character did the same thing to Giovanna, back in the States. Claimed he'd help her build her nonprofit, and then drained all the donation money out of the accounts for himself."

"Wait a minute." Elena turned to Zuniga. "You said Felipe bailed Jerome Haddad out of jail last night?"

Despite the warm, stagnant air inside Felipe's house, a chill crept over Victor Zuniga, like a ghost had passed through his body. The ashen-blue face of the dead woman found on Jerome Haddad's yacht haunted him. When he closed his eyes, the dead woman's face had changed to Giovanna's.

Janice and I both looked up as the black Honda Civic skidded to a stop in the circular drive in front of the Leisure Dreams property. Gravel crunched under the car's tires.

The driver's side door opened with a creak. A familiar, unwelcome figure unfolded himself from behind the steering wheel and rose to his full height beside the vehicle. He slammed the car door and swaggered toward us.

I felt my entire body tremble. I glared at Jerome, wishing my eyes could shoot venom like those poisonous frogs in the Amazon. "What are you doing out of jail?"

"This is private property," Janice snarled. "You're trespassing."

Jerome kept walking toward us. His pale blue eyes glinted like ice crystals. His tongue traced the curve of his thin lips like a viper preparing to strike. "We'll see about that. I think you have something that belongs to me."

"Get out of here, Jerry!" shouted Janice. "I'll call Security."

I looked around in alarm. Janice and I were alone at the front of the building. All the other guests and staff were in back by the pool, fawning over Tio Armando. The music in the lobby would drown out our cries. "You heard her, Jerome. You're not welcome here."

Jerome did not stop. He crossed into my personal space like a dog ignoring an electric fence. "How dare you, Gio."

I took a step backward to maintain some distance from him. "How dare I what?"

Jerome turned to Janice. "And you?" He gestured at our Leisure Dreams surroundings. "I guess *he* makes you happy?"

Janice lifted her pert nose into the air and looked down it with her ocean-blue eyes. "He has never once hit me."

Jerome clenched his jaw.

"He makes me happy," Janice sneered. "Happier than I ever would have been with you."

Jerome leaned his face close to hers.

"You're despicable," hissed Janice.

I watched, paralyzed. Jerome's eyes gleamed. It seemed the world had stopped spinning for a second, then resumed in slow motion.

Jerome and Janice froze in a stand-off.

"That's too bad," Jerome said. The hand at his side thrust toward Janice. "Maybe I can't have you, but neither can he."

Janice gasped. Her face whitened.

Blood reddened her beige knit shirt. She grabbed her side and stared.

"Jezebel." Jerome brandished the bloodstained knife.

I opened my mouth in a scream, but before the sound could escape, I felt Jerome's large hand cover my lips and the knife's point graze my throat.

Michelle handed Deborah's camera back to her. Deborah and Sue almost knocked foreheads peering over the camera's screen to approve the shot Michelle had taken of the two of them crouched next to Tio Armando. The giant tortoise had found more landscape vegetation to nibble on, and another green sprig hung from his mouth, making him look even more otherworldly.

"Great photo, Michelle, considering the human subjects you had to work with," Deborah said.

"Speak for yourself," said Sue.

"You both look smashing," Michelle assured her. She cocked her head. "Did you hear something?"

"What?" asked Sue.

"I thought I heard a scream." Michelle scanned the crowd gathered on the veranda.

"A bird," suggested Deborah. "I've been hearing a lot of different bird calls out here in the jungle. Maybe because it's so quiet otherwise."

Michelle wondered where Giovanna had gone. She didn't see Janice or the twins, either. She walked toward Jim; perhaps he knew.

Rafael stepped back onto the veranda and put his cell phone in his pocket. He strode over to Jim, reaching his side at the same time as Michelle. "Señor Roberts?"

Jim looked up from his conversation with Dieter and Helga. "Rafael?"

"The National Park Service is on its way to pick up Tio Armando." Rafael placed his hands on his hips.

Jim's face stiffened.

"I know you think you made an agreement," continued Rafael. "And everyone may still honor it. But until there is a proper enclosure for the animal, until the park service has inspected it, the Darwin Research Station will keep him for now. Professionals will care for Tio Armando and keep him safe." Rafael gave Jim's shoulder a tentative pat. "Until they decide what to do."

Jim swallowed. He turned back to Helga and Dieter. Their circle had grown as several other guests wandered over, listening to Rafael's words.

"Well now," said Jim, recovering. His public relations smile came out like the sun after a sudden storm. "How did everyone enjoy the preview of Leisure Dreams' coming attraction?"

Rafael looked at his watch. "The ship sails in one hour. We must get back."

The group headed inside the building. They crossed the lobby and exited the way they had arrived.

Michelle was the first to spot Janice, slumped against the front steps, covered in blood. Her eyes were slits, and she expelled weak, shallow breaths.

Jim was right behind Michelle. "Janice! Baby!" He rushed forward and gathered Janice into his arms, oblivious of the blood spreading to his tan silk shirt. "Janice, my Janice! My sweet baby. Don't leave me!" He looked at Michelle, his eyes wild. "Help! Somebody help her!"

"What happened?" cried Helga. She elbowed her way through the crowd and knelt beside the others.

"Oh, my gosh, that looks like a stab wound," said Michelle. "It's bad."

Someone appeared with a towel, and Michelle pressed it against Janice's side to control the bleeding. "Call an ambulance!" she cried.

"Gio," croaked Janice. "Giovanna."

For a moment of terror, Michelle thought Janice might say Giovanna had done this. *But how could that be?*

Jim shot a look at Michelle, then lowered his ear to Janice's lips. "What, Baby? What are you trying to tell me?"

"He . . . he took Giovanna."

Detective Victor Zuniga doubted it was protocol to allow Elena and Laurel to help him search Felipe's house. However, time was of the essence, and both women knew Felipe. They could better interpret any findings.

Felipe's cell phone lay under the coffee table. Victor retrieved it and verified that the last call received had come from Laurel's cell phone, which fit her story.

He'd placed his last outgoing call the day before, to the police station. *To inquire about bail for Jerome Haddad,* thought Zuniga. Before that one, he had called a local number, most likely a mobile phone. Zuniga pressed the number to redial.

Zuniga listened to several rings before his call went to voicemail. The greeting was a factory one, verifying only the number dialed. He hung up without speaking and pocketed Felipe's phone.

"I think Felipe had a visitor sleep here last night." Elena pointed to the pillow and rumpled sheet draped over the couch. "Not a close enough friend to share his bed."

Could the overnight guest have been Jerome Haddad? Zuniga wondered. It had been late when Felipe bailed him out of jail; perhaps it was easier to bring Jerome here than to find a hotel room. Because he'd been living on the yacht, Jerome would not have already secured lodging in town.

And if Jerome had been here . . .

Laurel located Felipe's computer in the bedroom. None of his documents were password-protected. "Here are the plans for the new reserve." She carried the laptop into the main room and set it on the dining table to show Zuniga and Elena.

Laurel opened the PowerPoint presentation. A series of slides summarized the reserve's objectives, facilities planned, costs to execute, and benefits of the project.

"Slick," remarked Zuniga.

"I can't imagine Felipe writing this," said Laurel. "Too high brow. It doesn't sound like the way he thinks."

"He's not that organized," agreed Elena.

"Here's the donor list." Laurel opened an Excel spreadsheet with columns of donor names and amounts. She whistled. "He has collected a lot of money. From all over the world. I didn't realize this reserve was such a big project."

"What's that document?" Elena pointed to a .jpg file labeled "Site" in the same folder.

Laurel clicked on it and they all watched it open. "Looks like a map of Santa Cruz."

"Is that where the reserve is supposed to be?" Zuniga touched an area near an intersection that had been circled.

Elena eyed the document. "That's right near Bellavista, where I live." She studied the map. "I drove by that corner this morning, on my way to the Darwin Research Station to meet the cruise passengers. Nothing's there."

"Well, it's not finished yet," said Laurel. "They're still raising capital."

"But there's nothing," said Elena. "It's a vacant lot."

"But . . ."

"No clearing, no signs, no—"

"No reserve," said Laurel.

Elena and Laurel looked at each other. "Remember what Giovanna told us about that partner of Felipe's," said Laurel.

"But if there's no reserve," said Elena. "Where is Felipe keeping Tio Armando? There's no room in his backyard. Why did he bring him over here already from San Cristóbal?"

Zuniga jumped as Felipe's cell phone vibrated in his pocket.

CHAPTER THIRTY

Jerome dragged me toward the car, arms pinned against my body, and left Janice slumped on the driveway, bleeding.

I squirmed and battled him with all my strength. I knew my chances of surviving a kidnapping were statistically better if I'd stay and fight. Allowing an attacker to take you to another location meant almost certain death. Crazy that I'd think about statistics amid an attack.

As my feet skidded along the gravel, I remembered the rush of gratitude I'd felt when Fernando pulled me out of the water, saving me from drowning in Gardner Bay—just a few days ago. I'd been so thankful I'd live to see my twenty-fifth birthday. Maybe that gratitude had been premature.

Sausage-size fingers covered my mouth. I chomped into them as hard as I could.

Jerome yanked his hand away from my mouth, shaking his fingers in the air. I glimpsed the purplish indentations my teeth had made. "You rabid bitch!" Before I could regain my footing and slip from his grasp, he grabbed my throat.

I jammed my elbow into his side, kicked at his shins. But Jerome was stronger than he looked, and the knife blade sharp and unrelenting. Every movement earned me a fresh nick on my neck. The more I fought, the more his grip tightened.

He kept moving me toward the car.

He doesn't have enough hands to force me into the car and hold onto me until he drives away. I can still escape.

Struggling less to keep the cuts to a minimum, I bided my time and pretended to cooperate as we approached the vehicle, planning how I'd twist away once he shifted his attention to opening the car door. But instead of taking me to the passenger door, Jerome headed for the trunk.

I panicked. *No!* I'd locked myself in a tiny closet once when I was a child, hidden there for hours before anyone found me, and I hoped never to be trapped in a small, dark space again.

As he inserted his key into the lock, I squirmed from his grip. I had almost wriggled away when he seized me by the hair and smashed my face into the trunk lid. My vision blurred.

Writhing in pain, I clutched at my nose. Jerome grabbed me around the waist and hoisted me into the trunk, bending my limbs like a pretzel.

I felt a whoosh of air as the lid slammed. The whole car shook.

The trunk was hot and dark, and it stank of mildew. It was worse than that closet, the smell worse than mothballs. My nose hurt. My face ached. Perspiration stung the nicks on my neck. My leg curled beneath my body in an unnatural position. I shifted my weight to free it.

Kick out the taillights, I thought, trying to get some traction with my feet and find the right spot to hit. I doubted my efforts would do much good in daylight. Would anyone even see us along the access road?

I fumbled for the trunk release. There was none. *The model is too old*, I thought.

I banged against the lid of the trunk. "Help!" I cried. "Somebody help me!" Where were Jim Roberts, my grandmother, and the rest of the cruise passengers? The hotel staff?

I heard the engine start.

Jerome's hands shook as he gripped the steering wheel. *Now what?*

"Stop! Help me!" came the muffled shout from the trunk.

That damn Gio is trouble. What was I thinking, taking her with me? Where will we go now?

Jerome had come to Leisure Dreams to see Felipe's deception for himself. To right a wrong. To make the arrangements to transport that big turtle to his buyer in Dubai. So he could get paid. That had been the plan all along, regardless of Felipe's delusions about building the reserve they had pitched to donors. *I can't show my face at Leisure Dreams now. Gio has ruined everything.*

Instead of closing a deal, he had hurt Janice and trapped an angry hornet. *Why can't I get away from Giovanna Rogers? What did I ever do to deserve her? When I left Georgia, I thought I'd never have to see her snooty face again.*

"Let me out of here!"

"Shut up, Gio!" He shoved his foot against the accelerator.

She was thrashing around in the trunk, unrestrained, creating a terrible racket. *Why didn't I think to bind her hands and feet? Knock her unconscious?* He doubted the trunk was airtight, so she wouldn't suffocate before she could cause him problems.

The car lurched as it hit a pothole. "Piece of crap!"

His flight from Leisure Dreams was unfolding in slow motion, like a nightmare in which his feet were tied to lead bricks.

I should have taken Janice. She belongs with me. She just... she made me so angry when she compared me to Jim Roberts!

"Let me out of here, you asshole!"

And now I'm stuck with that anal bitch, Gio.

More thumping against the walls of the trunk. More muffled cries.

Maybe I can make it to the airport and board a flight before the authorities find Janice. Or Felipe. Or realize Felipe's car is gone.

"Where are you taking me? You'll never get away with this!"

"I told you to shut your trap." *Can't this car go any faster?*

"What do you think Jim Roberts will do when he finds out you stabbed his wife?"

"Shut up, I said."

"I bet he's found her by now. And called the cops."

"Zip it!"

"Where the hell are we going? This is a small island. You'll never get away."

Jerome gritted his teeth. *Why couldn't that trunk be soundproof?*

"They're coming after you, Jerome. They know what you've done."

His eyes strayed to the rearview mirror. "You're a pain in the ass, Gio. But you can be my human shield if there's trouble."

Michelle gave up hope that Janice Roberts would say more about who had taken Giovanna, and where they'd gone. Janice faded in and out of consciousness and had not spoken again. Someone had called the authorities; Michelle prayed they'd hurry.

Kumiko had jumped into action, applying pressure techniques to control Janice's bleeding and barking orders to those around her. Kumiko, Michelle learned, worked in Nagoya as a critical care nurse, and prior to that, had spent twenty years in a hospital emergency room. Michelle had never had a long enough conversation with Kumiko during the cruise to ask much about her profession, but her serendipitous presence on the site visit might save Janice's life.

From her first-aid training as a flight attendant, Michelle understood the dangers shock presented to an injured person, even before Kumiko shouted for someone to get Janice a blanket.

While Kumiko worked on Janice, Michelle caught the eye of one of the hovering staff members who had been serving punch earlier. "Can we get some blankets to cover her?"

The woman gestured for Michelle to follow her.

They hurried back inside, crossed the lobby, and headed down a side hallway. The woman opened a supply closet full of linens.

The task made Michelle feel useful, but it was not enough to distract her from wondering what was happening to Giovanna. *He stabbed Janice, almost killed her. What is he doing to Giovanna?*

Michelle returned to the lobby with blankets in her arms just as the twins strolled inside from the terrace, tossing their long, blond ponytails and giggling.

"Where is everyone?" asked Jenny, her face flushed.

"We saw a mama seal and her pup down by the beach," said Jessy. Her blue eyes sparkled with delight.

Michelle swallowed and looked at the twins. Clutching the blankets, she wished she could hold onto the pain she was about to unleash on the girls, keep it inside, and obliterate it. But she couldn't. She spit it out. "Something terrible has happened."

Jerome did not remember the access road to Leisure Dreams being so long. *I must have made a wrong turn somewhere in this Godforsaken desert jungle.*

The Honda Civic bumped along like a Conestoga wagon on the Oregon Trail.

A low-hanging branch slapped the side of the car. Briars scraped the paint.

Giovanna kicked at the back seat. The trunk walls were not thick enough to mute her pleas and curses. "Help me! I've been kidnapped by a madman!"

How long will it take for her to shut up?

"Help!"

"No one can hear you, Gio. Save your breath. And my ears!"

"Asshole!"

"I should have slit your throat." *It would have been so easy.*

She fell quiet for a moment. Then, "Why?"

The car hit another pothole. He hoped Giovanna could feel the impact from the jolt.

Jerome steadied the wheel. "You have to ask?"

That shut her up.

But Giovanna did not deserve a quick death. She should experience excruciating pain. She should fear for her life, beg his forgiveness before he finished her. *I want to watch her plead for me to end her miserable existence.*

Like Connie. He had confided in her, entrusted her with his plans, and she had helped him grow his business. For years, they built a successful partnership, peppered with enough romance to make life enjoyable. But what a big mouth she'd grown! Addicted to social media, Connie spent more time on the computer than she did taking care of him, satisfying his needs. In the process of oversharing everyday minutiae, Connie divulged damaging secrets about their travels and his business activities. Jerome had not signed up for that. She had become dangerous.

Was Connie naïve, or had she sabotaged his business, leaving a trail for those who resented his profits?

Violence had never been his style—other than an occasional slap to punish disrespect—but Connie left him no choice. He could no longer trust her. He'd never meant to hurt her. But her betrayal made him so angry. The knife had been in his hand already and before he knew it…

Jerome shook his head to dispel the image, the horror on Connie's face. The end of their partnership.

Before the trouble with Felipe, Jerome had meant to return to the wreckage of the *Second Wind* to collect his other island specimens and personal belongings. And dispose of Connie. Erase that chapter of his life. Leave the islands as soon as he could close the deal with the buyer and transfer his funds out of the joint account Felipe had set up.

Most likely, Connie had led Gio to the Galapagos, to him. Gio and Janice had both followed him here, ganged up on him. Gio had poisoned Janice against him. Otherwise, he might have been able to woo Janice back. He'd become a player, on par with that smug Jim Roberts she'd married.

Gio was the biggest mistake of his career. *She deserves the worst kind of suffering.*

Thinking about how he would like to punish Gio calmed his nerves, took his mind off the trek down the rutted road, the mistakes he'd made in anger that might backfire and derail his plan. Maybe he should pull over somewhere and do her in right here...

Gio had been one of his few female business partners who'd refused to succumb to his sexual charms. That haughty rejection had always bothered him. Not knowing her biblically made him feel less in control of her.

Giovanna Rogers was not a classic beauty like Janice. Her face was ordinary and her hair a mess, but her body was smoking-hot. There was something sexy about her defiant, take-me-as-I-am attitude. Women who played hard-to-get whetted his appetite and challenged him to put them in their place.

At first, Jerome thought Gio's reticence derived from some misguided sense of loyalty. Loyalty to her wimpy fiancé Tim, and perhaps loyalty to Connie, who'd been Gio's friend in college. Gio had always taken care to never end up alone in a room with Jerome—at least not long enough for him to suggest mixing pleasure with business. His subtle innuendos and off-color jokes never registered even a smile from her. What did Tim ever see in such a killjoy?

One day they had taken a road trip together to meet with a potential donor in a town two hours away. Tim, that faithful guard dog, had planned to go along, but at the last minute, an emergency arose with one of his veterinary patients. At last, Jerome could spend some time alone with Giovanna.

On the way back, they stopped for a late lunch at a quaint country inn. The meeting had gone better than expected; they'd secured a donation even larger than they'd hoped. Gio was in great spirits. They celebrated with a small bottle of wine and pleasant conversation about their childhood antics. In her euphoria, Gio laughed at his jokes, and Jerome noticed for the first time what a pretty smile she had. The ice queen was thawing.

But when he suggested they delay their return for a few hours and check into a room at the inn, Gio froze. As if the music had stopped.

"Let's be clear," she said, sober as a nun. Her playful smile had vanished. "I have no intention of ever sleeping with you, so please respect my wishes and don't bring it up again."

That tease! How dare she humiliate me like that?

"And stop calling me Gio. My name is Giovanna. No one calls me Gio."

Jerome gritted his teeth at the memory. *Gio will pay.*

etective Victor Zuniga held Felipe's cell phone and listened. The man on the line was talking so fast and so low that he could only catch a few words. Confused, Zuniga asked, "*Donde estás?*"

There was a pause. "Leisure Dreams." The voice sounded stupefied, then suspicious. "Felipe?"

Victor was silent.

"Felipe?" the man's voice grew anxious.

"It's Victor."

"Victor?"

"*Un amigo de Felipe.*" Victor moved the cell phone to the other side of his head. "Can you please slow down and repeat what you told me?"

The man hung up.

Victor looked at Elena and Laurel. "Will one of you please try calling this number from your phone?"

"Who is it?" asked Elena.

Victor pointed at the number on the screen. "One of Felipe's contacts. It sounds like the man works at Leisure Dreams, or at least he's there now. And he was rambling about Tio Armando." He raised an eyebrow. "Maybe one of you can figure out what he's talking about."

Laurel's mouth popped open. She looked at Elena and then took out her cell phone. "What's that number?"

Zuniga showed Laurel Felipe's call log and then turned to Elena.

She held up her phone. "Before I do anything else, I have to call Daniel to let him know I'm running late."

"Good," said Zuniga. "Ask him if Giovanna Rogers made it back on board."

Elena suppressed a smile and patted Victor's shoulder. "Sure, Detective."

Michelle spotted the speedboat dispatched from town as it arrived at the Leisure Dreams pier to pick up Janice Roberts and transport her to the Puerto Ayora hospital. Staff members and cruise passengers lifted Janice onto a backboard and then carried her down the stone steps and onto the pier. Kumiko climbed into the watercraft with her.

Jim started to board the boat, but the operator held up his hand.

"Janice!" Jim cried, shaking, reaching for the sides of the boat.

Michelle and Helga held him back.

"You need to stay here for your daughters," said Michelle, as she led Jim toward shore.

"Kumiko will make sure they take good care of your wife," Helga assured him.

Weeping, Jenny ran down to the pier. Michelle stepped aside so Jenny could hug her father. "Mommy will be okay, Daddy. She has to be okay!"

Michelle spotted Jessy near the top of the hill, hanging back from the group. Jessy's body quivered from spasms of uncontrolled crying. Michelle went to her and held out her arms.

Jessy hesitated for a second, then allowed herself to tumble into Michelle's arms. "Take a deep breath," Michelle said.

Jessy obeyed, her sobs subsiding. Tears had soaked the front strands of her long blond hair.

Michelle stroked Jessy's ponytail and smoothed some escaped hairs behind her elfin ears. "They're doing everything they can for your mother. We have to have faith." *I hope the wound is not as bad as it looked,* she thought.

Jessy took more deep breaths, then sputtered, "Is she going to be okay?"

"Of course," said Michelle, almost as a reflex. "Everything will be okay." And then she prayed it was not a lie. For Janice or for Giovanna.

Back at Felipe's bungalow, Laurel stared at the digits she had typed into her cell phone. "I recognize this phone number," she said to Detective Zuniga.

"Who does it belong to?"

"Miguel Ruiz. He used to work at the Darwin Research Station." Laurel touched the transmit button and lowered her voice. "He got hired at the new Leisure Dreams resort."

"Miguel's a friend of Felipe's?"

"I think so." After several rings, her call went to voicemail. "He may not want to talk to me, either," she said to Zuniga. "He didn't like my findings about Tio Armando. Maybe Elena should try to call him."

Zuniga frowned. "Is Tio Armando at Leisure Dreams?"

"Why would you think Tio Armando is at Leisure Dreams?" Laurel asked.

"This Miguel . . . it sounded like he said Tio Armando was there. And that someone was coming to get him."

Laurel scrunched her face. "That doesn't make sense."

Elena had stepped to the other side of the room for her conversation with Daniel. She clasped the phone to her ear and paced.

When she hung up, the color had drained from her face. She looked at Laurel and Victor.

"What?" asked Laurel.

"Some of the cruise passengers went to visit the new Leisure Dreams resort. There was some kind of attack."

"Attack?" Victor's breath caught on the word.

"One woman was stabbed, and another was kidnapped."

"At Leisure Dreams?" Laurel's eyes grew wide. "How . . . ?"

Victor stared at Elena. "And Giovanna?"

Elena shook her head. "Not back yet. She was at Leisure Dreams."

The police radio on Zuniga's belt squawked.

CHAPTER THIRTY-TWO

R afael took charge of the traumatized tourists milling around the dock at Leisure Dreams. "Everyone, if you left any personal belongings on the bus, please make your way there now to retrieve them." He fluttered his hands toward the stone steps leading to the hotel. "The ship is sending one of its Zodiacs to pick us up, so please meet back here at the pier as soon as you're ready."

"I'm not leaving without Giovanna," Michelle declared.

"Señora, I've notified the police." Rafael shooed her up the steps like a child. "There is nothing you can do."

"Don't they want to interview us? Find out if there were any witnesses?"

Rafael had stopped listening to her and was urging the twins toward the bus.

Brooding on a large boulder, Jim stared out to sea, almost catatonic since seeing his wife carried away, perhaps forever. "Jim." Michelle touched his shoulder. "Who do you think did this? Could it have been an employee?"

Jim blinked.

"Think, Jim. Is anyone missing? Acting strange?"

He looked around and shrugged.

"Could someone be unhappy with the working conditions?" *Already?*

Jim sighed.

"Why would someone hurt Janice?" Michelle pressed. "And why kidnap Giovanna?"

Jim turned and looked at Michelle through bloodshot eyes. "I don't know. I'm sorry, but I have no idea who'd do this. I pay the workers well and they seem happy. I've accounted for everyone."

"No one has gone after the kidnapper?"

The blank look on Jim's face did not change.

Michelle raised her voice. "Why didn't anyone start looking for Giovanna immediately? Before Janice lost consciousness, she seemed to be asking us to go after Giovanna's captor." *But, amidst the chaos, no one thought to do that. Everyone hovered over Janice. Now there's no trail, no clues to pursue. The attacker could be anywhere by now. How will we ever find Giovanna?*

"Señora, did you leave anything on the bus?" Rafael interrupted. "We have to let the police handle this matter."

"The closest police unit is in Puerto Ayora," said Michelle. "They'll come here first and ask questions before they search for my granddaughter."

"Señora—"

"They'll lose valuable time. The kidnapper has already hurt someone." Michelle planted her hands on her hips. "Don't you think the police will want to interview us? We can't go back to the ship now."

"Señora, please. Go get your things off the bus."

In a daze, Michelle followed the others who had left items on the bus, through the lobby that only an hour ago had seemed so majestic. Down the front steps and across the driveway still stained with Janice's blood.

Such a peaceful island, where wild animals are not afraid of humans. How could such a horrendous attack happen here?

Deborah and Sue stepped down from the bus as Michelle reached it.

"Michelle, I'm so sorry about Giovanna." Deborah's face was somber, her color pale. "I hope they find her, and that she's okay."

"If there's anything we can do ..." said Sue.

Michelle nodded her thanks. *Deborah and Sue can't bring back Giovanna. Their empty words are what's expected, what people say to express concern when they know there's nothing they can do.*

Michelle was the last person to enter the bus. She made her way to the back row, remembering how happy she'd been to see her granddaughter join the group, board the bus from downtown Puerto Ayora, and walk down that aisle—less than two hours ago. Giovanna's backpack still rested on the seat. *Is this all that remains of my granddaughter?*

I may never see Giovanna again. I'm the one who persuaded her to come with me on this cruise, and then to join Jim's group today for the visit to Leisure Dreams. What have I done?

Some papers protruded from the partially-open backpack. Papers Giovanna had compiled about her former business partner. Michelle pushed them back inside so she could close the zipper.

Jerome Haddad. A chill crept down Michelle's spine as she remembered the man's unsmiling, glacial-blue eyes. *Is he still in jail?*

Michelle recalled how excited, how proud Giovanna had been that she'd told Laurel and Elena about Jerome's financial misdeeds. And how Laurel had rushed to warn Jerome's new business partner to scrutinize his dealings. *What if Jerome found out what Giovanna had done?*

Jim Roberts and his army of lawyers couldn't stop Jerome Haddad; why did Giovanna think she could do it?

What if Jerome got out of jail? If they only locked him up for damaging a reef, he might have paid a fine and secured his freedom.

Michelle stared out the window of the bus. Could Jerome have come to the Leisure Dreams site? But what would have brought him here? If he was after Giovanna, how would he have known she was here?

And why attack Janice? Michelle recalled the conversation she'd had earlier with Janice and Jim. How astounded she'd been that Jerome had also conned Janice. *Maybe there's unfinished business between Jerome and the Roberts couple.*

Michelle fingered Giovanna's backpack. Was Janice stabbed because she tried to intervene in Giovanna's abduction? Or had she been the intended victim?

Maybe they'd had a confrontation that went wrong?

Jerome's a financial criminal, not a killer. He has no history of violence. Or does he? Those soulless eyes . . . so evil.

Michelle sank onto the seat and buried her forehead in her hands. *What a nightmare this trip has become! If only I could wake up and start the day over.*

"Anywhere you want to go, Giovanna. It will do you good to get away."

"Anywhere? What about the Galapagos Islands?"

"The Galapagos Islands? Roberto and I loved our trip there. It's a magical place, a great place to heal."

"So, we can go to the Galapagos?"

"If that's what you want. Let's book it."

Little had Michelle known that her granddaughter's interest in traveling to the Galapagos had more to do with seeking revenge against her business partner than finding a magical place to heal.

Jerome Haddad. The more Michelle thought about it, the less far-fetched her theory seemed. *Jerome did this.*

I have to tell the police.

Michelle picked up Giovanna's backpack and her own handbag, then hurried down the aisle, off the bus, and back to the pier.

Jerome winced. *Make that goddamn banging stop!*

Giovanna pounded the back seat. Out of the corner of his eye, Jerome could see the cushion moving. He felt like a kid who had a wasp trapped under a jar.

"Cut that out, you skank!" he called.

How would he ever get her out of the trunk without losing control?

He wouldn't. He couldn't use the bitch as a hostage. She'd never let him use her as a human shield. If no one had tied him to Janice or Felipe yet, no one would interfere with his departure, and there'd be no need for a hostage. He'd abandon the car in the airport lot, parking as far away from other vehicles as possible. With any luck, he'd be on a flight back to the mainland, with a quick transfer out of the country before anyone discovered Gio in the trunk.

And then what?

Gio will still be alive. And she'll talk.

The flight from Baltra to Guayaquil takes about two hours. Even then, I'll still be in Ecuador. If Gio gets loose, the cops will grab me before I can board an international flight. How is it so easy for movie heroes to escape from trouble? Jerome had never needed tools like fake passports and disguises, but they would come in handy now.

The pounding was relentless. "Stop it, slut!" he snapped.

Left alive, Giovanna Rogers was dangerous.

Michelle tried to explain her theory to Rafael. She didn't have all the pieces to the puzzle, and she knew she sounded like the frantic grandmother she was.

"Rafael, you're the only one around here with a cell phone that works in the Galapagos. Will you please call the police again and let them know who they should look for?" Some of the staff had cell phones, too, but they had scattered.

Rafael looked skeptical. "Señora, I thought you told me this man was in jail."

"Please, call the police station," Michelle begged. "Find out if Jerome Haddad is still in jail. If he is, then some island madman did this, and we're back where we started."

Jim still sat on his rock, staring across the bay. The sky had grown overcast, which fit the mood. The twins had come by with their things but couldn't persuade him to follow them down to the pier.

When Michelle spoke, Jim turned toward her and Raphael. "Haddad!" he cried. "Haddad did this?" He raised his reddened eyes toward the gathering clouds. "Why didn't I think of that right away?"

Michelle sidled closer to Jim. "We don't know for sure, but I told Rafael it's a good possibility."

Rafael waved his cell phone at them. "I'm calling. But here comes the Zodiac, so gather your things and get ready to go back to the ship."

I had grown hoarse from screaming. We must now be far enough away from the resort that no one but Jerome could hear me. On the way in I hadn't noticed houses or businesses along the access road. I hoped the construction workers had returned from their *siesta*.

The trunk was dark and stuffy, and it was hard to breathe. Sweat soaked my clothes. I was using up precious air and energy with my screams and kicks. *No one is pursuing us; no one will force Jerome to free me.*

The worn carpet beneath me felt damp, and my perspiration made it soggier. My body was not accustomed to being coiled up like a magician's assistant in a compact box. Every pothole rattled my teeth. Something hard jutted into my back, aggravating the spot that I'd bruised when Jerome threw me into the trunk. *A spare tire?* Maybe there was a jack I could use as a weapon.

My fingers explored the wall behind the back seat. Did it fold down? At least on one side? Was there perhaps a center section that opened into the trunk?

I fumbled and shoved, stopped to catch my breath, and then pushed harder. Something started to give.

CHAPTER THIRTY-THREE

his Godforsaken road is endless, lamented Jerome. *Where the hell am I?* The Honda bumped along, its wheels thunked in and out of ruts. *At least it's not muddy.*

Another jolt. He clenched his jaw. *Piece of shit!*

Jerome had passed a construction crew on the way in. The workers had been doing more talking and smoking than clearing and paving. They'd given him directions to Leisure Dreams, which had been a great help. Now he hoped he would not run into them on the way out. He didn't want them to hear the ruckus coming from his trunk and ask questions. *My cargo is none of their damn business.*

Still, seeing the road crew would be a landmark, an assurance that he was going the right way. *Out of this miserable desert jungle.*

He reached a fork in the road. *I don't remember a fork. Where did I go wrong?*

How can I tell I made a mistake, though? All this scrub brush looks alike.

He glanced at the sun, cursed under his breath, and then took the left fork. *This must be the way out.*

Pop! The Civic lurched to the right and slowed even more.

Jerome gripped the steering wheel. He tried to keep the vehicle limping forward.

The Honda slowed. *What now?* Jerome thought. *What a piece of crap.*

The car listed to the right. The wheel rim scraped against rock.

Jerome pounded the steering wheel. *A fucking flat tire?* And the spare was in the trunk. With Gio. If there was a spare. And if it was even usable.

He floored the accelerator, urging the crippled car to continue. The vehicle inched forward.

Another clatter came from behind. His eyes shifted to the rearview mirror.

The rear seatback dropped forward. Like a dragon emerging from its den, Giovanna Rogers pushed her way into the car's interior. Through the mane of tangled hair, her eyes glinted with fury.

Zuniga rushed to the Puerto Ayora police station. He had to trust Elena and Laurel to lock up Felipe Santore's house before heading back to the *Archipelago Explorer*. Not standard procedure, but more pressing matters awaited him.

Detective Juan Estevez had returned from Puerto Baquerizo Moreno that morning. Estevez had been the one who called Zuniga about the situation at Leisure Dreams. It was serious, and Estevez insisted on doing everything by the book.

Jerome Haddad was armed and dangerous. Allegedly, he had stabbed three people. The woman found on the wrecked *Second Wind*, most likely Haddad's wife Connie, was dead. The two other stabbing victims were in critical condition. Victor could not go after Jerome without backup.

Victor understood the need for protocol, for safety. But he was growing impatient. Minutes ticked away while the team finalized their plans and briefed reinforcements. They had to alert authorities at the airport and at the ferry, where the fugitive would have to cross the Itabaca Channel to reach the airport on Baltra Island.

"They're already on the lookout for Haddad," Victor reminded Estevez. "We put out an alert this morning, right after we found the body on his yacht."

"But now we have a description of the stolen vehicle," said Estevez.

"*Vámonos!*" cried Victor. "Before there's another dead body."

Jerome Haddad had kidnapped Giovanna, and he had a motive to kill her. Maybe he had already. The perpetrator had nothing to lose.

Giovanna. Victor squeezed his eyes shut and clasped his hands together. *Please, let us not be too late.*

As I poked my head through the folded-down seatback, I glimpsed Jerome's frosty blue eyes in the rearview mirror. The slight movement of his shoulder told me he'd grabbed the knife.

Our eyes locked. *So much for the element of surprise.*

"Lonely back there, isn't it?" With a tight smile, he lifted the knife and let me see his firm grip on the weapon.

"Oh Jerome," I rasped. "You don't need that. We have a lot to discuss. Partner."

"Partner?" he scoffed. "What did you tell that crazy woman?"

"Crazy woman? You mean Laurel?" I forced a chuckle. "What are you talking about?" Dragging my torso with my elbows, I continued to wriggle through the gap between the trunk and the back seat.

Jerome glared. He kept one hand on the wheel, even though the car was hardly moving.

"I gathered pledges from a dozen new donors for our reserve here." I tried to project confidence and enthusiasm as I pulled my knees forward. "Don't you want to hear about them?"

"*Our* reserve?"

"You mean we're not still partners?" Pretending not to hear the skepticism in his tone, I straightened myself up in the back seat. "You and Connie left Georgia so fast, but I just figured . . ."

"What?"

"I mean, we worked so well together." My words came out too scratchy to be convincing.

"You still want to be partners?"

"Don't you?" I feigned more conviction.

"Why did you—?" His eyes flickered. "When you came to the jail last night—"

"Don't tell me I did all that work for nothing." I inched along the seat toward the car door. "In fact, they must wonder where I went. And why you haven't come to pick up Tio Armando yet."

"What?" Jerome turned to watch me. Was he buying it?

"Tio Armando, the famous giant tortoise. He's over one hundred years old, and the last of his species." I launched into my best sales pitch. "He'll make us millions. Except he's running loose at the Leisure Dreams resort."

"The turtle is there? At Leisure Dreams?"

"If we don't hurry, Jim Roberts will claim him. He's already telling people—"

"Jim Roberts!" Venom dripped from Jerome's voice.

"You came to pick him up, didn't you? I told everyone—all our donors—I was helping you save Tio Armando." I put on my sweetest smile and moved my hand toward the door handle.

"How did you—?"

I flung open the back door and propelled myself out of the car.

stevez and Zuniga sped through Puerto Ayora with lights flashing and siren blaring. Another police unit followed. Pedestrians and vehicles pulled aside.

Victor was glad there weren't many roads on the island. *Still, Haddad could be anywhere.*

With no new leads, no reported sightings of Haddad nor the stolen Honda Civic, they had no choice but to proceed to the last place where he'd been seen and search for clues, talk to witnesses, find his trail.

In minutes, they reached the private access road to Leisure Dreams. A sign reading *No Trespassing / Propiedad Privada* marked the entrance like an unarmed security guard; it had not kept Jerome Haddad away.

Around the first bend, they spotted a road construction crew taking a smoke break.

Estevez stopped the police car and rolled down the window. "Excuse me, *Señores.* Did anyone see a black Honda Civic come by here? Four-door sedan."

One worker nodded. "The driver asked us how to get to the Leisure Dreams resort."

"Which way did he go?" asked Victor, leaning over Estevez.

The worker pointed toward the resort.

"He hasn't come back this way yet?" Victor probed.

Two of the workers looked at each other and shrugged.

"Think!" Victor pressed. "It's a matter of life or death."

The other worker shook his head with more conviction. "No, Señor."

I stumbled as I sprang from the back door of the slow-moving Honda Civic. I scraped my hand when I landed on the sharp pumice gravel.

Cursing, I picked myself up and started to run.

The car lurched to a stop. *So much for a head start,* I thought, looking over my shoulder.

The car door slammed.

I had not run this fast since I was on the track team in middle school. Was I headed in the right direction, back to the resort? But the priority now was to put as much distance between Jerome and me as possible.

The vegetation on either side of the road was a blur: a mixture of ferns, scrub brush, and Scalesia trees. I could feel pebbles crunch beneath my tennis shoes.

Feet pounded behind me. Jerome was gaining ground.

I brushed against a prickly pear and tried to ignore its sharp scratches across my bare leg.

I pushed myself harder. If only the bus would come down the road, with the other tourists en route back to the *Archipelago Explorer.*

Except for Janice. What will happen to Janice?

I swallowed. My throat was raw from screaming.

The road didn't look familiar, but I knew the view from on foot would appear different than the one from the inside of a bus. *Was the access road we took to the resort this primitive or had we veered off it?*

Heavy breathing grew louder. Without turning around, I could sense Jerome drawing closer. A predator sprinting after his prey.

I tried to speed up.

And then I tripped over a protruding root. "Dammit!"

Again, I pulled myself up. I'd skinned my knee, but now was not the time to check how bad it was.

His hand grabbed my shoulder. I twisted to the side to deflect it.

He reached for me again.

Spinning around, I thrust out my leg and swung as hard as I could, like I'd seen actors do in martial arts movies. My sneakered foot missed his groin by less than an inch. I teetered on one leg to stay upright.

"Damn you! Bitch!" He grabbed his crotch and glared.

Before I could return my foot to solid earth and regain my equilibrium, he lunged at me like a wounded beast.

His weight crashed into me and I lost my balance. We tumbled to the ground, with Jerome landing on top, crushing me against gravel. Somehow, he still held the knife.

I opened my mouth and let out my most deafening scream.

"There's a car on the side of the road up ahead," said Estevez.

The two police units parked in single file behind the stolen vehicle. The officers jumped out, guns drawn.

Victor was the first to reach the black Honda Civic. Adrenaline surged as he peered inside. "It's empty."

"Check the trunk," said Estevez.

One of the other officers pointed to where the back seat had flopped forward.

His partner opened the rear door and stuck his head in the opening. "No one in there now," he reported.

Victor felt the hood. "It's warm. They can't be far away."

The other officer kicked at the flat tire. "Here's what stopped them."

"Fan out," ordered Estevez. "Radio check."

"Affirmative." Victor headed into the bush. The others proceeded in different directions.

And then a scream pierced the air.

I lay on the rocky ground, the sharp steel against my throat, staring into Jerome's icy blue eyes as he straddled me. I expected my life to pass before me, but I was too frightened to think about anything except how his hot, stale breath stank.

A savage smile slithered over his lips. "Well, Gio. What do you have to say for yourself?"

My body trembled from fatigue as much as fear. "What do you want from me?"

He shifted the knife's position, goading me with the blade. Most likely paying me back for my ill-advised visit to the police station the night before, where I'd gloated about seeing him behind bars. "Well, Gio. What do I want from you? Let's see." His thumb caressed the steel. "How about a partner who doesn't betray me? Is that too much to ask?"

I flinched. *Now might not be the best time to set the record straight about who betrayed whom.*

"Maybe there is something you could do for me before I slice you to bits and feed you to the sharks." With one hand still holding the knife to my throat, Jerome moved the other hand to his belt buckle. I could feel the bulge in his pants against my thigh. "You and I could have made a great team. A missed opportunity."

A wave of nausea swept over me. "What would Connie say? Does she know what you're doing?"

"Connie won't be a problem."

The look in his eyes transmitted pure evil. Ever since Victor told me they'd found Jerome alone on the yacht, I'd wondered what had happened to Connie. And after what he did to Janice . . .

"What did you do to Connie?" My heart beat like a bass drum.

Jerome grinned, relishing my discomfort. I'd never believed in the devil until now. "You were always such a prude."

I wanted to survive, no matter what it took. "Me?" I forced a sultry smile. "No. Want to get it on? Let's go."

Jerome blinked.

"But let's not do it out here on the gravel," I purred. "Let's get a room at Leisure Dreams. One with a big king-size bed and a mirror on the ceiling. Or we can do it in one of those two-person bathtubs with jets." I started to push myself up on my elbows.

Jerome shoved me back down. "Gio, you're a tease."

"No, I . . ." I squirmed and eased away a few inches.

He planted a foot on my knee. I couldn't move anymore without pain and serious injury.

A satisfied smile snaked across his lips again. He rose to a standing position and raised the knife.

I gulped. Out of the corner of my eye, I spotted a coconut-size rock just within my grasp. My fingers reached for it.

"Freeze!" The male voice sounded familiar but from my vantage point on the ground, I couldn't tell where it was coming from.

Jerome turned and glared, then plunged the knife toward me.

I had the rock in my hand.

A shot rang out.

I flinched, dropped the rock. Jerome toppled to the ground like a tree felled by a lumberjack. Blood splattered me, and the knife slipped from his grasp.

Was I cut? Was I shot?

I screamed.

Jerome did not move. One of his legs had landed on top of mine, a dead weight. I struggled to free my leg.

"Giovanna! Are you okay?" In a moment, Victor was at my side.

I exhaled. *Is he a hallucination? Did I die?* "You . . . you saved me." My eyes shifted toward the rock and then moved to his face. I knew he'd seen the rock, and me with it in my hand. "How did you find me?"

Victor lifted Jerome's heavy leg so I could extricate mine. Our hands touched as I reached to massage my knee, the same one I'd scraped when I tripped. Now blood smeared over both of us.

I stared at Jerome's motionless, blood-covered body. Yes, he was a human being, but I wasn't thinking of him in that way. "Is he... is he dead?"

Victor felt for a pulse and nodded.

Our eyes met. Relief washed over me. Not an ounce of sorrow for Jerome. Maybe for Connie's loss. No, wait... Connie was no longer around to feel grief. Jerome deserved to die, but at least I hadn't been the one to kill him.

Victor extended his hand. "Are you hurt? Here, let me help you up."

I gave myself a quick once-over. None of the blood on me poured from open wounds. Very little was even my own.

A smile covered my face, like a ray of sunshine. *Victor.* He was real. I accepted his hand, warm to the touch.

I'm alive.

He pulled me from the ground and gathered me into an embrace, indifferent to the blood, sweat, and dust that covered me.

I threw my arms around Victor's neck and ran my fingers through his thick black hair, tracing the moisture at his hairline. Our faces met, our lips found each other's and joined into a deep kiss. So pure, so passionate, like Buttercup and Wesley in the final scene of *The Princess Bride.*

For the first time since I'd started running, I heard the birds chirping in the trees.

"Ahem." The sound of Estevez clearing his throat interrupted us. He stood in a clearing about ten feet away. When Victor did not respond, Estevez launched into a barrage of rapid Spanish.

Our lips parted, but I still clung to Victor. "Is he talking about me? I heard him say *Señorita.*"

Victor flashed his impish smile and kissed me again. "Ignore him."

"You saved my life," I murmured. "You saved me from... How can I ever thank you?"

Victor curled his lip at the grotesque mound of flesh next to us. "Sorry he'll never face justice for what he did to your business, and to you."

I pondered his words for a moment. I looked again at the lifeless body of my treacherous ex-partner—my captor and tormentor—then back at Victor. "This is justice. He'll never hurt another person."

EPILOGUE

rom various sources, I learned that, after an extended hospital stay, Janice Roberts and Felipe Santore both recovered from their wounds and returned to their homes.

Laurel arranged for the transport of two female tortoises from Tio Armando's colony of relatives on Isla Isabela to join a captive breeding program at the Darwin Research Station, where Tio Armando now resides. Mating appeared successful, and both female tortoises have since laid fertilized eggs, so the future of the sub-species seems assured.

Jim Roberts offered me a job managing Leisure Dreams – Galapagos, which I accepted. The Leisure Dreams resort will provide free shuttle service to the visitor center at feeding time so guests can see Tio Armando.

I like it here. Perhaps because of a certain local detective who keeps an eye on the place. Within a few months, I got the resort project back on schedule and the budget under control. Michelle and Roberto will come down for the grand opening. She's glad I convinced Jim that his plans for putting in a golf course were not cost-effective. At least, for now.

Victor is helping me learn Spanish.

THE END

Acknowledgements

Thank you to the Peachtree City Writers Circle who critiqued this manuscript one chapter at a time, month by month, as the story developed. I also thank my beta readers: my friend and travel agent, Donna Pacho; fellow Atlanta Sisters in Crime Lisa Malice, Linda Sands, and Edie Petersen, as well as Writers Circle members Paul Lentz, Mark Myers, and Rosemary Walden. And of course, thanks to the team at Sunbury Press for bringing my book to publication.

I fell in love with the Galapagos Islands after taking a bucket-list cruise there in 2014. Although the setting inspired this story, the events are entirely fictional. I regret any incorrect assumptions or negative impressions I may have cast on any of its institutions, police procedures, cruise lines operating in the region, the Ecuadorian government or its people.

ABOUT THE AUTHOR

Sharon Marchisello is the author of *Going Home* (Sunbury Press, 2014) a murder mystery inspired by her mother's battle with Alzheimer's disease. Besides fiction, Sharon has written travel articles, corporate training manuals, screenplays, and book reviews, including regular contributions to the Killer Nashville online magazine. Her blog, *Countdown to Financial Fitness,* and nonfiction self-help book, *Live Well, Grow Wealth,* deal with personal finance. She earned a Master's in Professional Writing from the University of Southern California. An active member of Sisters in Crime, she contributed a short story to the Atlanta chapter's anthology, *Mystery, Atlanta Style.* Another of her short stories appeared in the anthology *Shhhh...Murder!* (Darkhouse Books, 2018).

Sharon grew up in Tyler, Texas, and earned her Bachelor of Arts from the University of Houston in French and English. She studied for a year in Tours, France, on a Rotary scholarship before moving to Los Angeles and then later, Seattle. Retired from a 27-year career with Delta Air Lines, she now lives in Peachtree City, Georgia, where she does volunteer work for the Fayette Humane Society and the Fayette County Master Gardener extension office.

If you enjoyed this book, I would be honored if you'll leave an honest review on Amazon or Goodreads so that other readers can find me.
www.sharonmarchisello.com
www.facebook.com/SLMarchisello/
twitter.com/SLMarchisello